Avery DeMarco

autumn's wish

autumn's wish

an **autumn falls** *novel*

BELLA THORNE

with **elise allen**

DELACORTE PRESS

Text copyright © 2016 by Bella Thorne
Jacket photograph © 2016 Howard Huang

All rights reserved. Published in the United States by Delacorte Press,
an imprint of Random House Children's Books, a division of
Penguin Random House LLC, New York.

Delacorte Press is a registered trademark and the colophon is a
trademark of Penguin Random House LLC.

randomhouseteens.com

Educators and librarians, for a variety of teaching tools,
visit us at RHTeachersLibrarians.com

Library of Congress Cataloging-in-Publication Data is available upon request.
ISBN 978-0-385-74437-9 (hc) — ISBN 978-0-385-38525-1 (ebook)

The text of this book is set in 12-point Chaparral.
Interior design by Heather Kelly

Printed in the United States of America
10 9 8 7 6 5 4 3 2 1
First Edition

Random House Children's Books supports the First Amendment
and celebrates the right to read.

I would like to thank all my fans, and the avid readers who have followed me on this journey. I never thought I'd have the ability to publish one book, let alone three, and it has been an honor and a labor of love to bring Autumn to life. I hope you all enjoyed reading the stories of these characters as much as I enjoyed creating them. From the bottom of my heart, thank you. I completely adore you.

1

september, senior year

"Some students have a background or story that is so central to their identity that they believe their application would be incomplete without it. If this sounds like you, then please share your story."

I stare at the words from the Common App prompt until they dance in front of my eyes. That doesn't take long. I'm dyslexic. If I don't focus, the dancy-swimmy thing happens pretty much right away. Especially if I'm looking at something that makes me want to hurl as much as a college essay prompt.

But, hey, I shouldn't freak out. It's only my future, right?

Sigh.

Fine.

When I was fifteen years old, my father died.

I know this doesn't make me special. Lots of kids' fathers die, and it's probably just as beyond-words awful for them as it was for me, but when I lost my dad, I lost everything. My mom plucked my brother and me from Stillwater, Maryland, and dragged us kicking and screaming to Aventura, Florida, a place so hideously foreign and humid that I knew it would never be home.

That's what I thought at the time. I was wrong.

Over the last two years, I've made a life in my new town. I still miss my dad every day so much it hurts, but overall I'm happy. I have friends I love, I'm close with my family, and I even have a mission in life—a "Thing," as I always called it when I was younger, though if I told you about it specifically you'd never let me into your school because you'd think I was crazy.

Point is, life is good. Finally. When I thought it never could be again. And yet just when I'm feeling great about things, just when I'm okay with who I am and who I'm with and what I'm doing, someone comes around to thrash my life all over again.

I'm talking about you, College. You with your big promises of sports and theater and independence and opportunities of a lifetime—you're the one who's yanking away the life I love. My friends are all scattering away next year because of you. And don't tell me it's okay and that I can go have the same great opportunities, too, because that's not what it's about. It's about change, and believe me,

College, I have had more than my share. I'm done with change, and if you don't mind me saying so, it's pretty crappy of you to dangle it like a giant chocolate cake in front of a bunch of kids who would otherwise be perfectly happy staying where they are.

And another thing, College, as long as we're talking woman to friend-stealing behemoth—

"Okay, time!" Reenzie calls as her phone alarm beeps. She's been sitting cross-legged on her family room floor with her laptop on the coffee table but now pops to her feet with a huge grin. She looks like a cheerleader when she jumps up like that. The stereotypical cheerleader, with the flawless face and perfect body and high black ponytail, but that's actually not Reenzie's scene at all. She's laser-focused on academics and the Future, which is why she has our whole group spending an otherwise perfectly good Saturday at her house practicing college essays.

"You can't call time," J.J. pipes up from one of Reenzie's puffy reclining chairs. His laptop is balanced on the arm of the chair because his lap is occupied by his girlfriend, Carrie Amernick. She's sprawled across him, her back against one arm of the chair and her legs dangling over the other. "You can take as long as you want to write a college essay."

J.J. is long, lanky, deathly pale, and freckled. There is absolutely no reason my stomach should flutter and flop when I look at him. Except it does.

3

"J.J.'s right, Reenzie," Carrie says. "This is crazy." Her blond bob sways as she kicks her legs playfully and musses J.J.'s hair. He smiles like she's the most adorable thing ever.

Now my stomach lurches. Hard.

It's totally not fair of my body to act this way. I *had* J.J. We were together. He was crazy in love with me and I was the one who let him go. Plus it's not like I'd take him back if I could. He has Carrie. She's totally great for him and I'm happy for them.

My stomach just needs to get the memo.

Jack, who's next to me on the sofa, is also watching J.J. and Carrie. He leans over and whispers in my ear, "See how she's always touching him? She does that to make me jealous."

"Keep telling yourself that," I whisper back. Jack has been obsessed with Carrie for forever. Amazingly, he still thinks he stands a chance.

"You're correct," Reenzie says, pointing a newly manicured finger J.J. and Carrie's way, "but this is essay *practice*. It's all about getting our thoughts together quickly and expressing them succinctly."

"Here's my succinct thought," Amalita says from her sprawled-out spot on the rug. *"No mas!"* She slams her laptop shut.

Unlike Reenzie, Ames does *not* look like the stereotypical cheerleader . . . even though she's head of the varsity squad, bendier than a pipe cleaner, and flippier than popcorn kernels in hot oil. Amalita's shorter and rounder than anyone you'd see playing the role on TV, but unlike most calorie-counting toothpicks, she has zero body issues. Guys love her.

As Ames sits up and stretches her arms over her head, all her bracelets jangle down. "This is boring. Besides, I gotta rest up. House party with Zander tonight. You guys coming?"

Taylor chokes on her tea. She carries the stuff with her at all times in a reusable water bottle she refills throughout the day. Ever since she read that TV and musical-theater star Kristin Chenoweth swears by tea to keep her voice at its best, she refuses to be without it.

"Tee?" Ames asks, referring to Taylor's nickname, not her drink. "You okay?"

"Totally," Taylor croaks, and it's a testament to her effortless grace and beauty that she still looks like an angel even when she's bent double in Reenzie's other recliner, red-faced and spluttering. "Went down the wrong pipe. Party sounds great. Sorry I can't make it."

She catches my eye and I grimace back. We don't like Zander, and we *really* don't like his parties. Just thinking about them sends a ball of smoke-and-stale-beer smell to the back of my throat, and I want to choke.

"Can't make it either," I say. "Sorry."

"Seriously?" Amalita asks. "None of you?"

When everyone grumbles in the negative, Ames shrugs. "Your loss. I'm gonna bail."

"Oh, come on!" Reenzie says as Ames heads for the door. "Don't you want to practice SAT analogies?"

Amalita doesn't even bother to answer. She holds up a hand and breezes out the front door.

"Reenzie!" Sean moans. "Enough! It's a Saturday. Let's do something else."

"Like what?" Reenzie asks.

Sean smiles wickedly and pounces off the floor, grabbing her around the waist and kissing her neck. Reenzie squeals and laughs.

This time last year, I'd have yanked out my own heart and eaten it if I'd seen them together this way. I didn't just crush out on Sean when I first moved here; I *pulverized* out on him. I couldn't even glance at his quarterback-muscular body, perfect brown skin, and dizzying blue eyes without melting into a puddle on the floor. Now . . .

Okay, he's still severely puddle-worthy, but I know he's wrong for me. He and Reenzie have been super-serious for practically a year now, so I don't even think of him that way anymore.

Much.

"Let's go swimming," Sean says. "It's hot in here."

"Yeah, it is," Reenzie says, eyeing him up and down. "But you didn't bring your suit."

"Who needs a suit?" Sean says with a smirk.

Okay, I might be over him, but I'm not a masochist. I don't need to keep watching.

"I'm out!" I say.

"Me too!" Taylor adds.

Carrie pokes out her lower lip and looks into J.J.'s eyes. "I wish you had a pool," she says, pouting. "Swimming sounds like fun."

"I have a pool!" Jack says. He leaps up from the couch so quickly his laptop smashes to the rug. "No suits required."

"We'll pass," J.J. assures him.

I'm not even sure Reenzie and Sean notice as the rest of us get up and leave.

The second we get outside, the heat welds my tank top to my skin, but after three years I'm used to it. "Who gets the privilege of driving me home?" I call. I'm the only one in our group who doesn't have some kind of car at their disposal. It's fine by me. I didn't even want to get my license last year. I finally did, and Mom lets me use the car when she doesn't need it, but honestly I'm happier without. If it's up to me, I'd much rather ride than drive.

"We'll take you!" Carrie chirps.

She's holding hands with J.J., and while I don't see him squeeze her hand, I do see her react to it and wheel toward him, a confused look on her face.

"I kinda had other plans for us and A Racier Sir Grace," he murmurs.

Carrie giggles and turns back to me. " 'A Racier Sir Grace,' " she explains. "That's 'Carrie's Carriage' with the letters rearranged. He's really good at that kind of thing— it's so cute!"

I smile through clenched teeth. I'm the last person

7

Carrie needs to enlighten about J.J.'s quirks. His car was named after *me* long before it was named after her.

"Sorry, Autumn," J.J. says. He faces me but looks somewhere beyond my left ear. I desperately want to dive into his sight line so he's forced to look at me, but I grab a strand of my humidity-limp orange hair and twirl it until the urge subsides.

At least he said my name this time.

That's my issue. It's not that J.J. has a girlfriend; it's that he acts like we barely know each other when we used to be best friends. I got it at first—he was hurt and he couldn't deal—but it's been eight and a half months since we patched everything up. Eight and a half months! Plus he's with Carrie—he has clearly moved on. We should be friends again, and it kills me that we're not.

"I'll drive you home," Jack offers.

I look at him. His round, freckled, smiling face and blond hair. His arms spread wide with generosity. His long denim shorts and faded *X-Men* T-shirt.

"Tee?" I ask.

"Sorry." Taylor winces. She's looking at her watch. "Didn't see how late it was. Voice lesson across town."

"Come on!" Jack complains. "You're acting like my car's the Sarlacc pit."

"Is that an *Avengers* reference?" I ask.

Jack's mouth hangs open and he stares at me like I just slapped his grandmother. "You're lucky I let you in my car at all," he says, then turns and stalks away. I roll my eyes and follow him. I open the passenger door slowly, a little bit at a time, wedging my body between the door and the floorboards so the sea of empty plastic bottles doesn't tumble onto the ground. Holding my breath, I squeeze myself as tiny as possible and slide in, pulling my feet onto the seat before I quickly slam the door shut.

"You shouldn't put your feet on the leather," Jack says as he turns on the car.

"If I put them on the floor, your trash would be up to my knees!"

"It's not trash—it's recycling!" Jack insists.

"Only if you take it out of your car and put it in a recycling bin," I retort. "Otherwise it's landfill!"

Jack suddenly lunges over me and buries both arms in the pile of bottles. I scoot back in my seat. "You don't have to get rid of them *now*," I say.

"Shhh, shhh," Jack says as he sits back up holding a pair of binoculars. He puts them to his eyes, looks out the windshield, and smiles. "This is good. Her shirt's riding up."

I follow his gaze to J.J.'s car, right in front of us. Carrie has climbed onto the center console and the two of them are making out like they need the oxygen from one another's lungs to breathe.

"Put those down!" I say, slapping the binoculars out of Jack's hands. "What is wrong with you?"

Jack shrugs. "Don't put on a show unless you want someone to watch."

He pulls away from the curb, but as he rolls up next to

J.J.'s car, he rolls down *my* window, beeps his horn, and shouts, "Nice technique, Austin!"

I bury my head in my hands as J.J. and Carrie stop what they're doing to stare at us, and I keep it buried long after Jack pulls away and zooms down the street.

"He's not happy," Jack laughs.

"Of course he isn't!" I snap. "That was totally obnoxious!"

I sound mad, but I'm not. Jack's Jack. He's gross and obsessed with sci-fi and comics . . . and I love him for it. Just like I love Amalita for her quick temper and constantly jingling jewelry, and Tee for throwing herself into all things dramatic, and Reenzie for her crazy-insane drive, and Sean for being so certain he's the hottest thing around, and J.J. for instantly knowing every anagram for any given phrase. I mean, I love them for their good traits, too, but their bizarro quirks make me even happier because . . . I don't know . . . they're my people. Loving them for their weirdness makes them feel even more like my people.

"Any chance we'll all end up at the same college?" I ask Jack.

He snorts. "You crazy? Reenzie's all Stanford. *Maybe* J.J. could get in there. But Sean'll go to some state school that gives him a huge football scholarship. Taylor'll be at some la-la theater school. Amalita wants somewhere 'exotic—'"

"Okay," I interrupt him. "But *some* of us might end up at the same school, right?"

"Doubt it. I mean, maybe Carrie and J.J., 'cause she's applying to all his same schools. Otherwise"—he turns and leers at me—"enjoy me while you've got me."

I roll my eyes, and even though we talk for the rest of the ride, I'm not paying attention. Instead I'm obsessed with finding out how many of her high school friends my mom stayed close with when she went to college and how many she's still friends with now.

"Mom!" I call when we get to my house and I run inside.

She doesn't answer. I look outside at the pool, but she isn't there, so I run all over the house, peeking into every room and calling for her until there's only one place left to look.

"Hey, Erick, have you seen—" I say as I throw open the door to my thirteen-year-old little brother's room . . . and choke before I can finish my sentence. The whole room reeks of boy sweat. The boy in question wears denim shorts and no shirt as he hoists himself again and again over a pull-up bar he begged Mom to let him install.

"One hundred eight . . . ," he croaks in his half-deep/half-high-pitched voice as he bobs his head above the bar, "one hundred nine . . ."

"Yeah, right," I say. "Try *eight . . . nine . . .*"

Erick grins. "Try *one*," he challenges me.

I grimace. I *did* try one when Erick first installed the bar. I did it when no one else was home, because I had a feeling it wouldn't go well. I gripped the bar, hung down,

11

and managed to bend my elbows a couple of very impressive centimeters before searing pain ripped through my biceps and I let go of the bar so fast I tumbled onto my butt. I shook it off and figured no one would ever know, but of course my film-obsessed brother had installed a motion-activated bar-cam to record his workouts, so now my athletic feat is immortalized on his YouTube channel.

"Have you seen Mom?" I ask.

"She's at work," he grunts as he dramatically squeezes out one final pull-up, then leaps nimbly to the ground. "She called and said we're on our own for dinner. I vote protein. Need to feed the furnace."

He flexes his biceps and kisses them, one at a time.

"Ew," I say. "Put those away."

"Wanna see me make my pecs dance?"

"Wanna see me lose my lunch?"

He makes his pecs dance anyway. I don't actually lose my lunch, but I do leave the room immediately. It's infinitely weird and disturbing to me that Erick is considered a "hot boy" at school, a fact I know from the pool party we had at the end of summer. A bunch of kids from his class came over, and all the girls were oohing and aahing over how much he'd changed over the summer. I have to admit it's true. He's as tall as our mom now, so just a little shorter than me, plus his braces are gone, and while I'd never tell him this, you can totally see all the work he puts in on his muscles.

Still, it's weird. Erick's not supposed to be studly. He's

my dorky, scrawny, film-obsessed little brother, and he's supposed to stay that way. Just like my mom's supposed to stay the kind of mom who's around all the time, instead of working so hard to open another branch of her successful animal-rescue foundation, Catches Falls. And just like my friends are supposed to stay right where they are, here with me, instead of going to new places where they'll meet new friends and forget all about me.

I lean against the hall wall and slide down it, disgusted by my own thoughts. I pull out my phone and text Jenna, my best friend from forever and the one person I'm still close to back in Maryland.

> I am a horrible human being. I want everyone else to fail just so things don't have to change.

Right there with you, Jenna texts back. Looking up black magic spells to make Sam tank his SATs. Come over and let's be horrible together.

Sam is Jenna's boyfriend. They're both track superstars, and while Sam could get a track scholarship to University of Oregon just like the one Jenna's after, he's a genius and has his heart set on MIT. A bad SAT would bump him out, leaving him free to join Jenna in a West Coast runners' paradise.

I smile when I read her text. I love Jenna. If someone as well adjusted and together as her can be just as insane as me, maybe I'm not so insane after all.

Or maybe I am and I just have good company.

Be there in 5.

I know it's a very weird thing for me to say to someone in Maryland when I'm in Florida, unless I mean five hours or five days. Which I don't. See, my dad left me this gift after he died. A couple of gifts, actually. The first one was a diary that made wishes come true. I know, it sounds crazy, but it happened and it was real and it worked . . . until all of a sudden it didn't work anymore. I thought that was the end of it, but then I found *another* gift—a dry-erase map of nowhere that existed in the world. When I write on the map, it takes me to that place. Like, I could write "Australia," and *bam*, I'd be hugging a koala. An *angry* koala, with my luck, and I'd end up getting my face scratched off. But if I use it carefully and really think about what I'm writing, it usually gets me exactly where I want to go.

Dad had left me both the map and the diary as part of my mission—to bring peace and harmony to my little corner of the world. I kind of made a mess of that last year, but I cleaned it all up by New Year's. And even though I'm all kinds of messed up in my own head about J.J. not being my friend anymore, and Mom and Erick changing, and everyone leaving for college in less than a year, that's all my own stuff. For my friends and family, things have been pretty peaceful and harmonious, so I haven't used the map except to see Jenna on a regular basis, because yeah, a magic portal to your best friend in the universe? Kinda the most amazing thing ever.

I go into my room and rummage through my school backpack until I find the pouch where I keep the map and dry-erase pen. I shut my bedroom door, plop down on my bed, and scrawl "Jenna" across the weird green landmassy blob in the middle of blue ocean.

And nothing happens. I'm still on my bed.

I peer closely at the map. Did I write her name wrong? It wouldn't be the first time I made a mistake like that, only I'm not sure how even with my dyslexia I could have messed up the letters in "Jenna" to make the word "home" or "my bed."

Nope, the name is fine. I wrote it the same way I always do.

Did I not press hard enough? Was I maybe not thinking about Jenna hard enough when I wrote her name?

My phone rings.

"Hey."

"Where are you?" Jenna asks.

"It didn't work," I say. "Let me try it again."

I lick a finger and start rubbing off Jenna's name so I can write it again, but then I hear her voice go all dark and foreboding in my ear.

"Is the *zemi* still there?"

I freeze, and not just because I realize I'm an idiot and Jenna is much smarter than me. I slip my fingers underneath the postcard-sized board. I raise it slowly and nervously, like I'm expecting a cockroach to scuttle out from underneath. Finally, I flip it over.

The back is plain blue plastic. No design. No *zemi*.
No spirit of my father.

"No," I say breathlessly. "It's not there."

"And that's why you're not here," Jenna says.

She declares it like it's a normal conclusion. A dry-erase board with a design on it? Of course it can totally take you magically anywhere you want to go. No design? Are you kidding? No way can you leap through space with something like that. For a super-logical girl like Jenna, it's a weird jump . . . except she and I have been through this before. When I first received the wish-granting journal, it had a *zemi* on the front—a design that looks kind of like a triangle with a face in it. My grandmother Eddy told me that my dad's ancestors, the Taino, said the *zemi* holds the spirits of the dead. A few years ago I'd have thought that was crazy, but now I know it's true. I'm not saying my journal and the map are *possessed* by my dad or anything, just that somehow, some way, a little piece of him is attached to those *zemis,* and that's why the magic works. He was looking out for me, making sure I accomplished what he knew I could do.

Last year, when the *zemi* disappeared from my journal, I was devastated. I felt like I'd lost my dad all over again. For a second I feel that same pang, but then my heart speeds up and I'm so buzzed with energy I jump to my feet.

"If it's gone from this," I say, "maybe it's on another gift. Maybe it's in a hidden compartment somewhere on the map!" That's how I found the map in the first place—it appeared in a hidden spot in the diary.

I shake the map by my ear and listen for anything rattling inside.

"Anything?" Jenna asks.

"A breeze," I say, fanning my hair out of my face. "A really nice breeze."

"But nothing inside?" Jenna prods.

"I don't think so," I say, "but maybe it's somewhere else. Maybe it's in my room. Maybe it's in another part of the house? Oh God, what if it's in Erick's room? I can't take any more body spray mixed with hormones mixed with sweat."

"Trying to ignore those words so I don't torture myself and imagine the smell," Jenna says. "But looking for it isn't the answer."

"It's not?"

"No," she says. "You have to go see Eddy. She gave you the diary; she clued you in on how to find the map. She'll know what to do now."

Jenna's right. If anyone will know what the spirit of my father wants next, it's my grandmother, Eddy.

Time to take a trip to Century Acres.

2

september, senior year

Eddy, my father's mother, is the main reason we moved to Aventura in the first place. She lived alone down here for years, but when she had a stroke and couldn't take care of herself, Dad moved her into Century Acres, an assisted-living home. The idea was the whole family would come down and help her, but . . . well . . . things changed. At the time I thought there was no way we'd move without Dad, and when we did I kind of resented Eddy for it. Like it was her fault Mom was ripping me away from everything I loved.

I don't feel that way anymore. Eddy's a little crazy and a lot embarrassing, but I love her. And I owe her a visit anyway, since I haven't seen her all summer. Jenna and I spent the summer as counselors at the sleepaway camp we've gone to since we were kids. We used to say we'd do that every summer until we were eighty, but Jenna already told me this was probably her last time. If she's going to run in college, she'll have to spend next summer getting in shape.

I think I handled the news well. I told her that would make her the first of my friends to abandon me next year, and for an entire week I had all the kids in our cabin refer to her only as Judas.

Point is, even though Eddy and I talked on the phone while I was away, I didn't see her all summer. Then when I got back I had to catch up with all my friends and cram in all the reading and assignments I'd ignored during vacation, and *then* I got busy with school, and now I'm a whole week in and I haven't seen Eddy at all . . . so I was planning to visit her soon anyway. Now I'm just motivated to do it right away.

I pound on my brother's blissfully closed door. "Erick! I'm running out for a sec! We'll order pizza when I get back!"

I half hear him shout something about "too many carbs," but I'm already heading for the garage. In a happier world I'd call J.J. for a ride. Instead I have no choice but to ride my bike three miles through the thick humidity and heat. By the time I get to Century Acres, my cutoff shorts and filmy tank are sweat-stuck to my body, and my hair clings like droopy orange noodles to my face and neck. I'm also wheezing a little. It's a good look for me, especially since there's a decent chance that my all-time pop-star

19

idol, weirdly now-kinda-sorta-sometimes friend, and oh-my-God-I-for-real-*kissed*-him bae Kyler Leeds could be inside.

The second I open the door, a *whoosh* of arctic-level air-conditioning freezes me solid, and my ears are assaulted by overly amplified classical piano music: the pre-dinner entertainment for the residents. I can see the pianist. He doesn't look much older than me, and I'm sure this is his good deed for the day, but he's not enjoying it. His forehead is a mess of sweat and he keeps glancing nervously at two little old women who won't stop heckling him. Their matching plush chairs are pivoted toward the pianist, so I can only see them from the side.

"Boo!" cries a tiny white-haired woman in a purple terry cloth tracksuit.

"You're no musician!" adds an equally tiny woman with thinning jet-black hair. "Play something good!"

"We want another song!" calls the first woman, and she climbs onto her seat and punches a fist in the air as she makes it a chant. "We want a-no-ther song! We want a-no-ther song!"

I sigh. This is my grandmother Eddy and her best friend, Zelda Rubenstein. I dart over to them and mouth "I'm sorry" to the piano player as I grab their attention.

"Hi, guys!"

"Autumn!" they cry in unison, and immediately forget about the piano player. Eddy throws her arms around my neck for a hug. It's a little strange because even standing on the chair, she's barely taller than me, and she's so light I feel like I'm hugging a child who I should pick up and set safely down on the floor.

"Oh, I missed you this summer, *querida!*" she coos, cupping my face in her hands. They're strong against my cheeks, and I remember she made her living as a potter for years when she raised my dad in Cuba.

"Hey!" calls Zelda. "Bring that *punim* down here too. I want in."

I have no idea which part of me is my *punim,* so I just bend down and lean toward her. She also grabs my face, but her hands feel like thin papery gloves. She pulls me close for a kiss that lands uncomfortably close to my lips, and I can feel the big red splotch left by her lipstick.

"Don't manhandle her, Zelda," Eddy says as Zelda wipes the mark off my face. "She's *my nieta.*"

"Well she'll be mine, too, once she marries my Kyler," Zelda counters.

"*Sí, sí,*" Eddy admits, "but I still say we have the reception down here. I don't trust the people in New York. They put things in the water."

"You're *meshuggeneh,*" Zelda says, waving her off. Then she turns to me. "And don't you pay attention to what you read on the Internet. Those supermodels are just a phase for Kyler. You're the one he'll come back to in the end."

"*Ai, mi carina,*" Eddy sighs as she sits dreamily back in her seat. "You'll be such a beautiful bride."

"Who says I'm marrying Kyler Leeds?!" I balk, even

though the real answer to that question would be *Me! I say it! Almost every day of my life!*

At least, I *used* to say it. Having my dream become Eddy and Zelda's dream is a total buzzkill.

"What, he's not good enough for you?" Zelda asks. "He's a big star."

Like I don't know that. My room was papered with his picture until we actually met and I felt weird having him stare at me all the time.

"And he got us the new comfy chair so we could both sit," Eddy adds, patting the armrests of her chair. "We owe him."

So I'm payment for a chair. Sometimes I wish Eddy and Zelda had stayed mortal enemies.

"Eddy, I actually have to talk to you about something." I glance over toward Zelda and smile apologetically. "Something . . . personal."

"*Haría cualquier cosa por ti.* Anything for you." She leans on the armrests and pushes herself up, then points warningly at Zelda. "Anyone touches my chair, you know what to do."

Zelda nods knowingly, patting her silver handbag. Then she leans as far back in her own seat as she can and stretches her legs so they extend onto Eddy's chair cushion.

"What is she going to do?" I ask as Eddy links her arm through mine and we start down the hall toward her room.

"Mace 'em," Eddy says. "Kyler got her a can for her birthday. She's just waiting for a chance to use it."

I shake my head and don't say anything else until we're inside Eddy's room with the door closed. I help her settle into her favorite chair; then I perch on the side of her bed.

"Is it the *zemi*?" Eddy asks.

I nod and pull the map from my purse. "It was on the back of this, but it's gone. I figure there's another one on something, like last time, but I don't know where to find it."

Eddy nods and takes the map in her hands. She rubs her fingers over the front of it, like a blind woman reading braille. Then she turns it over and does the same.

"It's not like on the diary," I say. "It was just printed on. You wouldn't feel it."

"Maybe, maybe not," Eddy says, but she stops feeling the map and instead holds it up to her eyes. She moves it closer, then farther away. She leans over and turns on her night-table lamp, then pushes the map right next to the bulb. "Ah," she says, smiling. "Reinaldo. He's still here."

Every hair on my body jumps to attention. Reinaldo is my dad. And even though I know she doesn't mean he's actually *here*, just the idea of it makes me ache so much I can barely sit still. "He's not, though," I say. "The *zemi*'s gone."

"*Almost* gone," Eddy clarifies. She motions me over to the lamp. "Look closely, *querida*. In the right light, you can just barely see it."

I get up and lean over the lamp. This close, the light's so

bright it burns my eyes, but I force them open as wide as I can and stare at the map as Eddy slowly tilts it back and forth.

"I see it!" I gasp. It's the triangle face of the *zemi*, right where it always was, but so faint that I don't know if it's really there or if my eyes are playing tricks on me. Before I can be sure, Eddy sits back, pulling it out of the light.

"Just enough," she says, "to help you find the thing you want most."

I smile, understanding what she means. I dig into my purse and pull out the dry-erase pen, then take the map from Eddy. I pause, my pen poised over the map. What should I write? Carefully, I spell out "My dad's next gift."

"Ow!" I shout as my shin hits something hard.

"Autumn? *Estas bien?*" Eddy asks, half rising from her chair.

That's weird. I'm still in Eddy's room, only I'm on the other side of her bed, next to the night table . . . which I think just gave me a nasty shin bruise. Immediately, I realize two things. First, whatever part of my dad is still in the *zemi* clearly lost its strength, because I didn't even make it out of the room. Second, for the first time ever, someone saw me travel by map.

Or did they? Eddy looks pretty nonchalant for someone who just saw the impossible.

"Eddy . . . did you just see me bounce across the room?"

"*Sí,*" she says, like it's a perfectly normal thing to witness. "So what are you waiting for? *Mira!*"

She nods to the night-table drawer, urging me to look inside.

"Your night table?" I ask. "Do you have something in there for me?"

Eddy rolls her eyes. "Me? No. Reinaldo . . ."

She scurries over to me and nods meaningfully at the night table. I frown at her. Is she serious? If my dad's gift for me was there, wouldn't she know it?

Or am I crazy for thinking logically when I just beamed across the room like a sci-fi hero?

Yeah, probably that last one.

I open the drawer. The inside is completely empty except for a circular, slightly tarnished silver medallion, about the size of a roll of Scotch tape. A thick silver chain lies through a loop on its top.

An antique necklace?

I pick it up.

"Ah," Eddy breathes next to me. "The *zemi*. *Te quiero*, Reinaldo."

Unexpected tears well in my eyes. The triangle-faced *zemi* is etched in deep, beautiful lines across the silver. I rub my thumb over the now-familiar face and imagine my father smiling through it.

"I wonder what it does," I say.

"Open it," Eddy advises, which is when I see a latch on one side of the medallion.

Is it a locket? Is there a picture inside? I imagine a shot of my dad and me together, maybe one of the ones from his phone that got lost in the accident. I eagerly press the latch and the locket snaps open.

Only it's not a locket. What's inside is an array of steampunkish open cogs that whirr and click and spin. On top of the cogs are four windows, one at the top and bottom of the locket and one on each side. The top window shows the number 10 in a blocky old-style font, the left window says "December," the right "19," and the bottom window . . .

I stop breathing and I nearly drop the medallion.

"*Dios mio,*" Eddy says softly. She crosses herself, and I know she sees it too.

The windows show a date. The exact date my father died.

"Why would he give this to me?" I ask, my voice shaking. "I don't want it."

Eddy pretends to spit on the ground. "*No.* You don't say that about a gift from the spirit world. If your father wants you to have this, there's a good reason."

That's what she says, but she starts pacing around the room, muttering prayers in Spanish.

Still, she's right. My dad loves me. No part of his spirit would come back to torture me with the day he died. There has to be another reason he gave me this thing. He has to believe it'll help me bring peace and harmony to my little corner of the world.

I peer more closely at the whirring gears and windows and realize that there are tiny metal wheels next to the left, right, and bottom windows—the ones controlling the date. I push my thumb down onto the bumpy metal next to the word "December" and roll it up.

"January," it says in the window.

My heart pumps faster. I'm getting an idea of what this might do.

I turn the wheel on the right, and the numbers spin up to 31, then start over at 1.

This thing . . . this *calendar* . . . it doesn't just show the date; it lets me *set* the date. And why would it let me set the date unless . . .

My heart is beating so fast now I think it'll slam out of my chest and hit the wall. I wheel to Eddy and grab her arms, stopping her in her tracks.

"It's time travel!" I shout, not even caring how ridiculous that sounds. "I can set a date and I can go there!"

But Eddy's still too upset from seeing Dad's death day to understand. She looks at me with unfocused eyes. "A date?" she asks. Then her face relaxes into a blissful smile. "Ah, I have a date. With Juan-Carlos Falciano. So *guapo* . . ."

Oh no. Eddy's lost in the past, dreaming about my grandfather.

"*Muy guapo,*" I agree. "Very handsome."

I get her settled back in her chair where she can daydream in peace and turn my attention back to the locket. I'm right about it. I know I am. The map took me to a place, and this watch-calendar will take me to a date. A date where I can bring peace and harmony to my little corner of the world.

My breath catches and I bite my fist to stop myself from screaming out loud because suddenly I get it.

I know *exactly* where to go. Or when to go.

I'll go to the day before my dad died. I'll convince him *not* to take the motorcycle drive that killed him. I'll stop his accident before it ever happens. I'll have him back.

My heart swells up and fills my chest. I love my dad so much. *This* is what he wants from me. This is what he's been building up to with the diary and the map. He wasn't supposed to die at all, and now I can make that right. I can bring him back and we'll have the life we were meant to have all along.

Fingers trembling, I carefully set the date: December 18, two years ago. There's no way to set a place, but it was kind of like that with the map too. When I wrote "Jenna," I went to *my* Jenna, not some other random person with that name.

My dad's spirit is in this locket. He wants me to do this. He'll know where I want to go.

I close the locket and grip it tightly in my hand. Squeezing my eyes shut, I imagine going to him. December 18. He'll be at our Aventura house, but it'll be mostly empty, because we'll still be in Stillwater. He'll have just come from Century Acres to check on Eddy. I'll appear in the family room and run outside to find him swimming laps in the pool, like he told us he did every day. And even though he knows I'm supposed to be back home, he won't be surprised to see me, because he'll just *know*. I'll make him promise he won't get on his motorcycle tomorrow, and when I come back to now he'll be there, sitting at the dinner table with Erick and Mom, just waiting for me to come home. I'll run into his arms and he'll wrap me in the tightest hug ever. "Thank you, baby," he'll say softly into the top of my head. "I love you." "I love you, too, Daddy," I'll say, and I'll squeeze him even tighter. And even though Mom and Erick will have no idea why we're acting like we haven't seen each other in ages, Dad will know I followed his mission for me and saved him. And I won't care if all my friends scatter for college and everything else changes because I'll have him back, and I'll know that everything else will be okay.

It's so real. I can feel his arms around me and hear his voice. My heart races again as I sense the change in the air and know that I've shifted somehow. I'm not where I was before. I'm there, at the house two years ago, and all I have to do is open my eyes to make all my dreams come true.

I fling my eyes open . . . but all I see is Eddy, asleep in her chair.

I haven't gone anywhere at all.

I haven't saved him.

He's gone . . . forever.

The pain slashes into me like a thousand knives. My legs buckle and I crumple to the floor, screaming down into the carpet. I cry until I'm completely wrung out.

At some point I hear the door click open.

"Autumn?" a kind male voice asks. "Autumn, is that you?"

The man crouches down next to me, and I swim through a foggy daze to understand.

"Autumn?"

It's Ezra, one of the aides at Century Acres. He knows me well because I volunteered a lot last year.

"I'm fine," I say. I sound like I'm talking through cotton, and my face feels stiff and swollen from crying. I can't possibly explain what happened, so I go for the one thing that usually stops guys from asking anything else. "Bad cramps. I curled up down here and I guess I fell asleep."

Ezra sucks in his breath and steps back. He might be a nursing assistant, but he's still male. "Eddy's out too," he says. "I brought her dinner. Should I leave it in the kitchen?"

The "kitchen" was a small counter with a sink, a mini fridge, and a few cabinets, but it was all Eddy needed.

"Sure," I say. "Thanks."

I wait for Ezra to leave before I get to my feet. I look longingly at Eddy's empty bed. It would be nice to crawl under the covers and stay there for a decade or two.

My phone buzzes in my pocket. I want to ignore it, but it might be Mom, wondering where I am, so I answer without even looking at the caller ID.

"Hey!" Jenna says brightly. "Did you go see Eddy? Did you get the new gift?"

I open my mouth to answer, but I just start crying again. Jenna doesn't push. She knows I'll tell her everything when I'm ready.

I must be completely drained of all fluid because the tears don't take long to stop. I tell Jenna everything, and she lets me spill it all without saying anything.

"So I was wrong," I finish dully. "The thing doesn't work at all. I can't bring him back."

When Jenna spoke, her voice was soft and gentle. "Autumn . . . of course you can't bring him back. You can't change the past."

"Then why would he give me this thing?" I wail. "It's not like I can change the *future*. It hasn't happened yet!"

"Right," Jenna says. "But if you see what's happening then and you don't like it, you can change things *now* to make the future better. Like . . . if you jumped forward and saw yourself actually married to Kyler Leeds, you could come back and change things up so you don't make such a hideously horrible choice."

"Ignoring that," I say. "So . . . you don't think Dad meant for this to bring him back?"

"That was never his thing, right?" Jenna says. "If it was, you could have wished him back with the diary."

My heart sinks a little because I know she's right. At the same time, I feel kind of better. The locket didn't fail. I didn't mess it up. I just didn't understand what Dad wanted me to do. But now that I do . . .

"Will you stay on the phone with me?" I ask Jenna.

31

"Are you going to try it?"

I nod, which is ridiculous since we're not on FaceTime and she has no clue what I'm doing. "Yeah."

"Totally," she says. "When are you going to go?"

"Right now."

"No," Jenna says. "I mean, you're going to go to . . . *when*?"

I bite my lip and think about it. I could go a few months into the future and see where we're all going to college . . . but what am I going to do, change where people want to go? I could travel twenty years into the future and see where we all end up . . . but that's so far away, and I don't think I could handle it if I see that something really horrible happens to one of us. I shudder. Maybe sometime I'll do that, but not yet.

"Three years in the future," I tell Jenna. "That's enough time for all of us to be settled into college, right? If we all grow apart . . . I'd see it by then, right?"

"Right," Jenna says. "But if you *do* see us growing apart, don't believe it. I promise I won't let it happen."

"Deal," I say.

The medallion is still on the floor, where I left it. I put Jenna on speakerphone and pick it up, gently rubbing my thumb over the *zemi*. I think about how sure I was that I could bring back my dad and I almost start crying again, but I don't. He wants me to do something else with this gift, and I won't let him down. I press the latch, flip open the locket, and set the dials. September 21, three years in the future.

"Okay, I set it," I tell Jenna. "Now I'm gonna close it up and see what happens."

"I won't hang up," Jenna promises. "I'll be right here."

I nod. I know she can't see me, but I'm too nervous to say anything else. I don't even know where I should wish to go.

I close my hand around the locket, squeeze it tight, and empty my mind of everything but one thought:

Take me where I should go, Daddy. Wherever I need to go.

3

three years later

My eyes are still closed when I hear the song "YMCA" by the Village People blaring far too loudly in my ears. Naturally, I assume I'm in hell. Or at a bar mitzvah. A bar mitzvah in hell.

I open my eyes just in time to see a short elderly woman in a purple silk dress fling her "Y" hand toward my head.

"Whoa! Hey! Look out!" I shout.

But she doesn't hear me. She smacks the back of her hand right into my face.

Literally. *Into* my face. Her hand goes *through*.

Or stops somewhere in the middle of my brain. I don't know. I can't see where it lands and I don't feel anything. I just see the hand zip toward my eyes, disappear, and then zip away again a second later.

Whoa.

I take a deep breath, although I have no idea if I'm actually physically breathing right now. I mean, if I had lungs,

I'd have a solid body . . . and if I had a body, the old woman would have smacked against it, right?

I drop to the floor as the Village People call out another "Y." Getting impaled might not hurt me, but it's weird enough to make me dizzy and a little nauseous. I'll avoid it if I can.

I reach into my back pocket to text Jenna what's going on, but then I remember I left the phone on the bed in Eddy's room. I also notice that the couple of dollars I had stuffed into the pocket aren't there anymore. The locket, however, is still tucked into my palm. I slip its chain over my neck and go over the three things I've learned in the last two seconds:

1. Wherever I am, people can't see, hear, or touch me.

2. Nothing comes with me but the clothes I'm wearing and the locket.

3. "YMCA" will never die.

Looking down, I'm not shocked to see I'm on a dance floor covered with boogeying people, so I crawl between them until I get to an open space where I can stand and check everything out.

It's definitely some kind of big-deal formal event. All the guys are in suits or even tuxes, all the women in gowns.

There's a stage at the front of the room where a DJ rocks out to the record, making all the arm motions and revving people up each time the chorus comes around, shouting, "Come on . . . you all know what to do!" The dance floor is crowded, but there are still plenty of people sitting at round tables scattered throughout the room. I scan them for someone I know, and maybe a clue about why Dad sent me here.

"Oh, hey!" I cry, waving my arm in the air. "Amanda!"

It's one of Mom's friends, her first employee at Catches Falls, and she's sitting at a table with a guy I think is her date and two other couples. She clearly didn't hear me, so I run over to her . . . and only remember I'm some kind of invisible ghost creature when a waiter with a tray of steak dinners walks right through me.

Mmmm . . . steak. It smells really good. And the fries with it are the kind my mom and I like best—thin and crisp and . . . I'm salivating right now, they smell so amazing. Seriously, no one would mind if I snuck one off a plate, right? They can't see me. They won't even notice.

I run up to the waiter and reach for the easiest prey—a French fry so long it sticks way off the plate. I can snag it without even shifting anything else. I pinch it between my fingers . . . but my fingers go right through. Of course they do. My fingers aren't really here. Neither is my mouth, tongue, or stomach. I need to lodge an official complaint with my dad's spirit. It's so not cool to let me smell amazing things and not taste them.

Giving up on the food, I turn back to Amanda. I stand behind her and try to get her attention, but there's no way. I can't even get a good look at her face or hear what she's saying because the room's too noisy and she's bent over in close conversation with the other people at the table.

Guess there's one way to change that. I move to the spot directly across from Amanda, take a deep breath, and walk *through* the table until I'm standing with the floral centerpiece lodged somewhere around my liver. I duck down lower so I can see Amanda's face more clearly.

"Hey, Amanda!" I say, even though I know she can't hear me. "You look amazing. You were so skinny before. Mom and I used to worry. But seriously, you're gorgeous. And is this your boyfriend? *Very* cute. So tell me, what's this party all about?"

I stay silent now and listen to the conversation around me. It's not much to go on. Gossip about people I don't even know. And while it's kind of fascinating to imagine which dance floor demon Leanna might be and why she's dating yet *another* married man, I have work to do. I'm about to leave the table and look around some more when Amanda looks beyond me and lights up, excited.

"Oh! Oh! It's happening!" she shouts. "I want to see this. Everybody be quiet!"

I wheel around toward the dance floor and stage and see that the rest of the room feels the same way. The dance floor is empty except for the DJ, who stands next to a giant tiered cake that someone rolled into place.

So it's a wedding, then. Got it.

My throat suddenly closes. Is it *my* wedding? Why else would Amanda be here if it wasn't my wedding? I mean, we're not super close but my mom would totally invite her to my wedding.

Why am I getting married in three years? I'll only be twenty!

Who am I marrying in three years?

I start to hyperventilate. I should probably breathe into a paper bag, but I couldn't grab one if I wanted to. Another note to Spirit of Dad: ghost body should not have freak-out abilities when there's nothing I can do about them.

"Ladies and gentlemen, it's time for cake!" the DJ cries cheesily. "You know what to do, happy couple. . . ."

He grins toward one of the tables, but everyone is standing now and even though I crane my neck, I can't see who's sitting there. Then I remember I'm Ms. Ghost Body with a centerpiece lodged in my abdomen and push my way forward, but I only get a few steps before I see the bride and groom. They're on the dance floor now, but the bride isn't me. I can only see her from the back, but she has brown curls. Did I dye and curl my hair? She also kind of looks shorter than me. Do I shrink in three years?

The groom turns first, and I'm sorry, but I ghost-vomit a little in my mouth. I don't want to be mean, but he's *old*. Like, older than my mom old. And he's not hot-older-guy old either. He's weirdly tall, with gangly alien-dude arms and legs and a bald spot so large and shiny you could burn ants with the light that lasers off it. The hair he lacks on his head is all over his face, in a bushy blond mustache and beard.

This can't be my wedding. Mom would never let me get married to this man. Not in three years. This is insane. I want to find her and scream at her to tell me what's going on, but then the bride turns around and the universe socks me in the stomach.

My mom is the bride. The beautiful, glowing, smiling bride. She's holding a piece of wedding cake just like the groom and they beam at each other as she reaches up and he reaches down to delicately feed each other a single bite, before the groom runs his finger through the frosting and dollops it on Mom's nose.

Everyone applauds and cheers, but I run to the stage and get in their faces.

"I object!" I scream. "I object on the grounds that you are married to Reinaldo Falciano and you *love* him!"

No one's paying attention to me, least of all my mom, who lets Ant-Burner-Head sweep her into his arms for a dance to some Frank Sinatra song, which is completely ridiculous because Mom *hates* Sinatra, and she and Dad always laughed that the whole Rat Pack thing was totally overrated, so why on earth would she dance to it at her wedding, especially when she's already married!

The dance floor is quickly filling up, but Gangly Limbs stands a full head taller than anyone else in the universe, so I still see him across the room. I stalk toward him, completely ignoring the couples I walk through on the way, until he and my mom are right in front of me. Mom's in his arms, smiling up at him like he's the dreamiest man alive.

Then someone in the room starts clinking a fork against their glass. I hear the *tap-tap-tapp*ing from somewhere behind me, and I freeze because I've been to a wedding before, and I know what that means. When the glass clinks, the bride and groom have to kiss.

"Hey!" I shout. "Who's doing that? Cut it out!"

But it doesn't stop. Soon the clinking sound rings out from everywhere. Mom and Giant Bobblehead tear their eyes away from one another to smile at the crowd; then he leans down and—

"Whoa!" I shout. "No! Cut it out! That's my *mom*! Get off her!"

I try to swat Mr. Scruffy Face away from her, but my hand flies right through his body. I'm whacking at air, while he and my mom lip lock for just this side of an eternity. Finally they pull away from one another and smile at the room. Everyone applauds and awwws.

"Uh-uh," I call to the room. "No aws. This is not an aw moment. You understand, people?"

Across the room, someone else clinks a glass.

"Are you kidding me?" I shout, wheeling in that direction. "They *just* kissed. Let the people breathe!"

The clinking continues.

"That's it," I say. "I'm confiscating silverware."

I march to the closest table and stop short. Three seats

are empty, but at the others are Reenzie, Carrie, J.J., Ames, some guy I don't know, and . . . is that Jack? It looks like him, but a really hot version of him. He's got to be around four inches taller than the Jack I know, and instead of baby fat and freckles he has cheekbones and manscaped facial scruff. He's even wearing a tuxedo, and as far as I can tell there's no Marvel character on it anywhere.

"You guys!" I cry. "It's so good to see you! If you're here, that means we're all still friends in three years! You all look amazing! You especially, Jack. I mean, like, wow! And you!" I add, turning to the guy next to Jack. "I don't even know you, but you look great too! Are you a friend of mine from college?"

He doesn't answer, which I forgive since of course he can't hear me. I actually seem to have arrived in the middle of some drama, because Reenzie looks furious enough to bite through a china plate.

"You had to know it was coming, Reenzie," Jack says. "Weddings are hookup central."

"I know," Reenzie says. "But he's supposed to be hooking up with *me*. He said we'd be here as a *couple*. And look— right in front of everyone! It's embarrassing!"

She looks over her shoulder and I follow her gaze to the next table. The only people sitting there are Sean and some girl I've never seen before in my life. I don't get a great look at her now either, since she and Sean are attached at the tongue.

Reenzie spins back around and rolls her eyes.

"Seriously?" I ask her. "Sean's cheating on you right in your face? Ew!"

"Drink," Ames suggests. She is wearing one of her skin-tight dresses, this one in bright purple. She's seat dancing while balancing some kind of frothy cocktail that sloshes a little as she moves. "Open bar. It'll make you feel better."

She takes a giant swig of the cocktail, and I notice everyone else at the table exchange glances.

"What?" I ask. "What's the deal? Isn't it three years from now? She's twenty-one. She can drink, right?"

Again I get no answer. Carrie puts her hand on top of Reenzie's. "I say you forget Sean," she says. "You don't need him. You're on different paths. You're top of your class at Stanford. You'll be president one day. He's a Division Two quarterback with bad grades and no future."

"Wow," I say. "Thanks for the update, but . . . harsh."

"Preach it, girl," Ames says. She raises her glass in a toast and downs the rest of the drink. Carrie shoots her an annoyed look.

"Okay, I get it now," I say. "Ames isn't just drinking; she's *drunk*."

Carrie turns back to Reenzie and continues her thought. "I'm just saying, high school relationships aren't meant to be forever."

"Ooooh!" Ames exclaims way too loudly, leaning heavily onto J.J.'s shoulder. "She just burned you!"

J.J. smiles tightly.

"Except *us*," Carrie clarifies to J.J. "We're the exception that proves the rule. Right, Forrvee?"

"*Forrvee?*"

I say it at the same time as the guy next to Jack. J.J. blushes bright red, and as I look at him, I notice for the first time that he's the only guy at the table not wearing a tux. He's in a suit that I'm pretty sure I've seen before, so he's had it for at least three years. And unlike Jack, who got more buff over the last three years, J.J. seems a little thinner than before, with dark circles under his eyes.

"J.J. came up with it, Nathan," Carrie explains. Not to me, of course, but to the guy next to Jack—Nathan! "It's an anagram for 'forever.' I love you, Forrvee."

She leans over and kisses J.J., and I'm very glad my actual stomach is three years in the past or I'd definitely vomit.

"Hey! How come you guys aren't dancing?" a voice asks, and I spin to see Taylor walking over from the dance floor.

"Tee!" I cry. "You look gorgeous!"

It's true. Unlike the perfectly styled Reenzie, Taylor looks naturally stunning. Her long blond hair flows halfway down her back, and she wears a simple cream-colored dress and heels.

"We're not dancing because the two of you look like Cinderella and Prince Charming," Nathan says. "The rest of us can't stack up."

"Two of you?" I ask. "You have a new guy?"

As I ask, a ridiculously gorgeous guy sidles up behind Taylor. "Aw, come on. You sell yourself short," he says to Nathan.

"You're Taylor's boyfriend?" I ask. I look him up and down and notice he's taller than Tee, even though she's in heels. He's also seriously polite. He holds two drinks but puts them down on the table so he can pull out a chair for her first. Before she sits, she wraps her arms around him and they kiss, and I'm blown away by how striking they are together. They're both beautiful, but there's also something about her pale skin, blond hair, and cream dress against his dark skin, hair, and tux that fits perfectly, like a yin and yang. And it's not just their looks. There's an energy between them that just feels right.

I lean my face right between them as they pull apart. "I like him!" I say. "Good job!"

"So I forget," Nathan says when Tee and her boyfriend are sitting. "How'd you two meet again?"

"Yeah, how?" I ask.

Taylor and her boyfriend share a giddy smile.

"You tell him," Tee says.

"No, you."

"No, you."

"Ugh, gag me," Reenzie moans. "*No one* tell him. I can't deal right now." She turns to Nathan. "Tee and Drew met senior year of high school. End of story."

My nerve endings all perk up. "Senior year? That's now! I mean . . . *my* now. I mean . . . cool!"

"I'm bored," Ames sighs. She grabs Jack's drink, climbs clumsily onto her chair, raises the glass in the air, and shouts to the room, "Gwen Falls just got married! *Conga line!!!!*"

She hops down, sloshing most of the drink onto herself, slugs down the rest, then congas her way onto the dance floor. Amazingly, a long line of people form a train behind her and join in.

"She is mortifying," Reenzie declares.

"She's Amalita," Carrie says, as if that explains everything.

"Hey, that's mean," I say. "She's drunk at a wedding. It's not like she's always like this . . . right?"

Then Carrie spins to J.J. "Let's join in. We haven't danced all night. It'll be fun."

J.J. raises his eyebrows. "You sure you're up for it?"

Carrie rolls her eyes. "Worry wart. Besides, she's in the mood to *move!*"

For a second I think Carrie's talking about herself in the third person. Then she pushes back her chair and stands and I see the giant pregnant belly stretching out of her dress. Carrie grabs J.J.'s hand and puts it on the ginormous lump. "See? She's already dancing! She just wants her mommy and daddy to join in!"

J.J. smiles, but his face pales.

"NO!" I gasp. "No-no-no-no-no." I walk through the table to get in J.J.'s face. "What did you do? I mean, I know what you did, but . . . seriously? Is this for real?"

The minute Carrie and J.J. are gone, Nathan leans across the table to Reenzie and drops his voice. "Okay, you have to spill. Jack tells it like it's a major soap opera. Is it true? She trapped him with the baby?"

"What, you don't believe me?" Jack asks. "She *totally* trapped him. And they weren't even together. He broke up with her six months before it happened."

"But it's not like he was forced," Taylor says. "He didn't have to—"

"He wouldn't have if he knew what she was planning!" Jack shouts a little too loud for the room, and Nathan puts his hand on Jack's arm. Jack looks at the guy . . . lovingly? Then he puts his own hand on top of the guy's.

My head is still reeling from J.J. and Carrie, but I lean down and put my face closer to the guys' so I can check this out. Something's happening here.

"Hold up," I say. "Are you guys . . . together?"

"Look, Jack," Reenzie says, "I'm with you. I think they're throwing their lives away. But it's their choice. How would you and Nathan feel if J.J. got all upset about your choice?"

Nathan smiles. "Did she seriously just say being gay is a choice?" he asks Jack.

"I warned you," Jack says, though he doesn't seem angry. "She and Amalita are the two."

"So you *are* together!" I say, grinning at Jack. "So all your jokes and lusting after Carrie . . . what was that, a cover? Why didn't you just tell us?"

A glass clinks across the room. I wheel to the sound

and expect to see my mom kissing Giganto Groom, but instead I see something worse. It's my brother, Erick, at age sixteen, and apparently he gets even more serious about the weight training, because his neck is as thick as a tree, with veins snaking up from his tuxedo collar. He's several shades too tan and wears a sleazy thin mustache. And mirrored aviator sunglasses. Inside. At his mom's wedding.

Immediately I know I must have gone away to college. No way would I let Erick do this to himself. And who's the bleach-blonde sitting next to him with the pushed-up boobs and spray tan? Don't even tell me that's his girlfriend. She has to be in her twenties! He's thirteen! Okay, *sixteen* since it's three years later, but still!

Erick's been talking, but I've been too stunned to pay attention. I start listening now and quickly gather that he's making some kind of toast.

". . . and it's a great thing to see our mom so happy. Autumn, you have anything to add?"

I freeze. I'm about to see myself, three years in the future! I'm about to *hear* myself make a toast! What will I say? Will I make a huge scene and scream at everyone for forgetting my dad? Or I bet I'll be cleverer than that. I'll say something that sounds nice and supportive. Only when everyone plays it back later in their heads will they realize how much I'm against this travesty.

I wait for me to stand up, but it doesn't happen. What's going on? Even Erick looks concerned. "Really, Autumn?" he asks. "Are you sure?"

Then I see me. I'm crouched low in my seat at a corner of Erick's table. I'm wearing a blue sheath dress that's so gorgeous I should totally be owning the room, but I shrink into it. I look thin, but not healthy thin. Gaunt. And my hair . . . it's not even orange anymore. It's mouse-poop brown.

Erick asks me again if I want to speak, but I shake my head, keeping my eyes focused on the plate in front of me.

Blood starts pounding in my ears. Something is terribly wrong with me. Am I sick? Am I dying? Did something bad happen to me? Why do I look like that? Why am I acting that way?

"I still can't believe that's Autumn," Nathan whispers to Jack. "That's not how you described her at all."

"She's different now," Jack says.

"She's been different for a long time," Reenzie clarifies. "Since that panic attack senior year. She was so freaked out about everyone splitting up and leaving, she lost it. Wouldn't send out any college applications. Which was stupid because then everyone *did* leave and she was stuck here alone."

"I told her she should go to community college and transfer," Tee says, "but she wouldn't. She got a job working the front desk at Century Acres and kind of fell off the grid. I haven't even seen her in a year. None of us have."

"Really?" Nathan asks. "But she invited you to the wedding."

Jack shakes his head. "I told you—*Gwen* invited us. She thought maybe seeing us all would help Autumn."

"*Something* better help her," Reenzie sighs, "or Gwen'll be stuck with Autumn living in her old room forever. Not what she wants with a new man in her life."

"Reenzie," Taylor scolds.

"What? It's the truth. Autumn's a mess. If you ask me, there's only one thing that could make it better, and that's . . ."

"What?!" I scream when she doesn't finish the sentence. "What'll make it better?!?!?"

4

september/october, senior year

"Ow, my ear!" Jenna wails. "Stop screaming!"

I'm hyperventilating. I know everything has changed, but it takes a second to make any sense of it at all. I'm on Eddy's bed. Eddy's still asleep in her chair. My cell phone's on the bedspread in front of me. That's where Jenna's voice is coming from.

I pick up the phone. "Jenna?"

"Of course it's me. I just said—" Her voice stops, and when it comes back it's breathy and excited. "Oh my God, you just went, didn't you? You went and it brought you back like a second after you left, so no time passed at all. What was it like? What did you see?"

The more I look around Eddy's room, the more everything I saw feels like a dream. Already, some of the details are slipping away, like my brain can't handle them and wants to pretend they never existed. I rush to say the details out loud, just to cement them all in my head.

"It was horrible," I say, and my voice sounds cracked and harsh. "It was my mom's wedding, and—"

"Your mom's getting *married*?" Jenna gasps. "In *three years*? Were you and I totally freaking out?"

"You weren't there," I realize.

"What do you mean I wasn't there? Why wouldn't I be at your mom's wedding? Your mom would totally invite me to her wedding!" She stops for a second, then squeaks. "Oh my God . . . am I dead?"

"You're not dead," I assure her.

"How do you know?! Did someone *say* I wasn't dead?"

"Jenna!" I snap. "Listen! You're not dead! It wasn't about that. It's everything else. It's all messed up."

I tell her everything I saw. Sure, there were some good things, like Taylor finding the perfect guy and Jack out of the closet and happy, but most of it was absolutely horrible.

"I don't get it!" I finish. "Why would my dad's spirit give me a locket that lets me know I'll be a complete loser?"

"He wouldn't," Jenna says. "We talked about this before, remember? It's why you can't use the locket to go back in time. The past is done. The future you can change. Your dad doesn't *want* your mom to marry this guy. He doesn't want you to be a complete loser. He doesn't want me to be dead."

"You weren't dead."

"You have no proof of that. What I'm saying is he showed you all that stuff so you can make changes now and stop all the bad parts from happening."

I nod, taking it in. "Okay. Okay, that makes sense. But what do I do first? Do I break up Reenzie and Sean so he doesn't cheat on her? Do I steal Erick's weights so he doesn't become a muscle meathead? And how do I get Carrie's tubes tied without her knowing it?"

"All good plans," Jenna says, "but maybe harder than you need. You know the butterfly effect?"

"Yes, it's a Kyler Leeds song," I say.

"Ew, really?"

"Come on, it's good! I have it on my phone; I'll play it for you."

"Please don't," Jenna says. Now that I actually know Kyler Leeds and he's done nice things for me, Jenna puts him down far less than she used to, but she still thinks his music's unforgivably cheesy. "The butterfly effect is that thing that says something tiny, like a butterfly flapping its wings, can have this huge domino effect of changes that makes things really different."

"So I need to get a butterfly?" I ask.

"No. You need to concentrate on one thing that's easy to change. Changing that will change everything else. Then the next time you go to the future, it'll be totally different."

That makes sense, and it's not hard to figure out the easiest thing to change.

"Reenzie said everything got bad for me when I freaked out about everyone leaving and I wouldn't apply to school. So I won't freak out. I'll make myself the perfect college candidate, so applying won't be a big deal at all."

52

"Yes. Excellent. Sounds perfect."

"You'll hold me to it?" I ask. "You'll make sure I don't slack off?"

"Of course I will. My life depends on it, remember?"

I don't bother telling Jenna again that she wasn't dead in the future I saw. She won't believe me anyway, and the truth is she's right—technically I guess she could have been. We talk for a little more and then I slip out, leaving Eddy asleep in her chair. I call the pizza place before I leave Century Acres, so Erick's and my dinner will show up soon after I get home. Before it does, I hop on my computer and sign up for the very next available SAT date, three weeks away at the beginning of October. I didn't do so great when I took the test last spring, but back then I figured I'd just let it slide and trust that I'd get in *somewhere*. Now I know that's not good enough. I want a *lot* of colleges to choose from. That's why I choose a test date so close—if I flame out again, I'll have time for another retest. I'd rather not do that, though, so I also sign up for an online prep class that practically *guarantees* at least a two-hundred-point jump in scores. Perfect.

By the time I'm done, our pizza arrives. Erick tells me to give his slices to Schmidt, our basset hound. Erick would rather make a smoothie out of some protein powder Mom apparently got him last week.

"Ugh, you sound like Jenna's last boyfriend," I say. "He was this total musclehead."

"Jenna likes guys with muscles?" Erick asks, intrigued.

"*Some* muscles," I say. "This guy was one of those work-out heads who got so huge he couldn't lower his arms all the way. And eating with him was a nightmare. He wouldn't put anything in his mouth but protein shakes. She dumped him after their second date."

"Really?" he asks, sitting down and grabbing a slice of pizza. "Even though he was ripped?"

I smile inwardly. The story's a complete fake, but Erick has always been disgustingly in love with Jenna, and if he thinks she doesn't like her guys bulked up, maybe it'll save him from his 'roid-rage future.

Mom gets home late, but I'm still awake, and she's thrilled when I tell her about the pizza. She grabs a slice and a diet soda and takes them to the couch. I curl up with Schmidt on my lap and sit with her while she eats. She's totally impressed when I tell her about my new SAT date and prep class; then she fills me in on all the construction drama at the new Catches Falls branch.

The whole time we talk, there's a question I'm dying to ask, but it's so the kind of thing I never thought I'd say to my mom that I can't imagine getting the words past my tongue. I have to stare down at her pizza and address the question to her uneaten crust rather than to her face.

"Mom . . . have you thought about . . . I mean, are you . . ." Ugh, even asking the crust is hard. I close my eyes and blurt it out. "You're not dating anyone, are you?"

Mom chokes on her soda.

"No!" she says. "Autumn, what would make you even ask that?"

Other than seeing her get married? "I don't know, I just . . ." Inspiration! "I had this weird dream that you were getting married again and—"

I don't mean to well up. I don't. I honestly have no idea it's coming. It's just that I see her in my head in that wedding dress with that strange guy, and from where I'm sitting I can see my mom and dad's *real* wedding picture on the coffee table in the other room, and the next thing I know I'm starting to cry and Schmidt's licking my face and Mom's running around to sit next to me and put her arm around my shoulders.

"Oh, baby," she says. "It's okay."

"I'm sorry." I sniff. "I don't know why I was thinking about it—"

I sob and Mom rubs my back.

"It's normal," she says. "It's totally normal to wonder about that. But look at me, Autumn."

I meet her eyes. They're reaching out to mine, full of strength and certainty.

"Your father was the love of my life. There's no one else, and I'm not looking for anyone else. I have you, I have Erick, I have Schmidt and Eddy and my work and my friends. . . . My life is full. Okay?"

I sniff again, and nod.

Later, while I'm brushing my teeth, I wonder if I already

changed the future. I didn't do anything big, just signed up for a test and a class and had a couple conversations, but maybe it was enough. When I get back to my room, I yank on the chain and pull the locket out from under my shirt. I open it and make sure it's still set for my mother's potential wedding day, but before I can snap it shut, I notice something.

The little number in the top window—the one that used to show a 10—now shows a 9. I can't imagine why. None of the other numbers in the locket have moved, and this one doesn't even have a dial next to it. The number changed all by itself, sometime after I made that first jump.

Chills crawl over my skin as I realize what it means.

"It's a countdown," I whisper.

It has to be. It was at 10, I made one jump, and now it's at 9.

The locket isn't like the diary or the map. I can't use it as much as I want. I have ten jumps and that's it.

I decide not to jump again just yet. If my jumps are limited, I need to use them more carefully. I need to accomplish more in the present before I check back in on the future. I need to make sure my life can't possibly turn out the way I saw.

On Monday I harass Erick to speed up his morning grooming routine—which these days takes *way* longer than my own—so Mom can drive us both to school early and I can visit the guidance counselor before classes start.

"Ms. Falls!" he cries when he sees me, and springs up

from the largest beanbag chair in the office. Mr. Winthrop had some kind of epiphany over the summer, I guess, and decided he'd get more guidance customers if he became a "cool" teacher. For him that meant ditching his desk and chair and replacing them with an assortment of beanbags, a thick plushy rug, and a giant chalkboard where anyone who comes in can scribble down whatever's on their mind. As far as I know, Jack and J.J. are the only people who use the board. They sneak in whenever Mr. Winthrop isn't there and write innocuous anagrams for the most disgusting phrases they can come up with. Today the board says "aging toad goon," but I can only imagine what the letters spell rearranged.

"After last winter, I thought I'd lost you," Mr. Winthrop says.

Last winter was the last time I tried to reinvent myself. I was dating J.J. and feeling suffocated, plus I wound up losing all my friends due to map complications, so I threw myself into becoming the best possible college applicant ever. I was pretty amazing at it and have a single semester of admissions office perfection to show for it. But then I got my friends back and wanted, oh, a life, so I fell off the wagon a little bit.

"You did," I agree, "but I'm back and I'm all in. How do I get colleges begging for me?" I tell him I'm already on the SAT part; it's the other things I need help with.

"Well," he says, "there's the obvious: grades and teacher recommendations."

"Study hard and kiss up to the teachers," I echo. "Got it."

Mr. Winthrop doesn't think "kissing up" is exactly right, but I'm still pretty sure it's what he means. For a second I consider giving a Catches Falls puppy to each of my teachers as a big win-win. The puppies find homes and my teachers love me for bringing them joy!

With my luck all my teachers would be allergic. Maybe I need a better plan.

"Beyond that it's your extracurriculars," Mr. Winthrop says. "Are you still following your singular life's passion to improve the lives of the elderly by volunteering at Century Acres?"

"Did I say that was my singular passion?" I ask.

"You're not volunteering there anymore?"

"I *was* . . ." Right up until I found out Lame Future Me works at the Century Acres front desk. Now I think I'm more likely to change my future if I avoid the place except for Eddy visits. I try to explain this to Mr. Winthrop without giving anything away, but he just looks at me like I'm crazy. Then he reminds me that colleges love "arrows," kids who follow one passion and see it through, no matter what. He urges me to come up with some kind of extracurricular that at least seems similar to helping the elderly, even if it's not at Century Acres.

I'm still thinking about the problem at lunch, and my plan is to bounce it off all my friends. But when I see them sprawled out in a circle on the lawn where we always eat, all I can think about is them at my mom's wedding. Sean in particular. He's sitting there next to Reenzie with his arm draped over her shoulders, but he's looking across the lawn at a bunch of way-too-cute freshman girls wearing tiny tanks and shorts.

"Seriously, Sean?" I ask as I plop down between Taylor and Amalita with my tray of barely edible cafeteria food. "Your girlfriend's right next to you. Stop looking at those girls."

Sean's blue eyes get scattered and confused. "What girls?"

"Belly shirts and navel rings? Hot new blood? It's totally not cool for you to scope out when you already have the hottest girl on campus." As an exclamation point I chomp into my hot dog.

Sean crinkles his forehead in a way that is empirically completely adorable, regardless of the fact that he's off-limits and a cheating cad.

"What are you talking about?" he asks. "I'm watching those guys throw the football."

He nods across the lawn and I see that just beyond the girl-candy are indeed a couple of freshman jocks tossing a football back and forth.

"I like that *you're* checking the belly shirts, though," Jack says with a wicked leer. "And I *really* like when you talk about how hot Reenzie is. Reminds me of a dream I had last night." He waggles his eyebrows lasciviously.

"Oh please," I shoot back. "Like you actually—"

I stop myself before I inadvertently out him right here

at lunch. Truthfully, I think he'd be happier if he just told us all the truth and stopped pretending so hard, but it's his choice and his timing and it's not my place to push him into anything. Instead I play along and grin right back. "Like you actually could handle Reenzie and me in the same dream."

"Ew. Tell you what. You stop dreaming about me," she says to Jack. "And *you* . . . ," she adds to me, "you can go ahead and remind Sean how hot I am anytime you want."

"You don't have to remind me how hot Carrie is," J.J. says, smiling down at his girlfriend.

"Awww," Carrie coos, "because you already know?"

"No," he deadpans. "'Cause you keep reminding me yourself."

Carrie gasps, offended, and stomps across the field. J.J. has to chase her down and beg her not to leave. "It was a joke, Carrie! It was a joke! I'm sorry! I love you! You're gorgeous! You're the most beautiful girl I've ever seen!"

I lean over to Amalita and speak softly. "You know she left her bag here."

Amalita rolls her eyes. "She was never going anywhere. She just likes him to chase her."

Ames takes a big swig from her water bottle.

At least, I think it's a water bottle. It's hot pink and I can't see what's inside it.

"Whatcha drinking?" I ask.

Ames grins. "Cosmopolitan. Want some?"

My jaw drops and I look around before I lean closer and hiss, "Amalita! The school has a zero tolerance policy! You could get expelled!"

"*Relajese,*" Ames laughs. "It's *agua.* You think I'm insane?"

J.J. and Carrie plop back into their spot, but this time Carrie uses J.J. as a human lounge chair, resting her back against his chest and her arms on his knees while J.J. wraps his arms around her.

"In case it wasn't clear," J.J. tells us all. "I was joking. Carrie never reminds me that she's beautiful. I know it for myself."

"Good boy," Carrie says, like J.J.'s a well-behaved pooch.

"So here's something interesting," I say as lightly as possible. "I read this thing in the newspaper about under-age drinking. Sobering stuff."

"Why are we having this conversation?" Reenzie asks.

"Why are you reading a newspaper?" J.J. asks. "Who are you and what have you done with Autumn?"

His voice is playful, and my heart jumps a little. It's been a long time since J.J.'s teased me about anything. We used to go back and forth all the time, and we knew each other so well we could say a million things with just a look. I catch his eye and he smiles, but it only lasts a second before Carrie senses his attention isn't completely on her and leaps in with a subject change.

"So, Autumn, I saw you come out of Mr. Winthrop's office this morning," she says. "What's up?"

Jack snorts. "Did you see the 'aging toad goon' on the wall?"

"I did," I said. "Quite lovely." Then I decide as long as I have the group here, I'll get their help. "Here's the deal. If I want a college to love me, I need a lifelong passion that I can suddenly discover, cram into the next three months, and make colleges believe I've been all about it forever. Extra points if it's not wildly different from helping the elderly so I look all arrowy."

"Pretty sure that's not how it works," Taylor says. "A passion is a *passion*. Like me and theater. Or Sean and football. Or Amalita and—"

"Zander," Ames sighs as she sprawls out on the lawn. "The way that boy dances, *Dios mio*. I can't believe none of you were there Saturday night."

"That's good," J.J. says. "Colleges would love it if Autumn's passion was some guy who cut all his classes and partied every night. She'd get in everywhere."

"Don't mess, J.J.," Ames warns, jangling as she points a finger at him. "I've known you too long and there's too much I could say."

"Hey, back to me!" I say, breaking in before Ames blurts something hideous about J.J. and Carrie. "I'm serious. I need a stroke of extracurricular genius."

"Join me on the Senior Social Committee!" Carrie says. "We plan all the parties and events for the year, and we could really use some help."

I wince. Everyone I know of on the Senior Social Committee is like Carrie: perky people pleasers who get *really* excited about things like shiny confetti in cutesy animal shapes. Nothing wrong with that, just not really my style.

"Come on, Autumn, it's perfect!" Carrie says. "Colleges love the Committee Girls. They know we're responsible and motivated, and we can lead. *Plus* a lot of our events raise money for charity—including *elderly* charities—so it helps you with your arrow thing too!"

I'm not entirely sure I love the idea of getting more Carrie time, but she makes some great points.

"Okay," I relent. "I'm in."

"Yes!" Carrie screeches. "Welcome to the sisterhood! You'll meet me after school for your first meeting. We've only been back a week, but we're *deep* into Halloween dance planning—it's less than two months away—and we need some serious answers about which looks better: fake tarantulas or fake black widows."

I think she's joking, but when I meet with the "sisterhood" that afternoon, I realize there is absolutely no humor in what they do. They discuss the pros and cons of candy corn versus mellowcreme pumpkins with the same intensity that my mom and Eddy bring to issues of human rights in Cuba . . . or the way Jack and J.J. debate the merits of the *Millennium Falcon* over the Starship *Enterprise*. There's also a guy in the sisterhood. Gus is gay, and I worry that lumping him in as a "sister" is completely insulting, but when I bring it up he scoffs. Not only am I being way too sensitive, he says, but we on the committee have bigger issues to deal with—like mylar versus paper streamers.

Seriously? This is what colleges are into?

Whatever. At least now I have a passion for them, and the sisterhood becomes part of my hard-core new schedule. It's kind of like where I was last spring, only this time it's better because I'm not keeping busy to avoid a suffocating boyfriend. Instead, I'm changing my life. School days are all about my classes, and I spend my free periods getting a jump on homework so I can go home after Committee and dive into SAT prep. When I realize I'm having major trouble with my American history class because I can't read all those dates without them getting jumbled in my dyslexic head, I don't do my normal thing and figure I can handle it myself. I don't even bring the problem to ADAPT, the group I go to for kids with learning issues. Instead I go right to my teacher, Mrs. Foreman, and ask her for help. Not only does she promise to find me a tutor, but she also says she's very impressed by my initiative.

"Thanks," I say. Then, as I'm about to leave, I point to the water bottle she always keeps on her desk—the one decorated with the U.S. Constitution—and add, "I keep noticing your water bottle. It's so cool! Did you order it online?"

This leads to a ridiculously long conversation about the amazing things you can find on Amazon. It completely eats into my free period and a chance to do homework, but

I leave knowing Mr. Winthrop would be proud. Kissing up to a teacher? Done. Mrs. Foreman will write me a killer college recommendation—especially when I use the tutor she recommends to kill it in her class.

When SAT day comes, I'm not even nervous. Mom drives me, since I'm the only one I know taking them right now. Reenzie's spring score was practically perfect, so she's concentrating on APs; Sean's was fine for his football scholarship, and Taylor's was fine for her theater schools, which are more about her audition. Amalita did okay but she says standardized tests give her hives, so she'll do what I once thought I'd do and just let it be. J.J., Carrie, and Jack *are* taking the tests again, but not until November.

Unlike me, Mom's insanely nervous. "I still can't believe they turned down our request for accommodation," she snaps as she drives me to the test. "It's not right that you're penalized for working hard to keep up with your class!"

Since my dyslexia means reading can take more time for me than for other people, I applied for extra SAT time. They turned me down, on the grounds that I take tests with everyone else at school, so I should be fine. Mom's still furious about the injustice, but I'm over it. Plus I'm prepared. I could nail the SAT in *less* than the allotted time.

Okay, turns out that's a lie.

I end up not finishing, and I walk out of the test with a sore pencil hand and a raging headache, but I think I did really well. In fact, I kinda can't wait for the next two weeks to zip by so I can find out for sure.

I expect my mom to pick me up afterward, but instead it's her friend Amanda. She looks really young to me, and I can't figure out why until I remember the last time I saw her was at my mom's wedding . . . three years from now. "Sorry, Autumn," she says. "Contractor emergency. Your mom had to run out and talk to them at the new place. Wanna come hang with me and the pooches?"

If Mom's out, I'm sure they're shorthanded at Catches Falls, and I can always use some puppy therapy, so I say yes, and the minute I see the place I'm thrilled I did. Catches Falls isn't huge. It's a single storefront in the middle of a strip mall, but Mom's a genius and put a puppy play area right by the big front window. People can't help it. They always stop, check out the pups, and most of the time come in. Even if they don't take a dog themselves, they volunteer or give a donation, so the place does really well. That's why she's working on the new location. It's not on a popular walking street like this one, but it can hold a lot more dogs, and it'll have a big outdoor area with a giant yard and a doggie swimming/wading pool shaped like a bone.

The current location isn't as plush, but it's still fantastic. It's clean and open, with separate play corrals for puppies and medium-sized dogs. The new place will be able to handle bigger dogs, too, but right now Mom finds foster homes for those. Between all the corrals is a retail area where Mom sells leashes, treats, and all kinds of other doggie merch that she totally admits is overpriced, but the profits go to the rescue dogs' care.

The minute Amanda and I get inside, I use the Purell wall dispenser and race into the puppy pen, then plop onto a low chair that would be right at home inside Mr. Winthrop's office. Immediately I'm inundated with puppies. Four of them jump onto my lap and jockey for space, while one keeps leaping into my face to lick my nose.

"Hi, babies!" I coo. "Yes, I love you too! I do! I love all of you!"

"Cute," a man's voice says from the other side of the low puppy pen wall. I figure it's a potential adopter, so I put on a big smile and turn to him, ready to make the hard sell . . . but instead I scream.

The man looks alarmed. "Are you okay? Did one of them bite you?"

"No, no, it's not that," I say. "It's . . ."

But then my mouth kind of hangs there, open, because I'm completely out of words.

I know this guy. I've seen his too-long body with its gangly limbs before. I've seen his shiny nearly bald head with the thin fringe of yellow fur that seems to cascade down his sideburns into his far-too-bushy blond mustache and beard.

He raises his yellow eyebrows and peers down at me. "Is everything all right?"

No, I want to say. *No, it's not all right at all, because you're the guy my mom's going to marry in three years, and I'm not okay with it at all!*

Then my heart starts thudding against my chest because I suddenly understand what's happening. This guy is here because *this* is the day he and Mom are supposed to meet! This is the moment I can change her future and make sure the wedding never happens! All I have to do is make sure the two of them never lay eyes on one another.

"Hey, everyone!" my mother's voice calls from the rear of the store. "I'm back!"

Seriously?!?!

Fate is moving faster than me, but it's not over yet. Mom will stop in the bathroom to wash up before she gets near the dogs. She always does that when she first comes in the store. That gives me about thirty seconds to make a move, because something tells me that if Mom and this guy even make eye contact, it's all over.

I leap to my feet and furiously scratch my arms and legs.

"The dogs didn't bite me," I explain. "It's the *fleas*."

"Fleas?" he asks, wide-eyed.

I cross my hands and rake my fingers up and down my arms, hopping from leg to leg like the itchiness is unbearable. "It's the worst," I say. "You're not feeling it?"

He reaches a hand to his bald head and gives a tentative scratch. I want to smile but instead scratch at my neck and bounce miserably. "Ugh, I can't even take it!"

"I think I see them jumping," he says, lightly scratching at his own neck. "Little black spots, right?"

I give a final all-over scratch and then shake my head. "I'm out. I can't deal."

I push out of the puppy pen and out the front door. I don't look back, but I can hear and feel him following right behind. I walk to the nail salon two doors down before I turn around and face him, still scratching at my arms. "Did you get bit?"

"Maybe," he says, absently scratching his forearm. "Glad to be out of there, though. Thanks for the heads-up!" He walks off the curb and into the parking lot, still scratching at phantom itches, and I keep watching until he gets into his car and drives away. Only then do I stop pretending to scratch my own fake bites and smile.

I have to say, it's been a pretty amazing day. No horrible new husband for Mom, doubtlessly stellar SAT scores for myself . . . How could it possibly get any better?

I grin as I think of a way. I glance around. There's a bunch of people walking to and from their cars and ducking in and out of the stores, but everyone's minding their own business. No one will notice if I pop out for a bit, especially since Jenna and I established that I won't even be gone for a nanosecond in their time. Still, just to be safe I push myself up against the brick wall between the nail salon and a Chinese restaurant before I tug on the chain around my neck and pull out my dad's locket. I smile at the *zemi* on the cover.

"I think we did it, Dad," I say. "I think we changed everything. Let's check."

I open the locket to make sure nothing shifted. It's still set for the exact same date as last time. Then I close the lid, grip the locket tight, and concentrate.

Show me what I did, Daddy. Show me how things are different than they were before.

5

three years later

I'm in a hallway. It's very stark and white. White walls, white shiny floor, white fluorescent lights. Lots of doors. The place is instantly familiar somehow, but I can't put my finger on why.

The loud *clip-clop* of shoes gets my attention, and I spin around.

"Yes!" I shout happily. "Look at you! You're gorgeous! You look amazing!"

I'm talking to myself, weirdly enough, but a me who looks a million times better than the frumpy folded-into-herself nothing I met up with last time. This me wears gorgeous dark-wash designer jeans, knee-high black quilted boots, and a fitted black leather jacket with zippers in places that don't even make sense but look seriously hot. I carry a small black wristlet, and my hair . . . This me is a girl who wouldn't dream of dyeing her hair a mousy blend-in brown. My hair is so vibrantly orange I swear it shoots off rays like the sun, and my makeup and jewelry are so perfect I could give tips to Amalita or Reenzie.

I race up to myself, beyond excited to see me.

"I'm so proud of you, girl!" I say, though Future Me is in a serious hurry and doesn't break stride for even a second. She just keeps on walking, so I fall into step next to her and just keep talking. "You totally pulled it together, didn't you? It was the SATs, right? And the Senior Social Committee, and I bet you totally nailed all your first semester grades. Amazing college, amazing new friends, amazing new life . . . So why do you look so serious? What's up?"

Future Me has her beautifully glossed lips pursed in a straight line, and her face is complete no-nonsense. She has the same determined look I've seen on every kick-butt action hero Scarlett Johansson has ever played, and for a split second I wonder if I really am a trained assassin on a case. Or maybe I'm in a movie *playing* a trained assassin on a case.

Of course, then there would be cameras and directors and other actors around.

"Oh, Autumn, thank goodness."

I'm so busy staring at myself I don't even notice my mom until I hear her voice. She's right in front of Future Me and me. She wears white pants and a button-down red shirt with a laminated tag pinned to it that says *Aventura Hospital Volunteer*.

Hospital! Yes, that's why this place looks familiar. It's a hospital!

"Awww!" I cry as I realize Mom's not alone but has a big, gorgeous, brown-black-and-white furry Bernese mountain dog on a leash. The dog wears a red therapy-pet vest and is so well behaved he stops and lies down when Mom stops. I automatically bend down to pet him, but my ghostly hand goes right through him. If this were a movie, he'd pick up on my presence, but the dog has no clue I'm even there.

When I stand back up, Mom's hugging Future Me.

I can't help it. I glance behind Future Me's back to check out Mom's left hand.

No wedding ring, no engagement ring. And here it is, what would have been her wedding day in the other future.

"Score!" I shout. Then I call out in case the spirit of my dad can hear, "Okay, I still don't know how this works, but I'm good to go. I totally rock, Mom doesn't have the loser, she volunteers at the hospital, I come visit her . . . I'm ready to go."

Apparently, asking to leave the future doesn't do anything because I'm still here. I watch Mom pull out of the hug, but she keeps her hands on my upper arms and rubs up and down. Her eyes are teary and sympathetic, and I'm suddenly glad I didn't zip away. A warning tingle buzzes my nerves.

"Is he okay?" Future Me asks, and the tingle starts to hum. I look back and forth from Future Me to Mom, looking for answers.

"Is *who* okay?" I ask them. "Not Erick, right? Tell me it's not Erick."

Mom smiles sympathetically. "I'll take you to see him."

"Take us to see *who*?" I ask again, but I know all I can do is follow them as they walk down the hall. Actually, I walk ahead of them, backpedaling so I can try to read their faces. Future Me looks grim and Mom sympathetic, but neither of us is crying. If it was Erick in the hospital, wouldn't we be crying?

Is it Eddy?

"I'm sorry I couldn't pick you up from the airport," Mom says. "I hate that you flew all the way down from school and had to take an Uber, but I couldn't get anyone else to cover the therapy dog shift, and . . ."

The good: Mom just confirmed I go to college somewhere a plane ride away from Florida and her gig with the therapy dogs is a regular thing, which I know she must love. The bad: She's babbling. She only babbles when she's really upset and doesn't know what to say. I'm starting to get really nervous.

Then Mom smiles at something behind me, and I turn to see we've made it to a waiting room. It's filled with rows of industrial chairs broken up only by low tables covered in ancient magazines and a counter holding old-smelling coffee and broken-up cookies.

"Hey, guys," Future Me says, and smiles for the first time.

Now I see them: Reenzie, Taylor, and Amalita. They're on three of the chairs, Reenzie in the middle, their heads all bent together as they talk in low voices. When they get up to hug Future Me, I check them out. Reenzie wears the kind of black silk power suit I imagine her putting on to stride into a courtroom, except it's rumpled and askew, like she slept in it for several days. Taylor's in yoga pants and a sweatshirt, and Amalita wears one of her more sedate purple sheaths. All three of them look like they've been crying, though somehow Amalita's makeup is still absolutely perfect.

Mom walks up to the group hug and puts a hand on Future Me's shoulder. "You're in good hands. I have to take the dog to visit more patients. I love you." She gives Future Me's shoulder a squeeze and walks off while the group hug continues . . . and continues . . . and continues.

So my mom's not crying but my friends are. It's not a family member in the hospital, then. Is it one of us? Jack? Sean? J.J.?

I break into a sweat and start shaking my hands just to move and do *something*. "Okay, you guys are freaking me out," I tell the group hug. "I can't wait anymore. You have to tell me what happened."

Finally, they break out of the clutch.

"Have you seen him yet?" Future Autumn asks the girls.

Taylor and Ames shake their heads no, but Reenzie nods. "I flew in from Stanford the day it happened, when they airlifted him in from Tallahassee."

Amalita pulls a silver flask out of her bag and holds it out to Future Me. "It's the only way to handle this."

Taylor tries to give Future Me a meaningful look, but

Future Me ignores it. Instead I take the flask and tip it back for a long swig before handing it back to Amalita.

"Okay," I say, putting it together, "so Reenzie's still at Stanford, and Ames is still drinking; that's the same. But my life is better and my mom's life is better and . . ." I can't even say the next part I'm thinking: *Is someone's life worse? Did one of my friends die?*

Future Me sits down with Ames, Reenzie, and Taylor. They tuck into a corner so they can face one another, and I sit on the floor in front of them to listen as they talk.

"Come on," I urge them. "Spill. What's going on?"

But my friends and Future Me aren't talking about whoever's in the hospital. They're giving each other the scoop on their lives. I get the sense that they keep in touch but haven't all been in the same room for a really long time, so they need to fill in the blanks. Tee tells the others about her boyfriend, Drew, and when she shows a picture, I lean in close to look.

"Yes!" I gush, relieved. It's the same Drew from the other future. "He's perfect for you. I totally didn't want you to lose him just because other things changed."

Future Me tells the others all about Jack and Nathan, who are apparently still a couple in this future too. It seems Jack has become my closest friend from high school, which I never in a million years would have guessed. He and Nathan go to school in Boston, like me, and the three of us hang out together all the time.

"They send their best," Future Me says. "Jack would have come down with me, but . . ."

"After the way he and Paul ended things? Awk-ward," Tee singsongs.

"Paul?" I ask out loud. Paul is Sean's next-to-oldest brother, and he's gay. Did he and Jack go out before Jack met Nathan? Paul's four years older than us, which I guess isn't *that* big a difference, but wow.

"How's J.J.?" Future Me asks. "I haven't heard from him in . . ."

Future Me lets the sentence trail. Apparently it's been too long to remember, and I'm surprised by the sharp pang of loss in my stomach. It only gets worse when Amalita rolls her eyes. "Oy," she says, then takes a long swig from her flask. "How do you think? Two babies, no college, married to a girl he hates but will never leave because if he does she'll never let him see his kids."

"*WHAT?!*" I burst. "*Two* kids?! And he never went to college? Are you *kidding* me?!"

"Are his parents talking to him yet?" Future Me asks.

"Little bit," Tee says. "They hate Carrie, but they love the kids."

"Maybe you'll see him at some point," Reenzie says. "He comes by when he can. It's just tough with work and helping Carrie with the kids. He doesn't have a lot of time."

I can barely take this all in before slow footsteps get my attention and I turn to see David, Sean's oldest brother.

Like Sean, all three of his older brothers were football players, and David's a hulking mass of pale, unshaven guy. He walks with his head down, an unruly three-day stubble crawling over his face.

So it's Sean. Whatever's going on here, it's happening to Sean.

I almost don't want to learn. I want the locket to zip me home before I find out what horrible thing happened to him in this new future I created.

Reenzie walks right up to David and gives him a huge hug. I'm not sure if she and Sean are a couple in this future, but it doesn't matter. Reenzie's and Sean's families are so close she's like a sister to him. After the hug, she takes his hand and he holds it gratefully.

"You can come in for a bit," he croaks. "Mom says it's okay."

I stick with the group as they follow David down the maze of white halls and through a door. I have a vague sense of chairs in the room, of Sean's dad, Paul, and his other brother sitting there, rumpled and gutted and devastated, but mostly all I can focus on is the bed.

Sean's there. He's covered in tubes. They attach to his chest, his throat, his arm, his face. His neck is wrapped in a thick brace. His eyes are closed, and he lies perfectly still. Future Me and my friends are gathering around the bed, but I walk right through them and get next to him. Tears fill my eyes as I lean down to his face.

"Sean?" I ask. "What happened?"

He doesn't answer. He's asleep. But Sean's mom fills everyone in, even though I'm sure everyone in this room except me already knows. It's like she has to say the words anyway, just to know they're real and this isn't some horrible nightmare that'll end any second. She stands by his head, on the other side of the bed from me, and pets his hair gently as she smiles down at him and strains through tears to speak.

"He was doing so well at FSU," she says. "Better than anyone thought. They were saying he could have gone to the NFL. Can you believe it? The sack he took . . . it didn't even look like anything on TV. They say he'll never move anything below his neck again, but we know better, right, Sean? We'll get you the best care, and you'll be up and walking again, no matter how long it takes."

She says something more, but I don't hear it, because suddenly I'm gone.

6

october, senior year

I gasp for breath and lean heavily against the brick wall, sliding down until I'm sitting on the cement. I probably look like I'm having a heart attack, but luckily Aventura's strip mall shoppers are too lost in their own heads to notice.

I have to undo what I changed, I think. *I have to find that guy and get him back to meet my mom.*

I jump up and race through the parking lot, ignoring the cars that pull out in front of me. They honk and swerve and it's amazing I don't get hit, but I'm not even paying attention to anything but the driver of each car, looking to see if it's him.

None of them are. He's long gone. I stagger back to the line of stores and pull out my phone.

"It's so bad, Jenna," I tell her when I get her on the line. I give her the whole story, then say, "I don't even get it!

Nothing I changed had to do with Sean at all! Why did everything get so bad for him?"

"It's that butterfly effect thing," Jenna says. "Everything we do affects everything else in ways we can't understand."

"Then I should just stop! I shouldn't change anything! It's too dangerous!"

"But you will," Jenna says calmly. "Just the fact that you saw what you did means you're going to act differently, and the future will change again. You could probably go back to that same date right now and it'll be different because you're on a different path."

"So how do I know what to do?" I wail. "This is crazy! And J.J.—I keep making his life worse too. What should I do to make it better?!"

"Think about your dad," Jenna advises. "He's the one who gave you the locket, remember? He wouldn't want to make you crazy, right?"

"No," I agree, and I smile a little as I recount again his mission for me. "He'd want me to use it to bring peace and harmony to my little corner of the world."

"Exactly. You make changes to fix what you see in the future; then you jump ahead to make sure you got it right."

"Eight more times," I say, and I tell her about the little dial window that numbers the jumps. "But what if I run out of jumps and the future's still bad?"

"Another gift?" Jenna suggests.

It's a possibility. My dad has been pretty regular about them so far. But I don't want to count on it. What I *can* count on is what I know about my dad. He loves me. He wouldn't send me on an impossible mission that'll make me feel hopeless and sad. No matter how hard these futures are to see, I can't panic over them. I have to think of them as helpful hints—signs about what I need to change today so the bad things don't happen tomorrow. Like with Sean. In my jump, Reenzie said they airlifted him in from Tallahassee. He's been saying FSU is his number-one pick for school. The one he's dying for but isn't sure he's a good enough player to get into. Well, I just have to make sure he doesn't get in. Or if he does get in, that he doesn't go. He was at a Division Two school and not paralyzed in the first future I saw. That's the one I need him to get.

As for J.J. and Carrie, I've now seen two different miserable futures for them. To save them I clearly have just one choice. I need to break them up. *How* I'll do that I have no idea, but three weeks ago I had no idea how I'd break up my mom and her bushy-beard husband, but I managed that, right?

In the meantime, I can keep an eye out to make sure all my friends and family stay on track for their *positive* futures. Mom using the Catches Falls dogs as hospital therapy animals is genius. If I have to help her come up with the idea, I will. Reenzie seems on track no matter what, so that's great. I'll keep an eye out for Drew this year to make sure Tee meets him, and if I have the chance to help Jack feel comfortable telling us the truth, that's great too. As for Ames, maybe I can work on the drinking thing with her so it never gets really bad.

These are all amazing goals, but I have no idea how to accomplish them until the next week at school. I'm in the Senior Social Committee room, which is really just one of the classrooms we're allowed to take over each afternoon. Carrie and the seven other girls sit at student desks, and Gus stands at the active board taking notes. I'm sprawled out on the teacher's desk, stomach down, feet in the air.

"Okay, seriously, ladies," he snaps at the room. "*No one* is excited for the Halloween dance. It's like not a thing, and it needs to be a thing. It needs to be a *huge* thing."

"It would help if we did it *away* from school," whines Meegan Rudolph. She winds one of her pigtails around a finger. "We're seniors. We're done with dances in the gym."

The pigtails and whining have to go, but Meegan's totally right. "Maybe we could rent a place," I say.

"No budget," Carrie says. "We don't want to charge too much, and we have to be smart this year so we have enough left over for our prom and the after-prom party. The parents' fund will help, but we still need money of our own."

"Then what can we do at the school to make it special?" asks Mariah Amhari.

Mariah fascinates me because she always sits or stands with amazing posture, like a ballerina. Every time I look at her I feel like a hunchback. I never noticed her until J.J. told me she's his favorite person in the world. I thought he had a crush on her, but he said it's just because her last name's an anagram of her first. He likes to call her Harami, another anagram that in his fantasy is her actual middle name. "We're already making it a costume party."

"Done to death. We need to do something better." Then I bolt upright as inspiration strikes. "Like turn the school into a giant haunted house! We'll theme it like a school from the turn of the century . . . for kids with 'special powers' . . . and as people walk through the rooms we'll have these tableaux set up with scary lighting and kids getting experimented on . . . like a walk-through horror movie—"

"Budget," Carrie says, cutting me off. "And creepy. But mostly budget."

Gus sighs. "Here's what I say. If I wasn't on the Senior Social Committee, the *only* way you could get me to a school gym dance is if you promise me I'll find the man of my dreams."

Everyone murmurs agreement, and even though I know they don't think they're being serious, an idea starts to percolate in my head. One that will not only solve the Committee's problem, but might also change the course of my friends' futures for the better.

"What if we make it a matchmaking dance?" I ask. " 'We'll match you with someone so perfect, it's *scary*.' "

"I *love* it, Autumn!" Swoozie Lyman bubbles. "But how do we do it? Just the ten of us pairing people up together?"

"No way," I say. "No one would go for that. They'd think we're messing with them. It has to be all computer. Secure website, questionnaires people fill out, the program matches them up based on interests and things . . . like a real online dating service, but just for the people coming to the dance."

Everyone smiles and buzzes, and I'm happy they're all into it. Only Carrie is frowning, and I'm not surprised when she tells us why.

"What about those of us already *with* our perfect match?" she asks.

I'm ready for the question.

"Most likely, the computer will pair you up!" I say. "And even if there's some glitch and it doesn't, we just make some ground rules. Like . . . you're not *forced* to be with your date—"

"Your Scare Pair!" Swoozie cries.

"Love it!" Gus seconds. "And yes to Autumn. Everyone gets a Scare Pair, but you don't have to be with them all night. You don't even get their name until you get to the dance, so no one's a jerk and doesn't show if they don't like the name."

"The Don't Be a Jerk rule," I second. "That's perfect. No—the Don't Be a *Ghoul* rule. And we'll have one song near the start of the dance that's specifically for Scare Pairs. It can even be a fast song, so no pressure."

"Exactly," Gus agrees. "And in the spirit of Don't Be a Ghoul, everyone has to dance with their Scare Pair partner for that one song. 'Cause seriously, I don't care who it is, it won't kill you. If the pairs want to hang more after, great.

If not, they don't have to. That way we get the singles and we don't scare away the couples. Carrie?"

Carrie's lips are scrunched all the way over to one side of her face. "I don't know . . ."

Kassie Cooper, one of Carrie's best friends and who looks almost *exactly* like a darker-skinned brown-haired Carrie, leans dramatically on Carrie's desk. "Cair. I get it. I want to scratch out the eyes of any girl who *looks* at Ty. But even I'm totally cool with him having one fast dance with someone if the computer fixes them up." Then she smiles. "Plus, I want to know who it'll give *me*. Aren't you a little bit curious? I mean, we're here for less than a year. Don't you want to know if there's someone you overlooked?"

Carrie meets Kassie's eyes and smiles, then glances nervously at me and shakes it off. "I know there's no one out there better than J.J.," she says. "But, yeah, I'm still curious what the computer would say. It's a good idea, Autumn. It'll get people to pay for the dance and show."

"So . . . how do we make it work?" Mariah asks.

Luckily—and shockingly to me, because she comes off as a complete airhead—Brody LeClair is a complete computer genius. She apparently takes college classes in coding and already has a side business building websites. She knows *exactly* how to make the program work and can get questionnaires sent out within the week. If we give people another week to fill them out, we'll still have time before the dance for the program to do its work and for us to get everything printed out gorgeously for the party itself. We decide that even though it's a senior event, we'll open it up to the whole school. Since everyone has to pay ten dollars to submit their questionnaire, we figure the dance will pay for itself, plus make a little money for our class's prom fund.

When the meeting is over, I corner Brody and strike up a conversation. I need to be close to her. I'm still not sure how I'm going to pull it off, but I do know I'm going to use this dance to save the future. No way will I let Carrie and J.J. get paired together. I'm going to make sure they not only get other people, but also people who will really tempt them. As for Jack, I want the computer to pair him with a guy. I know he won't ask for it on the questionnaire, but I can pass it off as some kind of computer glitch. But hey, if I choose the guy wisely, maybe it'll lead to something fantastic!

Brody sends out a teaser email about the Scare Pair dance that night, and by the next morning the whole school's majorly excited, but probably no one as much as me. I'm the only one who knows how important it really is. I spend the whole week watching Carrie, J.J., and Jack closely, hoping they'll betray their secret crushes, but I get nowhere. The only guy Carrie talks about is J.J., and J.J. gets glared at if he even *thinks* about a girl other than Carrie. This time last year he was secretly in love with *me*, but I don't think that's in his head at all. Even if it was, it would get messy. I need his *dream* girl—someone he's had a crush on since before I even moved to Aventura. I try asking Amalita about it one day as we walk to class together, but she just gives me the side eye.

"Why?" she asks suspiciously. "You want to fix him up with someone special for the Scare Pair dance?"

I'm shocked that I'm so transparent, but I think I cover well. I drop my jaw and throw out my arms in a scandalized, "Who, me?"

Maybe I don't cover that well. Ames rolls her eyes. "*Dejalo*. Leave it alone. The boy has a good thing going. I love you, Autumn, but I don't want you messing with him again."

She wouldn't say that if she'd seen J.J.'s future, but I can't tell her that. I drop the topic. If I want answers, I need to find them myself. Subtly.

"So, Jack," I say on Thursday at lunch. "I'm trying to figure out who I want my Scare Pair to be. What do you think?"

"I think I want Jennifer Lawrence, ideally in her Mystique costume," he says. "Can you make that happen?"

I roll my eyes. "I mean for *me*. If you were going to choose a good guy—for me, I mean—who would it be?"

Jack scrunches his face. "We don't choose people. We just answer the questions on the questionnaire."

"I know, I know," I say. "I'm just asking. If you *were* to pick a guy."

"For you?" Jack asks. "How about Alex Futterman?"

"Alex Futterman hasn't showered in three years!" I explode.

"Oooh," Taylor pipes up. "You could get Derek Montzer."

"Picks his nose, rubs it on desks," I retort.

"I say Wayne Jarvitz," J.J. adds. "He's a hottie."

"He's a *freshman!*" I yell. "He hasn't hit puberty!"

"You're getting a jump on the future," J.J. says.

"How did we start playing this game?" I ask. "I don't like this game."

Jack shrugs. "You started it."

"I think it's fun," J.J. adds.

"I hate you all," I say.

Sean and Reenzie come over, both smiling so hard their faces might break. "Guess what!" Reenzie cries. "Huge news!"

"Huger than Autumn and Wayne Jarvitz?" Jack asks.

Reenzie gets a condescending look on her face that makes me want to vomit. Of course she believes it's true. "Awwww, are the two of you together? That's so sweet!"

I roll my eyes. "Yes, it's very special. What's your big news?"

"A scout from FSU is coming to Sean's game tomorrow!!!!" she squeals. "Can you believe it?"

J.J., Carrie, Ames, Jack, and Taylor all smile and congratulate Sean. I try to paint on a smile, but all I can see is him lying in a hospital bed, unable to move.

"My brother had to beg the guy. If David wasn't an alum, it never would have happened. The coaches there don't think I have the chops for Division One, but they agreed to check me out. I kind of can't even believe it. If I got in there . . . it would be a serious dream come true."

"Would it, though?" I ask. "I mean, Division One . . . that's a lot of pressure, right? Wouldn't it be more fun to play Division Two . . . or Five or Six? I mean, that's easier, and you could probably get a bigger scholarship because you'd be the best guy on the team, right?"

All my friends are staring at me like I've sprouted a unicorn horn. Sean was elated a second ago, but now he's looking down at me, hurt.

"What are you trying to say, Autumn?" he asks. "You don't think I can handle the pressure?"

I give up. This isn't the way to change his future. I smile bigger than anyone else did. "Are you kidding? Of course you can handle it! This is perfect and I'm totally excited for you!!!"

Everyone seems to believe me, and soon we're all congratulating him again and he's telling us all about his plans to impress the scout, but I'm seriously distracted. At the end of the school day, I tell Carrie I'm sick so I can get out of Senior Social Committee, and I call Jenna while I walk home.

"I need a plan," I say after I fill her in. "I'll give you some options, and you say yes or no. Get him on a flight to Canada."

"I like it," she says, "but you'd have to knock him out first and he's too big for you to carry."

"Ooh, knock him out is good!" I say. "What if I give him sleeping pills before the game? Or I could trip him somewhere that I know he'd fall and smash his head and lose consciousness for a few hours!"

"I thought your purpose was to *avoid* getting him injured," she says.

"How do I stop him from getting injured without getting him injured?"

"Get him arrested?" she suggests.

"Yes! That's a great idea! How do I do that?"

"Autumn, stop, you can't."

"Why not?" I ask. "Locking him up would be perfect! Okay, I need a wicked witch and a tower."

"I'm hanging up now," Jenna says. "I love you. Good luck."

When I get inside, I'm surprised to see Mom's home. I'm even more surprised to see her climbing down from the attic with an armload of old dog beds.

"Mom, wait!" I run to her and take the beds out of her hands. The attic stairs aren't built-ins. They fold down when you open the door in the back hallway ceiling, so they have no arm rail and they're very rickety. The few times I went up there, I hated every second.

"Thanks, Autumn," she says, coming down much more easily now that her arms are empty. "The dogs have been going through our bedding and I knew we had some old

Schmidt beds up there." She folds up the attic stairs and uses the long wooden rod we keep by the washing machine to push the door shut. It creaks closed like the sound of a dungeon door . . . which makes me think of something.

"Mom?" I ask. "What if you're up in the attic and the door is closed? Would it just fall open when you step on it?"

"You *never* want the door closed when you're up there," Mom says. "There's a catch on it so it stays shut. If you're up there and it's closed, you'd need someone else to open it from down here."

"Got it," I say as the wheels in my brain turn with diabolical brilliance.

Okay, maybe not brilliance. More like complete insanity. But it's all I've got. I just have to make sure there's a chance it can work.

"It's great to have you home so early," I say. "Think you'll be home after school tomorrow too?"

Mom makes a sad face. "I'm so sorry, honey. I'm going to be with the contractors at the new location until after dinner tomorrow. Erick has a mall date, and I thought you'd be with your friends watching a football game. Will you be home alone?"

"No!" I assure her. "Totally doing the football thing. Not a problem at all." I'm glad to know she and Erick will both be out of the house, though. It'll make my crazy plan much more possible. "Oh, hey," I add, as if I just thought about it. "Have you ever thought about training the Catches Falls dogs as therapy dogs? Especially the older ones that maybe don't find homes right away?"

Mom smiles. "It's so funny you would say that, Autumn. I was actually thinking the same thing. We have so many hospitals and retirement homes in the area, and I think the dogs could really make a difference."

"You should pursue it," I say, as if I don't already know she will.

For the rest of the day and all Friday at school it's amazing I say anything intelligible, because I'm completely preoccupied with my plan for protecting Sean. I don't tell Jenna about it because I'm afraid she won't approve and she'll try to talk me out of it, but I can't have that since it's all I've got. I race home the second school is over—no Senior Social Committee on Fridays—and I'm thrilled that Mom's and Erick's plans held up and no one's home. I run to the back hallway, grab the wooden stick by the washing machine, and slide its hook end through the metal loop of the attic door. I pull the door down, then unfold the rickety wooden stairs.

Now for the first hard part. I find Schmidt curled up in his bed by the sliding doors to the pool. He likes feeling the cool glass against his fur while he basks in the warm sun.

"Up we go, Schmidtty," I say. I bend low and haul the dog into my arms. Schmidt is sixty pounds of unwieldy dog weight that has gone perfectly limp because he has no desire to go anywhere. I can barely straighten my legs while holding him, never mind walk all the way to the back hallway.

I can do this, I keep reminding myself. *My body works. But if I don't get this right, Sean's won't anymore.*

With the image of Sean in the hospital bed fixed in my mind, I haul Schmidt up the attic steps, one rickety stair at a time. Then I clamber back down, leaving Schmidt whining nervously at the top. I'm not worried he'll try to climb down and fall. He's too scared for that. I feel terrible, but it's for a good cause.

"Sorry, boy," I tell him. "It'll only be for a little while, and then I'll go buy you a burger, okay?"

The offer doesn't cheer him. I check the time. I'm cutting it close. On away game days, Sean would already be off with the team on the bus. For home games, the Aventura players have only a short window between the end of classes and when they have to be back with the team to get into their uniforms and warm up. I need to catch Sean *now*.

I call his cell. When he answers, I channel Taylor and give the performance of my life. It's not hard. I just think about how badly I want to save him from the fate I saw and the fear comes pouring out.

"Sean, oh my God, I'm so sorry, I need your help. I'm all alone and I think he's going to get hurt and I need a guy and I can't get anyone else and I know you're busy and I'm so, so sorry but pleeeeease can you come over?!"

"Is this Autumn?" he asks, confused.

"Yes, *please,* I'm so sorry. It's Schmidt. Someone left the attic stairs open and he got up there and he can't get down and he's really heavy and I tried but I almost fell and I don't want to hurt us both and—"

"Easy, easy," he says so soothingly that I almost hate myself for what I'm going to do. "Look, I have to get to school soon. Maybe I can call someone and get them over there."

"No!" Schmidt howls plaintively and I'm suddenly so frantic that this isn't going to work that my voice gets shrill and I start to cry. "Schmidt freaks out if someone he doesn't know picks him up. He'll start flailing and moving and the guy could drop him and—"

"I'll be there in five minutes," he assures me. "I just have to be quick."

"Quick is great," I sob. "Quick is perfect."

I hang up and grab some of Schmidt's favorite dog treats. When I hear Sean's car outside, I run up to the top of the attic stairs and throw a treat to the farthest corner of the room. Schmidt bounds after it and I dart quickly back down the stairs.

"You're here!" I gush as I open the door.

Sean's wearing denim shorts and a T-shirt that shows off all his muscles, and for just a second I forget not only why he's here, but also why I ever stopped liking him. He pushes past me before I can gush. "Where's the attic?"

"That way," I say. I point him to the back stairs, and as I follow behind him, I lightly pull his phone from his back pocket and set it on the floor. He doesn't notice. "You are the best friend in the world and a true savior of dogs in need."

He turns and flashes his melt-worthy smile. "I'm a savior of ex-girlfriends in need," he says. "I don't like to hear you cry."

It seriously kills me that if all goes well he's going to hate me in about five minutes, but I remind myself I have no choice. This is my Dad-given mission, and even though Sean will never know it, *I'll* know I saved his life.

Sean jogs up the rickety stairs, and I follow right behind him. Our attic is unfinished. It's all wooden beams and a zillion random things we stored up here after the move. Thin, high windows let in the sunlight, and Sean bounds toward Schmidt, still in a far corner munching his treat. With Sean's back to me, I reach into my pocket and toss another treat to the other side of the room. Schmidt bounds after it.

"What was that sound?" Sean asks.

"I don't know!" I shout in fake panic. "Schmidt, no! Don't run to the stairs!"

Schmidt's not running anywhere near the stairs, but I pretend I don't know that. I pull on the attic stairs, folding them up and pulling the door shut as if in a panic. When I hear the door latch, I don't know if I'm relieved my plan really worked or terrified about what'll happen next.

A minute later, Sean walks over with Schmidt in his

arms. "Okay, Autumn," he says. "I've got him. You can open the door."

I nod and press down on the door, as if I don't know it doesn't open from inside. Then I push harder. I aim for a confused look on my face.

"Autumn?" Sean asks.

"I don't get it," I say. "It's not opening."

"What do you mean it's not opening?"

I push down on the door more frantically, then look up at him as if I've just made a horrible discovery. "I don't think it opens from the inside."

"No," Sean says. He puts Schmidt down and starts pushing on the door. "No, no, no, no, no. This isn't possible. I have to get out of here." He reaches for his back pocket. When he speaks next, his voice is shaky. "Where's my cell phone?"

"You don't have it?"

"I *had* it. I don't *have* it."

"Did it drop?"

We retrace his steps through the attic, even though I'm just doing it for show. No shocker, the phone's not up here.

"Are you kidding me?!" he roars. He looks frantically around the attic and grabs a giant golden goblet that was some hideous gift my mom and dad got for their wedding and kept because it was so hysterically awful. He runs it to the attic door and starts pounding the goblet down.

"Stop!" I scream. "You'll break it!"

"That's the point!" he yells back. "I need to get out of here!"

"You can't break a hole in my mom's ceiling to do it!" I yell.

That calms him down. A little. Or at least it stops him from destroying things. Sean's a good guy. He wouldn't hurt anything that wasn't his. Instead of pounding, he just paces the room like a caged animal. "Why did you close the door, Autumn? Didn't you know it locked from this side?"

I want to tell him I had no idea, but if my mom ends up saving us, she'll spill the truth.

"I wasn't thinking," I moan instead. "I was just so scared that Schmidt would run down and hurt himself."

"I have to get out of here," Sean says. "If I don't get to warm-ups on time, Coach won't let me play. If I don't play, the FSU scout won't see me, and there's no way I'm getting into the school."

"I know," I say. "I'm so sorry."

Sean paces some more, then lets out a visceral scream that I'm surprised doesn't get the attention of everyone else in the neighborhood. Sean seems to think the same thing, because he runs to one of the windows and tries to open it.

"I don't think they open," I say.

He cocks his fist and looks so furious that I worry for a second that he'll punch it open . . . but then he just sighs and sits down on one of my mom's big storage trunks. Sensing sadness, Schmidt trots to his side. Sean scratches his head. My heart completely breaks for Sean. He knows every second he's here, his dream is closer to slipping away, but he's not taking it out on me, or on Schmidt, or on any of our stuff. He's just dealing with it.

I move to him and sit down next to him on the trunk. "I'm sorry," I say, and put my hand on his arm.

"Don't touch me," he says dully.

Okay, maybe he's taking it out on me a little bit.

We don't talk while we wait. Sean sits and stews, only moving to look at his watch every few minutes. When we finally hear noise downstairs, Sean leaps up and yells down at the door. It clicks open, and as it folds down we see Erick. Sean races downstairs and pushes past him. I follow, but Erick stops me at the foot of the stairs.

"'Accidentally' locked yourself in the attic, huh?" he says with a knowing leer. "Been meaning to try that one myself."

"Shut up," I say. "And go get Schmidt. He's in the attic." I grab Sean's phone from the floor and race out the door. He's already in his car with the engine on, but I tear open the passenger side door and dive in.

"Get out," he says.

"I found your phone," I retort. "And I'm coming with you. I want to help explain to your coach."

Okay, the truth is I want to put on a good show so Sean and the rest of my friends don't completely despise me, but I'm secretly hoping nothing I say will make a difference to Sean's coach.

He drives full speed, his mood getting lighter every second. There's still a full half hour before the game, so Sean thinks the coach might take pity on him, especially with the scout in the stands. "Thanks for coming with me, Autumn," he says. "I think it might actually help."

"Hope so," I say, though I'm not sure I sound convincing.

We screech into the parking lot and run to the stadium, where Sean immediately finds the coach. In a wild rush, he explains everything that happened and urges me to back him up. I try . . . but the coach doesn't want to hear it.

"Rules are rules," he says. "You're not playing."

"But, Coach!" Sean objects. "You can't! Not this game. Suspend me for a different game. The FSU scout—"

"Is something you should have thought about before you went to play hero," the coach says. "You're out."

The coach walks away. Sean looks after him, mouth open, like he can't believe the conversation is actually over. Then he deflates.

"Sean . . ."

It's a sentence I start with absolutely no idea how I'll finish, which is fine because Sean doesn't let me.

"Autumn, don't," he says. "Please. Just go."

I sigh and look down at the ground as if I'm intensely depressed, when I actually want to skip out of the stadium.

I saved Sean.

I think.

I need to be sure.

The second I'm out of the stadium, I pull the locket out

from under my shirt. I open it up and think a minute, then set it for June, four and a half years from now. That's right after our senior year of college. If Sean's okay by then, I'll know for sure he's safe.

I close the locket and squeeze it in my hand.

Show me what I need to see, Dad. Let me know if Sean's okay.

7

june, four and a half years later

"Heads up!" Sean cries.

I look up to see him run to the edge of the pool—*my* pool, in my backyard at home—and execute an absolutely gorgeous dive. He hits the water and I squeal and cringe away as it splashes over me, but of course I don't feel it or get wet at all. I run-dance with joy as I trail him while he does a perfect crawl stroke across the pool and back again, then hoists himself out.

"You're moving!" I scream. "You're okay! You're—"

I take a second to notice his perfectly chiseled body, covered only by a tiny black speedo.

"Practically naked!" I gasp. "Since when do you wear a bathing suit like that? I mean, I'm not complaining, you totally pull it off, but . . . seriously?"

"Seriously, Sean?" Future Me echoes from a chaise lounge. She's on our deck with Taylor, Jack, and Reenzie. "Get back in the water!"

I walk over to Future Me to check her out. She's wearing a turquoise bikini and funky round sunglasses that are so super-cute, I kinda can't wait the four and a half years until I can buy them. Big smile, long orange hair, great makeup, hanging out with her high school friends . . . This is looking good!

Reenzie picks up a bottle of iced tea from our outdoor table. "A toast—to all the graduates!"

Jack, Taylor, Future Me, and Sean grab bottles and clink.

"So we all graduated," I say as they drink. "That's excellent!"

"Is it horrible that I'm kind of glad Amalita isn't here?" Reenzie says as she lowers her bottle.

"Yes!" Taylor admonishes her.

"It's not that I don't want to see her," Reenzie clarifies as she sits back on her chaise. "It's just that it was so hard watching her fall off the wagon again and again. It's exhausting."

"Her parents say the place she's in this time is really good," Future Me says.

"Third time's the charm," Sean says, perching on the end of Future Me's chaise. She smacks him on the arm. "No, I mean it!" he insists. "I hope she gets better this time."

"Okay, I get it!" I shout to the universe in general. "I need to deal with Ames and the drinking thing. I'll get her away from Zander and the parties. That'll do it, I know." I move to Taylor and sit down on her chaise with her, and it's only a little awkward when she stretches out so her legs go right through me. "So tell me," I say to her. "Are you with Drew? Did that work out?"

"Hey, everyone! Are we too late?"

The voice is weirdly singsongy, and I turn to see J.J. coming in from the back slider. He's bent practically double and holds the hands of a very small person with dark hair just like his. The baby toddles along on wobbly feet and knobby legs, and I'm pretty sure he'll topple if J.J. lets go.

I rest my head in my hands. "J.J., tell me that's not your and Carrie's baby."

"Hi, Uncle Jack!" J.J. says, waving one of the baby's hands. "Hi, Uncle Sean! Hi, Auntie Autumn and Auntie Reenzie and Auntie Taylor!"

Everyone coos and calls their hellos, and Taylor and Jack get up to play with the kid on the lawn, which I now realize is scattered with baby toys. Why? Does J.J. bring his kid here all the time? I remember the other future, where J.J.'s parents didn't have a lot to do with him. Is it like that here too? Did my mom take him under her wing? I wouldn't be surprised. She's nuts for babies.

I, however, am *not* nuts for babies, either now or apparently in the future. Future Me is all about lounging with Reenzie and Sean and isn't even looking at the baby on the lawn.

"Hey," Reenzie says. "Have you guys seen the Keith Hamilton billboards?"

"*Keith Hamilton* billboards?" I ask. "What's he on a billboard for? Did he invent something?"

"Yes!" Taylor cries from the lawn. "I cannot even deal with how hot he is!"

"Seriously?!" Future Me and I ask at the same time.

"Oh, Autumn, you have missed out," Jack says. "Boyfriend is an *underwear* model."

"He is *not*!" she and I again say at the same time.

Jack grabs his phone and finds something online, then shows Future Me. I, of course, check it out too.

Wow. The Keith Hamilton *I* know is cute enough, but he's a goofball. He's super smart and, as far as I can tell, hangs out with his group of all-guy friends in the halls, quoting movies that make them laugh. Oh, and he's in the school a cappella group. But *this* Keith . . . this Keith is shot in moody black-and-white, looking sexily at the camera, wearing an open button-down that shows his entire *eight*-pack and, of course, his Calvin Klein underwear.

"Keith Hamilton," Reenzie says in disbelief. "Who knew?"

"Carrie did," J.J. calls from the lawn. "She had a *huge* crush on him. To the point where if he'd shown any interest at all . . ." He leans closer to his son and says in a high-pitched voice, "I don't know that you'd even be here, little guy."

My pulse speeds up. If Keith Hamilton had wanted Carrie, she'd have chosen him over J.J.? I can make that happen! I can make Keith her Scare Pair!

"I totally get why Carrie would have a crush on Keith Hamilton now," Taylor says, "but *then*?"

"Come on, look at her taste," Jack says. "She had a huge crush on *J.J.*"

"Thanks," J.J. says. "You're a good friend."

"Hey, we all had crazy crushes in high school," Future Me says. "I liked Sean."

Reenzie raises her hand. "Guilty."

"Doesn't count as a crazy crush when you've both been back to the well within the last year," Sean counters.

"Ew," I say, but Future Me and Reenzie just look at each other and shrug, admitting he has a point. Clearly what Sean said isn't news to either of us.

"I had a *major* crush in high school," Jack says.

"Somebody ask him who!" I shout to all my friends. "I need to know for the Scare Pair!"

"Well, yeah," Reenzie says, rolling her eyes. "You were in love with Carrie."

"Hello! Do I need to come out to you again? Carrie was a cover!" Jack says.

"For who?" Taylor asks. "Who did you have a crush on?"

"Thank you, Taylor!" I proclaim. Then I move closer to Jack to make sure I hear it right.

Jack gets a dreamy look in his eyes and smiles. "Tom Watson."

"Tom Watson!" Future Me and I shout together. I feel good that I seem to have so much in common with my future self. Then she continues without me. "You could have totally had him! He was out!"

"Yes, but *I* wasn't," Jack says. Then his smile widens. "He made me wish I was, though."

I grin right back at him. I'm totally going to make his high school dreams come true.

"You know my big high school crush," Taylor says. "Mr. Ryan Not-Gay-at-All Darby."

"Oh, he's gay," Jack says matter-of-factly. "I ran into him at a gay bar in Boston."

"I knew it!" Reenzie crows. "Up top, Autumn."

Future Me and Reenzie are about ten feet away from each other but lift their hands in an air high five.

"I had a crush in high school," J.J. says.

Future Me echoes me again as we both turn bright red. Reenzie rolls her eyes. "Yeah, we know."

"No," J.J. says. "Other than that. I never told any of you guys. Mariah Amhari."

"You totally told me that!" Future Me says. "But you said you just liked that her name was an anagram."

"Because by the time I told you that, I had *other* crushes," he says pointedly. "Freshman year before I dated Carrie? Major Mariah obsession."

"Were you still interested in her senior year?" I ask. "Enough to leave Carrie if Mariah was your Scare Pair?"

"Hi, everyone!" calls an absurdly high-pitched voice. It's Carrie coming out the back slider. Carrie plus thirty pounds. Which I guess makes sense because while J.J. has one baby, she's holding *another* one!

"Twins?!" I roar. "Seriously with this?!"

Fraternal twins, clearly, because the two babies look nothing alike. The one Carrie holds has wispy orange hair and pale white skin. Honestly, she looks more like a baby J.J. would have with *me* than with Carrie.

"Ellie!" Future Me cries. She bounds out of her chaise and practically runs to the baby, gently taking her out of Carrie's arms. "Did you miss Otis? Did you want to come out here to play with him?"

Future Me—who totally ignored the first baby who came outside—is now on the lawn making squeaky noises to this second baby. The one who has orange hair like ours.

All the happiness I felt at learning everyone's crushes? Gone now. My skin's crawling, and I walk slowly to the lawn. It *would* make more sense to have baby toys here if the baby was mine. . . .

I shake my head. It's impossible. I graduated college! Future Me said so! And I'm not great with baby ages, but this one has to be around a year old, and no way could I graduate college and have a one-year-old. Plus, if this is Future Me's baby, what was she doing in the house without me? Wouldn't I want to be with her?

I get chills as I think of another possibility. Maybe I had the baby but gave it to my mom to raise because I wasn't ready to be a mom. Or maybe . . . Oh God, didn't I say I hooked up with Sean our junior year of college? What if *he and I* had a baby and we gave it to my mom?!

Future Me is on her knees on the lawn, playing peeka-boo with baby Ellie.

I stare at Future Me's stomach. It's perfectly flat. Would it be perfectly flat if I had a baby a year ago?

"Anybody hungry for snacks?"

I look up at the sound of the male voice, and my head actually explodes.

Okay, not really. But kinda really.

The man emerging from my house no longer has a bushy blond beard and mustache, nor does he have a fringe of blond hair. He is entirely bald now, like a too-large lolli-pop on an ultrathin stick. His glasses are as round as his head, and he grins like someone too oblivious to ever have an unpleasant thought in his life. He holds a tray of mini sandwiches with the crusts cut off and sets it on the table; then he beelines for the lawn.

"Ellie-belly, your sister's trying to have big-girl time with her friends," he says, scooping up the orange-haired baby and swinging her high into the air. The baby laughs.

"It's okay, Glen," Future Me says, holding her arms out to take the baby back. "Otis is here. I'll take her. We can all play."

"Little Ellie will never have to worry if her family loves her, that's for sure."

It's my mom's voice, and I turn to see her coming

outside with a tray of two lemonade pitchers and a bunch of glasses.

"Mom! Stop carrying stuff!" Future Me jumps up and grabs the tray from my mother.

Which is when I notice she's *very* pregnant.

8

october, senior year

At this point Jenna never turns off her phone, because she's dying to hear what I'll call with next.

"His name's Glen," I say.

"Who?"

"Balloon-head man. Mom's new husband."

"I thought you got rid of him," Jenna says.

"Me too!" I cry. "But he's back! And they have a baby! And she's pregnant with another one. *Glen!*"

"Glen and Gwen?" Jenna asks.

"Thank you!" I shout triumphantly. "See? It's ridiculous. And babies? Mom should be *done* with babies."

"Did you see anything about me?" Jenna asks.

I sigh a little. Jenna has become obsessed with her own mortality ever since that first jump when she wasn't at the wedding. "No. But you're alive, I'm sure. You're just not in Florida. I see or hear about the crazy-dramatic stuff. I'd know."

I fill Jenna in on everything else I saw as I make my way up to the stadium stands and hang up when I find my friends in our usual section. They're quieter than normal, and when I look at the scoreboard I see why. It's only the first quarter and we're down by fourteen points. Someone should probably tell Ames and the other cheerleaders down on the field. I know it's their job to be peppy no matter what, but it seems crazy for them to be so peppy and excited for a game this bad.

"Where have you been?" Taylor asks.

"Something's up," Reenzie adds. "Sean isn't on the field. And the scout's here."

"I know why," I say, and do my best to sound very believable and contrite as I tell them the whole story. I feel like I do a really good job, so I'm surprised when they all look at me like I've been speaking Spanish.

Was I speaking Spanish? They look really confused.

"Why would you call Sean to get Schmidt?" J.J. asks. "I live way closer to you."

"I don't know," I fumble. "I figured you and Carrie would be busy with . . . something. . . ."

Carrie smiles. "We *were,* but we still would have come over to help you."

"You could have called *any* of us," Taylor says. "You knew Sean had to be here on time."

"I didn't think the time was a thing!" I counter. "I didn't plan on getting locked in the attic!"

Jack snorts. "It sounds like you're the one who locked

you both in there. Trying to rekindle a little old flame? Should Reenzie be jealous?"

"Yeah, Autumn," Reenzie asks. "*Should* I be?"

I'm pretty sure Jack was just teasing, but Reenzie is *not*. Her jaw is set and her eyes have turned to steel. It constantly amazes me that someone as gorgeous and together as her thinks that *I'm* any kind of a threat to her relationship, but I guess that's Sean's fault. He waffled between the two of us long enough that he made her permanently neurotic about me. It's amazing it hasn't stopped us from being friends.

"Reenzie, seriously?" I say. "I was freaking out about my *very heavy* dog. Totally freaking out. Sean's the strongest. That's why I thought of him. And for real, if I had any desire to try and hook up with him—which I don't—would I do it when he'd miss the biggest game of his life? He wouldn't even *talk* to me when we were stuck in the attic, that's how mad he was."

Reenzie thinks about it a second, then smiles like it's her birthday. "You're right. He probably hates you now. We're good."

She swings an arm around my shoulders and pulls me to the seat next to her, where we watch the rest of the game. It's a disaster, and we lose by thirty points, so we spend the time concentrating on stadium snacks, selfies, and talking. Jack and Taylor pump Carrie and me mercilessly for information about the Scare Pair dance. They're wondering if they can put in requests and if we can rig the program to get them with someone fabulous. We both say it's completely out of our hands and all about the computer, but I'm smiling inside because I know I have plans.

After the game we pile into our separate cars—I ride with Taylor—and we go to the Shack at Deerfield Beach, where at least half the school always ends up on home game nights. The Shack itself is exactly what it sounds like—a little stand on a wide grassy lawn just off the beach that serves some amazingly greasy snacks and the best soft-serve ice cream in the universe. We all park at one of the always-empty motels down the street, but the minute we get out of the car, we hear the sounds of the party. People talking and squealing and laughing, music blaring from Bluetooth speakers, the people who always come with their guitars and drums and play music on the sand. As we walk closer and all the people start to take shadowy shape in the moonlight, I feel this rush of happiness and sadness at the same time. Maybe it's because I keep visiting the future, but it's like I'm suddenly aware this is all so temporary. After this football season, I'll never be at a beach party with these same people ever again. Even if I come back and visit as an alum, it'll be different. I won't be a part of it; I'll be on the outside. And suddenly I want to hug everyone, even the people whose names I don't even know.

I'm flying so high on euphoria, I don't think twice when I see Sean standing with a bunch of the other football players. I shout his name and throw out my arms like I'm going to hug him. Which I don't, because when he sees me his face gets all Hulk Smashy. Then what's spookier is that he smiles really wide and puts out his arms too. Just not for a hug.

"Autumn Falls!" he shouts loud enough for everyone on the lawn, on the sand, and in every motel room on the beach to hear. Then he climbs onto a picnic table and raises his voice even more. "If anyone's wondering why we were slaughtered today, Autumn is the reason! She locked me in an attic. Can you believe it? Locked me up so I couldn't play and we tanked the game! Oh, and while she was at it, she killed my future too. So if you want someone to blame, please, blame Autumn Falls."

He hops down from the picnic table and stares at me, the eerie smile still on his face. I don't have to look around to know that every pair of eyeballs in the crowd is on me right now. I can feel their hatred through the semi-darkness.

Maybe I should have just let Sean go ahead and have a paralyzed future.

No. He has every right to be mad. He doesn't know I did him a favor. And I've already seen evidence that we're good friends again by senior year of college. *Junior* year of college, since we apparently hook up then. So he'll get over this. And I'll live beyond this night and *not* be murdered in cold blood by the entire football-loving population of Aventura High, even though that part's a little hard to believe at the moment.

I turn to my friends, all of whom have their mouths open in shock. Except Reenzie. She's smiling, though to her credit she changes that to a frown when she realizes I'm looking.

Taylor moves closer to me. "If you want to go home," she says, "I'll totally drive you."

She's not trying to get rid of me. She can feel the angry mob brewing, too, and she wants to help me. But I'm not ready to leave. Even if everyone here hates me, it's still true that I have a limited number of these Shack/beach parties left. I want to stay. I just maybe want a little more distance between myself and the immediate crowd of bloodthirsty natives.

"I'm good," I say. "I'm just going to take a walk."

Tromping through the lawn is the worst. With every step, I hear a low hiss of angry voices. Most of them blend together, but I make out the occasional "Loser!" The farther I get from the Shack, the darker it gets, so I also can't tell people have started throwing their ice cream cones until they splat into me.

By the time I get to the beach, my legs are spackled in chocolate, vanilla, and sprinkles. If the crescent moon was just a little bit smaller or if I had just a little less pride, I'd consider licking it off. The Shack ice cream is that good, and I didn't have a chance to get a cone of my own. Instead I kick off my sandals, hook them over my fingers, and wade into the water up to my thighs. I stand and wobble with the waves, watching them stretch out to infinity.

A minute ago I wanted to hug everyone; now I feel very alone. I consider disappearing into the future for a bit. It would remind me that anything I go through now will be worth it in the end. I only have seven jumps left, though, and I want to save them for things I really need to know.

I'm up early the next morning, and the smell of baking pumpkin lures me downstairs. I find Mom in her favorite red robe, pouring batter into our waffle iron.

"Mmmm," she says. "I knew this would get you. Pumpkin has always had a near-mystical power over you."

"Pumpkin waffles especially," I say. "Do we have pumpkin butter?"

Mom scoffs and points to the little round jar on the counter. "What am I, an amateur?

"So I have to tell you the funniest thing," she says as we tuck into plates of perfection. "Remember how the other day you told me you were so happy I was home early in the day? Well, it made me worry that I wasn't spending enough time at home these days—"

"That's not true!" I assure her. "You're getting the new place off the ground. It's amazing!"

Mom smiles. "Thank you. But that wasn't my point. Afterward, I decided I wanted to do nice for you, so I went to Trader Joe's and bought them out of pumpkin foods, and it was the silliest thing—I wound up getting into this giant conversation with a man who had *his* cart full of pumpkin foods! He couldn't choose between pumpkin scones or pumpkin macaroons. He didn't want to get both, and he wanted me to help him decide because I was clearly a pumpkin connoisseur."

She's getting very girly as she tells this story, and the hairs on my neck are tingling. I have a strange suspicion I'm never going to want to eat pumpkin anything ever again.

"Are you saying you . . . *like* this guy?" I choke out.

"Autumn!" Mom looks at me openmouthed, like I shocked her, but there's still that thing dancing in her eyes.

"What? It's a question!"

"No," she says emphatically. "Glen is a *friend*. I just thought it was funny—I've never met a friend at the supermarket before, and now we're meeting tomorrow for coffee!"

I choke on my waffle. Mom runs and gets me a glass of milk.

"I shouldn't have told you," she says gently. "I can tell you're jumping to all kinds of conclusions. You shouldn't. He's a friend. It's nice to make new friends. I don't have a lot of friends apart from the ones I met at the rescue. It's not like when you and Erick were little and I met all my mom friends through you."

She's crouched down so she can look me in the eye while I sit and drink my milk. The sunlight streaming in through the back sliders lights her brown curls like an angelic aura. She's absolutely telling the truth. To her this is just a friend thing and she doesn't want me to worry, but I know better, and I nearly choke again as it all comes together.

This is why I saw her and Glen together in my last jump. It was the conversation I had with Mom that sent her on her pumpkin-product spree and right into Glen's waiting shopping cart. I did this. I got them back together.

Then I'll just have to get them apart again.

I wish Mom was going to the Scare Pair dance. It would certainly make my scheming easier.

At least the rest of the weekend is great. Ames and Taylor stay over on Saturday. Amalita partied too hard at the beach, so we all let her veg in my room and basically sleep it off all day while Tee and I make pit stops at Taylor's and Amalita's houses for their stuff, then hang in the pool. Sunday Amalita's feeling better, but we still go low-key. We're in our pajamas all day except when we're swimming, we do our homework together, and it seems like Taylor and I talk Amalita out of ever seeing Zander again. She definitely doesn't call or text him the whole time we're together, so that's huge. I'm tempted to jump ahead to the future, because I have a good feeling that the drinking thing won't be an issue for Amalita anymore. But with seven jumps and a lot of work to do still, I figure I'll wait.

Monday morning I have an email from Mrs. Foreman, my history teacher. She says she found a tutor for me and would like me to meet him in her office after school. I know Carrie and the rest of the Senior Social Committee won't like it because we're only a week away from the dance and are in the thick of shopping and planning and prepping. Even though she got me into the "sisterhood" for Get-Autumn-into-College purposes, I know she'll say tutoring isn't a good enough excuse to miss a meeting, at least not this week. Instead of trying to explain, I text her and say I have family stuff I got roped into, and I have to be at Century Acres after school with Eddy. She says it's fine, but I can hear her passive-aggressive guilt-trip voice and heavy sigh even through the text.

I bring a protein bar and Diet Coke in my backpack so I can hang in the library for lunch. It serves a double purpose. It keeps me away from Carrie so she can't try to convince me to blow off my plans, and it keeps me away from Sean. Most people are already thinking about next Friday's game and don't care anymore that I'm a football saboteur, but Reenzie keeps texting me giddy updates about how he can't even hear my name without punching something. So far it's been mainly pillows, and I'm pretty positive he'd never actually get violent with me, but better to give him another day to cool down.

When school ends, I wait until I'm sure the entire Senior Social Committee will be safely ensconced in their classroom before I zip down to Mrs. Foreman's office.

"Sorry I'm late!" I say as I race in. "I came as soon as I—"

Mrs. Foreman's office holds her desk, a massive library of books, and a couch with a low coffee table. The couch is right against the door side of the office, so I can't see who's sitting there laughing with Mrs. Foreman until he leans forward and turns at the sound of my voice.

It's J.J. And he's gaping at me like a fish out of water.

"Oh. Hi," I say. "I'm sorry, I thought I was meeting my tutor here."

"You are!" Mrs. Foreman chirps. "Autumn Falls . . . J.J. Austin."

I purse my lips together. Some teachers at Aventura are really into knowing every detail about students' social lives. They seem to know even before us who's going to break up and who's getting together. I've heard some of them even run pools. Then there are the teachers like Mrs. Foreman, who believe students only exist inside their classrooms.

"We know each other," I say.

"Oh good!" Mrs. Foreman says. "That's even better. And did you know that J.J. took my AP U.S. History class last year?"

Yes, I could say. *I believe that may have come up in the middle of one of our make-out sessions when we were going out last year. Tough to be sure, though, with his tongue down my throat and all.*

Instead I just smile. "Really? No, I didn't."

"Indeed," Mrs. Foreman says. "He was my top student and plans to major in the subject in college. I honestly can't think of a better person to hold your hand through this course."

J.J. smiles grimly, and I almost laugh out loud. I'm pretty sure the last thing in the world J.J. wants to do is hold my hand through anything.

"I'll leave you to it, then," she says. "I figure you'll use my office today; then you can figure out your own schedule from there. Don't forget, Autumn—our first test is next week. I expect great things now that you'll be tended to with such delicate skill."

Mrs. Foreman floats out of the room on a cloud of self-satisfaction. The minute the door closes behind her, J.J. buries his face in his hands.

"Got any anagrams for 'awkward'?" I ask.

"'Skywalker . . . and woe,'" he replies.

"'Skywalker and woe'?" I say. "Really?"

J.J. shrugs. "Technically that's 'so keenly awkward.'"

"Yeah, okay. That works better. And points for the *Star Wars* reference. Jack would be proud."

J.J. smiles weakly, and I lean on the arm of the couch. After a moment I ask, "Why didn't you tell me Mrs. Foreman wanted you to tutor me?"

"I didn't know. She just asked if I'd tutor one of her students. She's my main teacher recommendation, so I said yes."

"She is?" I ask. "And you really want to major in history? I thought you wanted to major in English lit."

J.J. looks me right in the eye. "Things change," he says.

I can't hold his gaze. I look down at my chipping nail polish. "Right."

Neither one of us says anything for a while. It's so bizarre. We're with each other almost every single day, but I can't even remember the last time we were alone together. Probably it was the day he broke up with me, almost a year ago. I can't even believe it's been that long. If you'd asked me then, I'd have sworn we'd be back to normal within a couple months—by last year's spring break at the latest. Instead we kind of found a new normal, and judging by the futures I've seen, we don't really find a way out of it. We stay friendly . . . but not super-close friends.

"You lied to Carrie," he says.

I'm so caught up in my own thoughts I don't know what he means for a second, but then I remember my story about Eddy. "Yeah," I admit. "I didn't think she'd approve of school over Senior Social Committee."

"Good call," he says. "I won't tell her."

Another minute of complete silence. I'm just about to tell him this is crazy and we should tell Mrs. Foreman it won't work out when he says, "Okay, then. Let's get started."

My test is on the American Revolution, and J.J. spends a half hour trying to drill facts and dates into my head. I'm concentrating hard, I really am, but the more he spouts, the more it all sounds like noise to me. Even when he writes everything down on notecards for me, the dates just blend together and dance and mix up on the page and in my head.

Finally he sighs heavily, and I feel terrible because I'm not getting any of this at all.

"I'm calling it," he says. "Elephant in the room."

"Oh!" I jump in my seat. "I know this one! Republican party!"

He scrunches his eyebrows, then laughs out loud. "Okay,

yes, that's the symbol for the Republican Party, but that happened about a hundred years after what we're studying. I meant *our* elephant." He blushes a little and looks down at his hands. "You know . . . us."

My heart gives an extra beat. I'm nervous, but I'm not sure why. What do I think he'll say?

He's looking at me like it's my turn to say something.

"Right," I offer.

"If I'm going to tutor you, we have to be normal. You can't be weird around me."

I'm so stunned it's like he threw a bucket of cold water on my face. "Me weird around you?! *You're* weird around *me!*"

"Seriously?" he snorts. "You barely say two words to me. Ever."

"You barely even look at me! When we're all hanging out, I could whip off my shirt and run around swinging it over my head and you wouldn't even notice."

The sides of J.J.'s mouth curl up in a smirk. "Pretty sure I'd notice if you took off your shirt and swung it over your head."

"I'm not so sure."

"Wanna try?" he asks. "I'll prove it."

I wad up one of his notecards and throw it at him.

"Hey! Tutor abuse! I could get a lethal paper cut!"

"Only if I use the cards like throwing stars." I pick up a notecard and fling it so it smacks point first into J.J.'s chest. He watches it hit its mark, then slowly gets up, raising a single eyebrow.

"I see you underestimate my ninja skills," he says. Then, in a flash, he whips the rest of the cards off the table and flings them at me in lightning-fast succession, while I race around the room screaming and dodging away. I end up taking cover on the far side of Mrs. Foreman's desk . . . which is right by her box of recycling. Score!

"Bombs away!" I shout as I crumple a sheet of paper and lob it at J.J. He counters with a mad volley of notecards.

Soon it's an all-out paper war, with each of us diving for the other's used ammunition as we dodge and attack. We leap on Mrs. Foreman's couch, duck under her desk, and roll her desk chair like a moving shield, shouting and squealing with every throw and hit.

Until the door opens. We freeze—sweaty, tousled, and panting—as Mr. Winthrop leans his head in. He looks angry at first, but then his expression widens into a knowing smile. Unlike Mrs. Foreman, Mr. Winthrop prides himself on keeping up with all the student social drama, so J.J.'s and my past is no secret. "I heard shouting," he says. "Everything cool in here?"

"We're good," J.J. says.

Mr. Winthrop smiles wider. "Glad to hear it." He winks and shuts the door . . . and two seconds later J.J. and I collapse onto the couch laughing.

"Did he seriously *wink*?" I ask.

"'Skywalker and woe'—next thing I'm writing on his board."

"'So keenly awkward,'" I agree.

We sit there for a second, shaking our heads and bursting out with another laugh every time our eyes meet.

"I've missed you."

I say it without meaning to, but once the words are out, I feel this deep pain inside because I realize how much I mean them. I've missed J.J. desperately. There's no one else I'm this goofy and happy and easy with—not even Jenna. And all of a sudden I'm terrified and can't look at him because I'm afraid I ruined it and he'll pull back into himself like before. Finally I risk a look at his face. My heart thumps when I see his eyes. Even though he's smiling, his eyes are deep and serious, and he doesn't take them off me.

"I've missed you too."

The deep pain inside me explodes into happy fireworks and I want to throw my arms around him for a huge hug, but I don't. I just look at him with a dopey smile on my face. Maybe not quite as dopey as the one on his . . . but yeah, probably the same.

"Okay," he says, pounding on the couch, "let's get you tutored up. We're out of time today, so we'll start tomorrow after Senior Social Committee. I'll come to your house."

"Really?" I ask. "I thought you always see Carrie after Senior Social Committee."

"I do," he says. "But this is to impress Mrs. Foreman and improve my college recommendation, so it takes precedence. Carrie'll understand."

I raise my eyebrows. "She'll understand you're hanging out with me instead of with her?"

"Not a chance," J.J. admits without hesitation. "But she will understand 'a nun's magnificent speeds.'"

I don't even ask. I just wait until he translates.

"An unspecified assignment," he says. "Doesn't make sense to get her upset about nothing."

"Right," I say. And while keeping the tutoring a secret from Carrie makes it seem like it *is* something, I totally agree with J.J. Much as Carrie and I are pseudo-friends, she's very aware that I'm the only other girl J.J. has ever dated at Aventura High, and she'd be freaked by us hanging out alone together. Especially during time that's supposed to be theirs.

Of course, if I have my way, this won't be an issue after Saturday's Scare Pair dance. Carrie will be off with Keith Hamilton, and J.J. will be floating in anagram splendor with Mariah Amhari.

The next day, J.J. does exactly what he promised. He shows up at my door moments after I get home from Senior Social Committee.

"No books?" I ask when I answer the door and see he's empty-handed.

"No need," he replies. He beelines for my couch, picks up the remote, and starts surfing through all the TV menus. "I know you. Books won't get this stuff into your head. If you're going to learn about the American Revolution, you have to become interested in the characters. So here," he says, nodding at the TV, "characters."

He presses a button and we start watching a movie

called *The Patriot*, which is about this guy who reluctantly joins the Revolutionary War, alongside his ridiculously hot son. The movie's not bad. Lots of action, and of course the hot son, who dies in his dad's arms. When it's over, J.J. starts telling me all the ways the movie is historically wrong. He brings up a bunch of things we've talked about in class, but while they were just dizzying dates before, now I feel like I can ground them in some kind of reality. I can imagine the people he's talking about, even if they weren't in the movie, and it all feels more alive. I'm shocked when my mom comes home with Erick and says it's already eight o'clock—I had no idea we'd been studying so long. Mom makes a huge fuss over J.J. when she sees him—she always thought he was great—and when she hears we haven't eaten, she insists on making us a meal, which we eat while we talk about school, and our friends, and our lives, and the best things each of us has been watching online that we can't believe the other one hasn't seen. We show them to each other and laugh like crazy until my mom boots him out because it's a school night and she insists I get some sleep.

It feels so much like we're back to normal that I half expect him to pick me up for school the next day, but of course he doesn't. I do see him at lunch. It's my first day braving our circle since I saved Sean's future by destroying it, and he's handling it reasonably well by pretending I don't exist and cringing whenever anyone says my name. As for J.J. and me, we act more or less the same way we have all year. Friendly, but in a cool, sorta distant way. It's only when something comes up that reminds us of one of the YouTube bits we saw last night that he catches my eye over Carrie's head and we both start laughing.

"What?" Carrie asks, already joining in and giggling. "Share with the rest of us."

"It's nothing," J.J. says. "I swear."

"Hey, Jack," I say brightly, fake-changing the subject. "What do you know about Skywalker and woe?"

It's a bogus question, meant only for J.J., but Jack takes it seriously and rambles on about the emotional state of the *Star Wars* character through all the movies. I force myself to look very interested and nod a lot, but really I keep glancing at J.J. His lips are pursed and he keeps looking down, trying to hide his smile.

That evening it's the same as the night before. He comes over—with a pizza this time—and we watch another movie. This one's called *1776*. It's a *musical* about the Declaration of Independence with some songs so truly dippy that I have to stand on the couch and make up my own words as I sing along.

"Come on!" J.J. laughs. "You have to listen to the words."

"My words are better," I say. "You're just jealous 'cause you're not as quick."

"Seriously?" J.J. asks, and of course the next second he's on his feet, too, killing me with his own version of the song that's all about Mr. Winthrop and his quest to be the coolest teacher at school. When the song's over, I bow to his superior songwriting skill and we plop back down to watch the rest of the movie.

At least, I'm *supposed* to be watching the rest of the movie. Instead I'm suddenly very aware of the inches between us on the couch. It feels solid, like the space between two magnets, when they're so close you know if you bring them even a millimeter closer they'll snap together. And even though I'm watching John Adams sing and dance, I'm seeing J.J. and me the way we were last year over Thanksgiving break. When he'd come over and we'd watch movies right here on this couch, only he'd have his arm around me and I'd lay my head on his shoulder. When it was good between us, before I got all mixed up with Sean and didn't want J.J. anymore.

Was that a mistake? I mean, I was totally wrong about being with Sean. Was I wrong about *not* being with J.J.?

I push the thoughts out of my mind and try to concentrate on history, but the same thing happens Thursday night. I try to concentrate on the movie, but all I can think about is the way J.J. looked at me the first time he said he was crazy about me. The way it felt when he surprised me with our first kiss.

I wonder . . . as long as I'm mixing things up for the Scare Pair dance, why don't I pair myself with J.J.?

No. That's insane. I messed J.J. up big-time when we went out before. We're finally friends again. I'm not going to risk that. I can't even dream about possibly, maybe, in the slightest, tiniest way even hinting to him that I'm feeling this way unless I know it's real and deep and about more than just loving him as a friend.

Still, I can't help but wonder . . . if my plan works and he and Carrie break up . . . will he end up with Mariah, or is there a chance he could end up with me?

I know one way to find out. That night in bed, I pull the locket from underneath my giant T-shirt and open it up. I set it for five months from now. That'll be next year, so I flip the year wheel as well, only I accidentally spin it way too far and have to spin it back to get to the year I want. Then I snap the locket closed, hold it in my palm, and concentrate on J.J. and me and what's to come.

9

✦✦✦✦✦

march, six years and five months later

I'm standing in the middle of an island. Not a desert island, a kitchen island, which I realize when I look down and see my stomach end in a slab of granite countertop. It's disconcerting, but only slightly less disconcerting than hearing my own voice behind me.

"You're sure it's not horrible we're crashing your anniversary?"

I spin around, the counter still bisecting me, and I gasp.

It's not that seeing Future Me is a shock. It's not, not anymore. What *is* a shock is this particular Future Me. She looks way older than me five months from now. Did I set the locket correctly? I yank on the chain and pull it out, then open it up and examine the date. The month and day are right . . . but when I hold the locket close and squint at the year I see it's not set for next year at all. It's *six years* from now. Or from *then,* when I left. So assuming Future Me went to college, she graduated two years ago.

I examine this Future Me for any clues about her. She looks a little different than other Future Mes. More professional and less casual, but maybe that's because this is the oldest I've ever seen her. Her orange hair is shorter than I wear it now, just above her shoulders. She has bangs, and her hair hangs so straight I know we're nowhere near Florida and its humidity. She wears jeans with a funky dark blue/light blue patch pattern on them and a giant brown sweater that looks so cozy I want to climb into it with her.

"It's our *dating* anniversary" comes a reply, and I finally rip my eyes away from my future self to see who I'm talking to.

"Jenna!" I scream. "See? I *told* you you're alive! And you're beautiful! Look at your hair!"

I run through the kitchen island and reach out to play with the blond corkscrew curls that sprout out of her head and hang down to the middle of her neck, but of course my fingers pass right through them. Jenna would lose her mind if she knew she'd traded her eternal ponytail for this cut. She'd totally freak out if she saw her always-bare face painted with red-red lipstick, blush, and eye shadow, even though the effect is completely subtle and sophisticated. At least she'd be happy with the outfit. I could see her in these heather-gray leggings, boots, and oversized off-white cable-knit sweater.

"You're killing me with this," I tell her. "I would literally die to get a picture of you right now and show it to you when I get back."

Future Jenna grabs a bottle of white wine from the refrigerator. As she uncorks it, she says, "Dating anniversaries only matter until you're married and have a *real* anniversary."

Future Me rolls her eyes. "You just got married six months ago. You haven't even *had* a real anniversary yet."

"Wait, *what?!*" I shout. "You're *married?!* Who's the guy? Is it Sam? Are you with Sam?"

"Doesn't matter," Jenna says. "Dating anniversary still loses. Besides, no way was I going to let you come to Colorado and not stay with me."

"Stay with you?" I echo. "This is your *house*?" I look around the gorgeously huge kitchen, with its stainless steel refrigerator and wood cabinets and giant island that served as my skirt when I first appeared in the room. Jenna's not only alive in the future, but she's also kicking butt.

She pours herself and Future Me a glass of wine and grabs two extra wineglasses; then I follow them into the living room. It looks like a ski lodge, complete with a sloped wood-beamed roof, a giant fireplace with a crackling fire, and sink-in couches. I listen in while Jenna and Future Me talk, but I also snoop around the room so I can soak up all the information I can. From what I gather, Jenna's married not to Sam but to a guy named Simon. They ran together in college, and I figure out it was the University of Oregon because I see an afghan with the college logo on it draped over another couch. There are pictures on the wall of Jenna and Simon's wedding. He's exactly her type: tall and athletic-looking, with sandy-blond hair and striking blue eyes.

"Jenna! He's so cute! And look at us!" I gush, pointing to another picture of the two of us grinning and mushing our cheeks together. She's in her bridal gown and I'm wearing a gorgeous baby-blue dress. There are other girls wearing a similar dress in the background of the photo, but mine has a slightly different neckline, like it's supposed to stand out and be different. I gasp. "I was your maid of honor, wasn't I?"

Jenna doesn't answer. She's still talking to Future Me, and I realize I'm missing valuable intel, so I move closer and listen in. Future Me is asking Jenna about business, and I get that Jenna and Simon are all outdoors, all the time. They run a ski camp in the winter and a kids' adventure camp in the summer, and spend spring and fall just enjoying themselves and prepping for the other seasons. They don't make a ton of money, but Simon's family bought them the house as a wedding present, and they make enough for everything else they need.

"Jenna, this is perfect," I gush. "I promise you, back in my time, you and I are going to work together to make sure all this comes true."

Just then, Future Me, Jenna, and I turn at the sounds of jingling and footsteps outside the front door. Jenna grins to Future Me. "The boys are back."

"The boys?" I ask. Then I remember the two extra wineglasses Jenna brought in from the kitchen. It would have to be her husband, right? And . . .

"Hey!" Simon calls as he opens the door, and I'm surprised and thrilled to hear his British accent. His cheeks are red from the cold and he's bundled in a thick coat, but I only glance at him before I'm completely distracted by his two giant black Labs. They bound inside and race up to Future Me, tails wagging furiously.

"Adorable accent . . . and *dogs!*" I squeal it to Jenna, but she's already up off the couch and out of my sight, I assume off wrapping herself around Simon. "I can't even deal with the level of perfection."

"Hey."

The voice comes from behind me. It turns my whole body to liquid, and my blood rushes closer to my skin.

I'm afraid to turn around, but I don't know what scares me: being right, or being wrong. Instead I keep my eyes on Future Me. She looks up toward the sound of the voice and smiles. It's a smile that's familiar, but I've never seen it on my own face. It takes a second before I recognize it. Future Me has the same look on her face that my mom and dad had whenever they looked at each other.

Okay, not *whenever* they looked at each other. That would be weird and kind of disturbing. But it would happen a lot. Not just in romantic moments like when they were toasting their anniversary or he heard a song they loved on the radio and swept her into his arms to dance, but little nothing moments like when he'd make a really dumb joke or when she came in from gardening all dirty and disheveled. They'd just look at each other with this doe-eyed expression that said nothing in the world meant as much to them as one another. Erick and I used to roll our eyes and make gagging noises whenever we caught them at it, but we both secretly loved it. We knew it meant they were crazy in love . . . just like Future Me is crazy in love with the voice behind me. The voice I know too well to second-guess.

I don't have to turn around to see. J.J. Austin walks right through me on his way to my future self. He looks like himself . . . only better. His jeans show off the muscles in his legs, and his shoulders are broader underneath his blue tucked-in button-down shirt. His face is more chiseled, and he has a light scruff of facial hair that I never would dream would work on J.J., but it totally does.

It's not just his body that's different, though. It's the way he carries himself. He moves like he's completely confident and comfortable in his skin. He sits down next to Future Me and kisses me . . . *us* . . . effortlessly, like he does it all the time. It's a take-it-for-granted kiss, but not in the kind of blow-off way we shared when I felt smothered and I wanted to get out. Our lips linger together, and when we pull away we're both smiling like nothing in the universe could make us happier than staring into each other's eyes forever.

"Enough!" Jenna declares from the couch opposite us, where she and Simon sit close together. She has her knees curled up onto the couch and Simon's arm is around her, but she ducks away just long enough to fill everyone's wineglasses and hand them out. "You get each other all the time. We only get to see you when you visit. Tell us everything."

Future Me and J.J. do as she asks. The two of them—the two of *us*—talk animatedly, bubbling over one another and finishing each other's sentences, but never rudely. Each interruption only picks up the story with more energy, and whichever one of us is cut off just smiles at the other, fascinated, as if hearing the next part of the story for the first time, until we're inspired to jump back in. All the while, we're constantly in contact. I reach out and touch his knee. He puts his hand on my back. We lace our fingers together. We do it all automatically, like we're moving together as a single being, with no boundaries between us.

I don't get our whole history from J.J. and Future Me. They recap some things Jenna has to already know but leave out big obvious things like when we got together. I have no idea if it was at Aventura High or in college. I don't even know if we went to the *same* college. What I do learn is that we must have been together at college graduation, because that's when we decided to pool any money presents we got and put them into a joint savings account we opened just for this purpose. It doesn't seem like we lived together after graduation, or even lived in the same city, but we both had jobs and put part of our paychecks into that account every month. Finally, after we'd saved for a year and a half, we each wangled four months away from work to empty out our vacation account and take a massive road trip around the country.

"Like the road trips you planned for us when we first went out," Future Me says, grinning at J.J., and I'm stunned because I was thinking the exact same thing. I'm even more stunned that J.J. doesn't seem upset by the memory. I mean, our first time going out wasn't exactly a huge success. But I guess since everything ended with us together, it's all just part of our story.

"And we're the last stop?" Simon asks. "We're honored."

"Beyond honored," Jenna seconds. She raises her glass. "A toast!"

"Wait," J.J. says. "I think you'll want to hold that a second."

He pales a little and swallows hard, and for a second I see the quirky, skinny, sunburned boy I met on my first day at Aventura High. Then he takes a deep breath and gets down on one knee.

My heart thuds so loud I'm sure everyone can hear it.

He's down on one knee. Is he . . . ?

I look at Future Me to see what she thinks. Her eyes are wide and her face is flushed. She stares down at J.J. with this weird mix of elation and fear, like she can't actually believe he's about to do what it seems like he's about to do.

I move right next to her. I want to move *into* her, so I'm looking through her eyes and seeing what she sees, but no matter how much I want to, the idea totally weirds me out, so I just get as close as I can.

J.J.'s trembling. I can see his hands shake as he reaches up and takes the hands of Future Me.

"Autumn," he says, "I fell in love with you the first second I saw you, and I've loved you ever since. No one else in this world makes me as happy as you. No one makes me laugh as hard. And when things are bad, you're the one who makes them better. When I think about my life, I think about you there, next to me, always. I can't even imagine me without you, and I think I knew it even then, the day we met. Autumn . . ."

His voice cracks and he gives a nervous laugh. It's so sweet I can't help but smile, and I guess Future Me does the same thing because he smiles back, more relaxed. He swallows and takes another deep breath. When he finds his voice again, it's soft but strong.

"I love you. I love you more than I can ever say in words . . . and I'm really good with words . . . but they're not enough. None of them are. Except maybe these."

He reaches into his pocket and pulls out a black velvet box. His hands are steady now as he opens it to reveal a beautiful round diamond on a delicate platinum band. He looks back up at me—at us—and his eyes shine with tears.

"Autumn Falls," he says. Then he grins wickedly.

"J.J.," Future Me says with a jittery laugh, "I swear to God if you anagram now—"

J.J. grins wider. "Autumn Falls . . ."

A dramatic pause. He can't stop smiling and neither can I, but I'm dying to hear him say it. Then he stops smiling. He looks up at me, completely open, sincere, and vulnerable.

". . . will you marry me?"

"Yes."

10

october, senior year

My voice is soft when Jenna answers the phone. I can't help it. I'm completely in awe of what I'm about to say. "Jenna . . . I'm in love with J.J."

"You are?! What happened?"

I tell her everything, and when I'm done she screams. "This is *amazing*! I don't even care if Sam goes to MIT. I have perfect-Brit-boy Simon waiting for me!"

"Yeah," I say, "it's amazing. For both of us. But the future keeps changing. What if we mess it up?"

"You won't," she assures me. "*We* won't. The future you saw is based on what's going on *now*, right? So all we have to do is stick with that and everything will work out the way it's supposed to. I stay with Sam, and you keep going with your plan to break up Carrie and J.J. at the Scare Pair dance."

"But what about J.J.?" I ask. "The way I feel . . . it hurts to have it inside like this. I just want to run over to his house and tell him!"

"No," Jenna says. "That's off-plan. Off-plan changes the future. Break him and Carrie up, then let it happen naturally from there."

"How?! How do I wait that long?"

"Future You did, right?"

"I don't know! I don't when J.J. and I got together. They didn't say. What if they got together after I saw this future and then ran to his house and told him how I feel?"

Jenna's silent for a moment, but I can hear her breath speed up the littlest bit as she paces her room. "No," she finally says. "I get what you're saying, but it doesn't sound right. Every time you've made a move based on what you've seen, it changed the future. I don't think you can risk it."

"You're just saying that because you want to meet hot-boy Simon," I grouse.

"*Yes!*" she retorts; then she pauses a second. "Wait a minute . . . when you were at my house, did I look for you at all?"

"Why would you look for me?" I ask. "I was right next to you."

"No, I mean *you*. Past You. 'Cause you're telling me this now, so when I'm actually there in the future, I'll remember this is the moment you told me about and I'll look for you, right?"

"I guess . . ."

"And you'll look for you too!" she shouts. "Which will be even weirder because now you'll know J.J.'s going to propose before he actually does it, which could change everything . . . unless the Future You that you saw *already* knew he was going to propose because she had once been *you* you and had seen it all before. . . ."

"Okay, you're making my head hurt," I say. "I've got to go."

"No off-plan!" she calls just before I click off. "Simon and I are counting on you!"

Once she's off the line, I stare at the phone.

I really want to text J.J.

Like, *really* want to text J.J.

Would it really hurt things if I texted J.J.? We're friends again now, right? We used to text all the time.

I surf the Net until I find the perfect thing to send: an episode of *Drunk History* about Baron von Steuben getting Washington's army into shape. I copy the link and text it to J.J., then wait an agonizing thirty minutes until he texts back:

☺

"That's it?!" I scream to my phone. "A smiley face?!"

I throw my phone onto the bed and throw myself down after it.

I suck at being patient.

I'm convinced there's no way I'll ever get to sleep. I do,

but I dream about J.J. and me on our amazingly perfect four-month cross-country road trip, so I'm completely miserable when I wake up and realize I have to wait six years for that to happen.

As if to rub in my trauma, there's an email from Carrie on my phone. It's for the whole Senior Social Committee. Tomorrow's the Scare Pair dance, and tonight we have to put all the date cards together. It's all about the last minute, because Carrie had the Senior Social Committee extend the questionnaire deadline until the end of the school day *today* so we get as many people as possible. Carrie's plan is to have all eight of us in the sisterhood meet at Brody's house right after school. That's when Brody will stop the server from accepting any more questionnaires, run her program, and print out the results onto fancy cards that we'll stuff into envelopes and label.

I have only the vaguest idea of how I'll sabotage the Scare Pairs and make them what I want. I'm hoping it'll all come together at the last second.

School is all about dodging J.J. There is no way I can handle our kinda-sorta not-really-around-other-people friendship right now. Just before lunch, there's a horrible moment when I see him walking down the hall toward me with his arm around Carrie. He's smiling down at her with his forehead close to hers, and even from twenty feet away I can tell they're all flirty and whispery, and I know if he looks up and sees me my chest will open up and my heart will flop onto the floor in a pool of horror.

He starts to raise his head, but I duck into the library. Clearly it's a Quest Bar and Diet Coke by myself day.

When school ends, I desperately wish I were meeting J.J. for another tutoring session, but I'm also desperately glad I'm not. I don't think I could sit two inches away from him and not say something stupid or try to curl into his arms. Instead I ask Brody LeClair for a ride to her house. Better to ride with her than with Carrie, who would be telling me all kinds of cute stories about her and the guy I'm supposed to marry.

Brody's house is huge. There are four giant bedrooms upstairs, and since she's an only child and a tech genius, one room is her "office." It's filled with computers, scanners, printers, and machines I can't even comprehend. I wouldn't be surprised if she could control a manned space flight from here. The one machine I *do* understand is the giant wall-mounted TV at the end of the room. In honor of Halloween, we're going to have a Tim Burton film fest while we work, starting with *The Nightmare Before Christmas*.

Brody and I are the first to arrive, which gives her a chance to stop the questionnaire site and start her pairing program. Carrie and Gus are the last to show, but we're all happiest to see them because they bring the pizzas, drinks, and snacks. Their timing is close to perfect, because the Scare Pair program finishes up just five minutes before they arrive.

"Okay, here's the deal!" Carrie says after we lay out all the refreshments. "Eat and drink all you want, but don't get the date cards or envelopes dirty. Brody just printed out labels for everyone coming to the dance. Now she's printing out the Scare Pair cards." She reaches for the humming printer and pulls out one of the freshly printed cards. It's thick stock and about the size of an iPhone 6 Plus, with a fancy orange and black border around the edge. The envelopes match perfectly.

"Ouch." Carrie winces as she looks at the card. "This one's for Steffi Aaronsen and it pairs her with Wayne Jarvitz. She won't like that at all. See?"

Carrie holds out the card. It has Steffi's name in huge drippy-blood font. Below that, it says, *shall meet her Scare Pair* in italics. Then, in a smaller version of the drippy-blood font is Wayne Jarvitz's name. Since Steffi's name is the big one, this is her card. Wayne's will have the same information, but the other way around. Beneath the smaller name it says in smaller italics, *Don't like what you see? Give it just one dance. Don't be a ghoul—that's the rule.*

"Brody's awesome and already printed out eight stacks of label sheets, one for each of us. The whole student body is there alphabetically, so you'll find who you need. Everyone start grabbing cards as they come out of the printer, stuff them into the envelopes, label the envelopes, seal them, then put them into one of the two plastic bins. When we have enough, the envelopes should stand upright in there. Just please try to keep them all in alphabetical order. The time we spend now is time we save at the start of the dance."

We all set to work. Despite the efforts of each year's Senior Social Committee, dances don't usually get big crowds. The computer thing helped, though. We have around two hundred people coming—two hundred envelopes to stuff with cards for one hundred Scare Pairs. For a high school dance, that's huge. It's also a ton of stuffing/labeling/sealing work, but it helps that we're all snacking, watching the movie, and squealing about every pair we read.

"No! Way!" Gus shouts as he looks at one of his cards. "I got Doug Church! I didn't even know he was out!"

"But you knew he was gay?" Meegan Rudolph asks.

"Oh, please," Gus says. "Everyone knows he's gay. He's as gay as Kyler Leeds."

"Kyler Leeds is not gay!" Carrie and I shout at the same time. We catch each other's eye and smile, and for a second I forgive her for wanting to steal my perfect future.

We all gab about most of the pairs we read, and though I keep an ear out for my friends, I know it's actually better if I don't hear their names. Then only one person and not all eight of us will know I changed things around. And maybe one person will think they remembered it wrong.

"YES! Brody, your program is a genius!" Carrie cries, waving her card in the air. "I got J.J.!"

"Of course you did!" Kassie dolphin-squeals back. "You guys are MFEOFAETLND!"

My head throbs, and it's not just because Kassie's screeching nonsense letters in a register high enough to break glass. My life jut got a lot harder. I can still change

Carrie and J.J.'s Scare Pairs—I have to more than ever now—but everyone's going to know someone swapped them. If I'm lucky, they won't guess it's me.

A few minutes later, Mariah Amhari holds a card in front of her face and moans. "I got Keith Hamilton."

Carrie wheels in her seat to face Mariah. "Seriously? Want to trade?"

I don't move a muscle, but inside I'm turning cartwheels. *Yes! This is perfect! Switch!*

Then Carrie laughs. "Just kidding. I'm taken. Keith's a cutie, though. You should work that thing."

Mariah sighs but dutifully stuffs and labels her Scare Pair envelope, then shoves it in place among the others.

"Zander Grigsby's coming?" Swoozie Lyman says a little later. "I didn't think he did school dances."

"Who's he paired with?" Brody asks.

Carrie's on her way back to her seat from the pizza table and looks over Swoozie's shoulder. She grimaces, then looks at me. "It's Ames."

Crap. No. No way. I've worked too hard to fix Amalita's future. She's avoided Zander since the football game—hasn't called, hasn't texted, hasn't anything. Not a chance I'm letting this dance push them back together.

"Ooooo," Gus singsongs a little bit later. He dances a card in my direction. "Someone else got a dream date."

"Is it me?" Meegan asks.

"Am I looking at you?" Gus retorts. "It's Autumn. And she's with dreamy Sean Geary!"

"Seriously?" I blurt.

"What? He's hot," Gus says. "And weren't you guys a thing last year? Now's your chance to get him back."

"Sean *hates* Autumn," Carrie informs him, then lowers her voice. "Didn't you hear what happened at the football game last week?"

"Carrie, I'm eight feet away from you," I say. "I can hear you."

"I can't," Gus says. "The minute you say 'football,' my ears shut off."

With two hundred envelopes to stuff, the party will go on for a while. That's good. I need the time. If I do everything at once, people will get suspicious. The helpful thing is that all of us are constantly up and down, moving between the printer, our chairs, the snacks, and the plastic bins. We're also all continually riffling through the two bins of envelopes to get everything in alphabetical order. Added bonus? The movie at the front of the room means everyone's attention is partly distracted up there. So here's what I do. All Brody's computer papers are superorganized in a bunch of baskets in a far back corner. In one trip around the room when no one's looking, I snag a sheet of blank label paper and stash it in my backpack. During another trip I grab a few extra blank cards and envelopes and shove them in the backpack as well. My next tasks are harder, but Tim Burton's totally in my corner. Everyone's so loving the end of *Edward Scissorhands* that they don't even notice me sift through the finished Scare

Pair envelopes, grab the ones I need, and stash them in my backpack.

When all the stuffing's done and the movies are over, we clean up Brody's office and load the bins of Scare Pair cards into Carrie's car so she can keep them safe until the dance.

"Autumn!" she calls out the window once she's in her car. "You need a ride home, right? I'm going that way anyway."

Of course she is. She's going to see J.J., which is the last thing I want to think about tonight. I was hoping to get a ride with a different member of the sisterhood, but I can't exactly say no now.

"So," she says once we're on our way, "tonight's the anniversary of J.J.'s and my first kiss."

"Really?" I say, then quickly change the subject. "So decorating the gym'll be fun tomorrow, right?"

"Our first kiss from the *first* time we dated," Carrie clarifies, totally ignoring my question. "Back in freshman year."

"Got it," I snap. "So . . . decorating."

"His parents are going to be out late tonight," Carrie says, "so we'll get to do something special to celebrate." She smiles, and her eyes dance with anticipation. "I even bought a costume."

I'm dying to clap my hands over my ears and scream *LA-LA-LA-LA I CAN'T HEAR YOU!,* but I grit my teeth and control myself.

"Sounds . . . fun," I manage. "Ooh, I love this song!"

I crank up the radio and sing along as best I can to some hip-hop song I've never heard in my life. I leap out of the car while it's still rolling toward my curb and run.

Immediately, Erick and some girl spring away from each other on the couch.

"Ew," I groan. "Where's Mom?"

"At the new site," Erick says.

"Hi!" The girl waves. She's cute and blond and disturbingly disheveled. I can't even. I nod to her but keep talking to Erick.

"Does Mom know you're here with her?"

"It's Lori," the girl says. "Lori with an i. And the o's really a heart."

"Okay, you need to stop talking," I say.

"She thinks we're at the movies," Erick admits. Smart kid. He knows if he hadn't said it I'd have found out later and totally blown his cover. "You won't tell, right?"

"Not if you do me a favor." I turn to Lori-with-an-i. "I'm borrowing him for a minute. If you take the opportunity to reconsider your life choices and run, I totally understand."

"Autumn!" he whines.

"Come on!"

I drag him upstairs to his room, where I leave the door open and immediately fling open every window. It doesn't do much to mitigate the body odor/body spray combo, but every little bit helps. I swing off my backpack and pull out the label sheet, blank Scare Pair cards, and envelopes. When I explain what I need, it doesn't take him long. The hardest thing for him is finding the drippy-blood font, but then it's a snap. He prints me out eight new Scare Pair cards, each of which I seal in an envelope and label. Mariah Amhari and J.J. are now a pair, and I've put Keith Hamilton with Carrie Amernick. Yes, the girls will totally know the pairs somehow changed, but ideally they won't suspect me.

I also have cards for Jack and Tom, pairing them with each other. Jack's original card, which I didn't know till I opened it, paired him with Denise O'Bryan, and Tom's original card paired him with Steve Consuelas. Now Denise and Steve will still have Jack and Tom and things might get confusing, but I'm doing the best I can. At least maybe I can get Jack and Tom talking, and they can take it from there on their own.

I had a similar but different problem with Ames and Zander. I needed to give them new dates, even though the dates are already paired with other people. For Zander I chose Corbin Foster. No doubt. She's tall, dark, and so gorgeous she could be a model. I feel pretty confident that if Zander sees her name on his card, he'll follow her around like a puppy all night. As for Ames, I give her Michael Watley, and Ames is usually a sucker for athletes. It'll totally work.

With everything printed out and ready, I release Erick

to Lori-with-an-*i*-and-horribly-low-standards and stash the envelopes in my room. Then I plop onto my bed and yank the locket chain, pulling it from under my shirt. I'm not going anywhere; I just want to look at the *zemi* carved onto the case. "I'm doing it, Dad," I say. "I'm making the future a better place."

I stare at the *zemi* a little longer; then I tuck it away. I suppose I should go to sleep, but I keep thinking of what Carrie said about her and J.J.'s anniversary. Ugh.

I'm relieved when my phone rings and blasts the image out of my head. It's Taylor. "Tell me you want to pick me up and do something fun," I beg as I answer.

"I do!" she cries. "Boca Community College, midnight showing, *Macbeth*."

"Is that a movie?"

"*Macbeth*," Taylor reiterates. "The play. By Shakespeare?"

"Never heard of him."

I'm lying, of course. I just like to make Taylor crazy by not getting ninety percent of her theater references. Of course, eighty percent I genuinely *don't* get, but this isn't one of those.

"It's supposed to be seriously dark and bloody," she says. "I saw pictures on Instagram. Actual beheading."

"*Actual* beh—"

She doesn't let me finish. "Actual *stage* beheading. Right in front of the audience. And we're up close and personal, in bleachers on the stage. Tell me you want to go!"

"I totally want to go!" I say. "Pick me up in five."

I hang up, fluff my hair, put on a little makeup, and head outside just as Taylor pulls up. We have some time before midnight, so we stop and get late-night breakfast food first. I'm dying to talk about J.J., but I have no idea how I'll explain what's going on with me. No one even knows J.J.'s hanging out with me for tutoring. If I tell her how I feel, she'll think I'm insane.

So I don't bring it up. We talk about other stuff, take goofy selfies we post to Instagram, and then go see the play.

I'm not a theater person, but the play is seriously cool. Taylor wasn't exaggerating. We sit right onstage with the actors. Everything's dark and shadowy, and there's this freaky music that makes me feel like something terrible's about to happen any second. By the time intermission comes, my heart's pounding so hard I feel like I've run a marathon.

"This play totally counts as aerobic exercise, right?" I ask Taylor, but her head's in the program.

"The guy who plays you-know-who is incredible, isn't he?" she asks.

"Voldemort's in this play?"

She glances out of the side of her eye. "Are you messing with me?"

I assure her I seriously have no idea what she's talking about, and she tells me you're not supposed to say the name "Macbeth" in a theater. Which seems kind of ridiculous when you're *watching* Macbeth and want to discuss the lead character, which Taylor does.

"Drew," she says.

Immediately, my ears perk up. Drew is the name of Taylor's dream man. The guy I saw her with in my first jump forward.

The guy she's supposed to meet senior year of high school!

"Drew?" I echo curiously.

"The guy who plays"—she looks at me, then rolls her eyes—"Voldemort. His name's Drew."

I stare at the fuzzily xeroxed picture in the program. "Yes! It *is* him! I didn't recognize him with all the blood spatter!"

"Recognize him?" Taylor echoes. "You know him?"

"No!" I quickly correct myself. "I just mean I didn't recognize him . . . in the show . . . as this guy in the picture."

Taylor looks at me like I'm a complete fool. "But it says his character name right there. It says he's Mac—" She stops herself and makes a face at me. "You're just trying to get me to say it, aren't you?"

"Totally," I lie, then quickly get back to what's more important. "But this Drew guy . . . you're right, he's really good. And cute, too, don't you think?"

Taylor blushes. "*Ridiculously* cute."

"You should talk to him after the show! The actors will

come out after, right? Like when we wait for you after your shows?"

"I guess," she says, "but why would he want to talk to me? He's in a college production. I'm just this high school fangirl."

Among the many things I love about Taylor is she has no idea how gorgeous she is. Reenzie might get all the hot-girl cred, but it's only because she knows how good she looks and struts around like she expects everyone else to know it too. Honestly, though, Taylor's even prettier. She's like the definition of classic all-American beauty—tall, long blond hair, blue eyes, fit but curvy. If she weren't my friend, I'd find her annoyingly perfect. And it's not like she's not confident or doesn't know how to dress herself. She is and she does. She just has zero clue of the effect she can have on people.

I don't try to convince her. "You're like the *opposite* of a fangirl; you're a fellow actor. You can talk to him intelligently about theater. He'll love that."

"Maybe," she says, but she looks dreamy and chews on her lip and I know she's pretty much convinced.

The second half of the show is even bloodier than the first. I'm sure I'd love it if I were paying attention, but I'm not. I'm watching Taylor watch Drew. She looks smitten, and even though I'm sure she thinks it's just because he's amazing-looking and super-talented, I know it's more. They fit together, but right now I'm the only one who knows it. I have so much energy I can't wait for the show to end, and when it does I'm the first to pop up and give it a standing ovation. Taylor's the second, and I totally see Drew do a double take when he notices her in the crowd.

"He's looking at you!" I tell her. "You see that? He's smiling right at you!"

"He's smiling because we're giving him a standing ovation," Taylor says. "I'd smile too."

Whatever. I make it my business to ask around and learn where the actors are coming out; then I drag Taylor outside to the stage door, where we wait to accost him.

He comes out so quickly, I have a sneaking suspicion he's racing to try to catch Taylor.

"Hey!" I shout. I wave my arms obnoxiously and flag him down. There's no room for subtlety when you're building someone's future. He shoots me a weird scrunched-faced glance, but when he sees I'm with Taylor his whole face opens in a wide smile.

"Hi," he says in a deep, mellifluous voice. I don't even care that he's talking right to her when I was the one who waved, because this is clearly history in the making.

"Hi," Taylor says breathlessly. "I'm Taylor. You were . . . magnificent out there."

"Thank you," Drew says, not ripping his eyes from Taylor's for a second. "Thanks for coming. I'm Drew, by the way."

"I know." Taylor giggles; then she bites her lip before adding, "I hope you don't think I'm a pretentious theater geek or anything, but the choices you made . . . I love the way you stalked the stage, like a wild animal caught in the cage of your fate."

She sure sounded like a pretentious theater geek to me . . . but Drew eats it up. He smiles even wider and nods with his full body, like he can't contain his excitement in one appendage. "Yes! That's exactly what I was going for!"

And they're off. I'm so invisible, I may as well be on one of my future jumps. I'm not complaining. Getting these two together is definitely part of my peace-and-harmony-to-my-little-corner-of-the-universe mission. Still, it's two-thirty in the morning and I have to be at the school gym in less than eight hours to start decorating for the dance.

"Hey," I say. "I'm so sorry to butt in, but Taylor's my ride and I have to get up kind of early, so . . ."

They both look heartbroken, but they hide it well.

"Oh, sure, no problem," Drew says. Then he relocks eyes with Taylor. "It was incredible meeting you, Taylor."

"You too," she says. "Maybe . . . we'll see each other again sometime?"

"I'm just going to step in here," I say, then lean in toward Drew. "We're seniors at Aventura High and there's this big dance tomorrow night. It involves computer dates, but the Don't Be a Ghoul rule only requires Tee to spend one song with the guy. Will you go with her as her guest?"

Drew looks confused. "Um . . . are you asking me out . . . for her?"

"No," Taylor says. Then she smiles. "*I'm* asking you out."

It's a moment of pure fiercetude, but then her insecurities creep back in. "I mean . . . unless . . ."

"I would love to," Drew says, and for the next bit of forever they do nothing but smile and blush.

Seriously, I could hold out a paper cone and get cotton candy from the sweetness.

"Great," I say. "So . . . um . . . maybe you guys swap numbers so you can figure everything out in the rapidly approaching morning?"

They do, and then he gives her an adorably awkward hug good night and calls out the same to me. Once Taylor and I are in her car, I kick back and soak in her happiness as she gushes about the guy I know she'll be with forever.

When I'm back home in bed, I pull out the locket again and talk to the *zemi*. "I totally get why this is our mission," I say. "We're pretty darn good at it."

I kiss the *zemi*, then fall fast asleep.

11

✿✿✿✿

I wake up two seconds later.

Okay, it's six hours later, but it feels like two seconds. I'm crazy tired, but I roll out of bed, stuff myself into drawstring shorts and an old T-shirt, twist my rumpled hair into a messy low bun, and schlump my way downstairs. I have to shield my eyes from the bright streak of my mom. She zips around the kitchen in a blazing-yellow dress. Her makeup's already done, her hair hangs in loose curls, and she floats around the kitchen like a cartoon princess singing with woodland creatures.

"You're sunny today," I say. "What's up?"

"Everything!" she chirps as she hands me a mug of pumpkin tea latte. "I have two wonderful kids, *two* wonderful branches of Catches Falls, and it's a gorgeous day today. Here." She opens the toaster oven, wraps a pumpkin pie Pop-Tart in a napkin, and hands it to me. "We should get going if you need to be at the gym by ten."

I'm glad she remembered. I'd much rather get a ride than zombie-walk. Still, she's awfully dressed up just to drive me to school. And she's feeding me a lot of pumpkin stuff. I look suspiciously at my mug and Pop-Tart, then try to sound casual. "So your Trader Joe's friend . . . the pumpkin guy . . ."

"Pumpkin guy?"

I grimace. Am I crazy, or is her voice oddly high-pitched right now?

"Yeah," I say. "What was his name? Len? Ben?"

"Oh, *Glen*!" she says, still whizzing around the room and wiping down counters.

"Right. Glen. Did you ever end up meeting him for that coffee?"

"We did," Mom says. "It was nice. It's always good to make a new friend. You ready?"

I raise an eyebrow, waiting for her to elaborate, but she doesn't. I want to ask if she's seeing him today, if that's why she's so dressed up, but I don't bother. I'll deal with her and Glen, but today I have other futures to mold.

The sisterhood of the Senior Social Committee spends the whole day transforming the gym into a spooky paradise. Lots of spiderwebs, colored lights, black lights, fog machines, Japanese lanterns shaped like jack-o'-lanterns, and *actual* insanely creepy jack-o'-lanterns that Swoozie Lyman—who is apparently a genius artist—carved over the past week. It'll all look a million times better at night, but it still comes together really well, and I have so much fun with everyone that I quickly forget how tired I am. There's only one hellish moment when I pass too close to Carrie and Kassie while they're speaking in low voices to one another, and I hear Carrie say, "We *just* made it out of sight before his parents walked in. I swear, if they had walked in one second earlier . . ."

She doesn't finish the sentence, just raises her eyebrows meaningfully. From that moment on, I'm tortured by an endless stream of way-too-vivid visions of what those raised eyebrows didn't say.

At four in the afternoon, the sisterhood takes off so we can get dressed and ready. We're supposed to come back at seven—an hour before the dance starts—to put out food and drinks and turn on all the lights, the fog machine, and the music. Before Carrie can offer, I pounce on Gus and ask him to give me a ride home. If Carrie's going over to J.J.'s house before the dance for more of what happened last night, I don't want to know about it.

The dance is semiformal, no costumes. Personally, I *love* Halloween costumes. Halloween was my dad's favorite holiday, and the four of us always went all out with themed costumes and decorations. But whatever—the senior class didn't want costumes, so we're not having them. Instead I put on an off-white over-one-shoulder dress, with a wrap top and flowing skirt that drapes to mid-thigh. It has excellent spin properties, so it's perfect for a dance. The locket isn't exactly the ideal accessory for the dress, but no way am I leaving it home. I throw it over my head and tuck the *zemi* medallion down the front. I wear my hair long, with just a little curl, and add a wide silver bracelet and funky hoop earrings. My silver heels won't be comfortable for dancing, but I fully expect to kick them off when the party gets good.

My oversized pink shoulder bag looks nothing but weird with the outfit, but I need someplace to stash my Scare Pair cards. I also toss in some lip gloss, my wallet, and my phone and I'm ready to go about five minutes before Gus—who agreed to grab me on his way back to school—honks his horn.

My heart thumps as Gus and I clomp our way down to the gym, our shoes echoing down the nearly empty halls. What if I don't get the chance to put my Scare Pair cards in with the real ones? What if someone catches me when I try?

I don't have to worry. Gus and I are the last to arrive. Carrie and the other six girls are already in the gym working, and the two low plastic bins of stuffed Scare Pair envelopes are already set out on a card table outside the main doors.

"You're late!" Carrie cries when she sees us. "Autumn, make the punch. Gus, start working on the fog machine."

"On it," I say. "I'm just going to ditch my bag back in my locker."

"Just toss it down somewhere!" Carrie retorts.

"Two seconds," I assure her. "I don't want to have to think about it later."

I kick off my heels and trot out the doors, then quickly peek back inside to make sure everyone's hard at work and concentrating on their own thing. Once I'm sure they are, I yank out my eight altered Scare Pair envelopes and very quickly slip them into—or *near* to—their rightful alphabetical spots. Then I sprint down the hall, ditch my bag, and sprint back.

I'm a little surprised none of my futures have shown me as a super-spy. I think I'd be really good at it.

We're still working on the room at seven-thirty when the first people start to show up. It's insanely early for a school dance, but we figure people are stoked about their Scare Pairs and want to find out right away. Carrie sends Kassie and Brody to hand the cards to early arrivals, then shuts the gym doors so we can finish up in peace. By the time we emerge at eight o'clock to start the party for real, there's a big crowd. Some of them have their cards, some need them, some are already laughing with or chatting up their computer dates. Everyone seems so buzzed and energized I get all wrapped up in the excitement.

"They like it!" I say, nudging Carrie. "It's a huge success!"

Carrie grins back and all eight of us start handing out cards as fast as we can, then urge people into the gym where the music blasts, the fog seeps across the floor, and recorded screams and maniacal laughter keep making people jump.

J.J.'s the first of my friends to come in. My breath catches when I see him. He's wearing black suit pants and a black button-down shirt and carrying a sport jacket slung over one shoulder. He walks down the hall toward me, a slow smile on his face. I smile back and almost say something, until I realize he's not looking at me at all. I'm standing right next to Carrie. The smile and intensity are all for her.

Ignoring everyone else, he wraps his arm around Carrie's waist and kisses her for just this side of an eternity. I tell myself to look away, but I can't—not even when it feels like my toenails are being peeled off my feet one by one.

"Do you have a card for me?" he asks her, still not even looking in my direction.

"I do," she says flirtatiously. "And I think you'll like it."

She flips through the envelopes, frowning when J.J.'s isn't exactly where it's supposed to be. Then she flips around some more and pulls it out. She watches J.J. with a knowing smile as he opens it and pulls out the card.

"Mariah Amhari?" he asks.

For a moment, Carrie looks utterly perplexed. Then she beams. "Yes! Isn't that fun? And since Mariah and I are both on the Senior Social Committee, we think we should set a good example and actually spend some time with our Scare Pairs. Mariah!"

Carrie moves to Mariah, who's on my other side and a little bit behind me. She leans in close and rises onto her tiptoes so she can whisper into Mariah's ear, "You actually switched! You are the best!!!!"

"What?" says Mariah, but Carrie's already leading her to J.J.

I'm just as surprised. I had no idea Carrie would think Mariah was behind the swap. This is perfect!

"Here you are!" Carrie says, presenting Mariah to J.J. "Go on in and have fun!"

Mariah still looks like she's about to object, but I'm ready. I've already pulled her envelope and I hand it to her now. "Can't forget *your* envelope!"

She opens and reads it, then looks curiously at Carrie. Carrie literally needs more face to contain her smile. Mariah shrugs and takes J.J.'s arm, but she raises an eyebrow to me before they go in, and I can't help but grin. It's pretty clear Mariah thinks *Carrie* made the switch so she can be with Keith. As for J.J., he still looks completely confused, but he's a true gentleman. He gives Carrie just one searching look, then turns his full attention to Mariah, chatting her up as they make their way into the gym.

"I don't know how she did it," Carrie says, "but I'm soooo glad she did."

I wheel around. Carrie's back is to me and she's talking to Kassie, but Kassie gives a warning nod. Carrie wheels around and blushes when she sees I've overheard. "N-not that . . . ," she stammers. "I mean . . . I don't . . ."

Entertaining as it is to watch her struggle for an explanation, I need her to relax and have a good time. "You don't have to explain," I assure her with a smile. "It's a fix-up dance. It's fun."

Carrie visibly relaxes. And when Keith Hamilton shows up a few minutes later, she sprints to him to give him his envelope. When he opens it, he looks as happy as she does. Carrie links her arm with his and calls out to the rest of us, "The remaining cards are all yours, sisters! I'm going inside to make sure everything's okay!"

"Right," Gus says once she's gone. "If by 'everything' she means Keith Hamilton's scrawny body. Hashtag-whatever, hashtag-breeders."

"You never know," I say. "He's scrawny now, but one day he could be an underwear model."

Gus, Swoozie, Brody, Kassie, and Meegan just look at me; then we all burst out laughing.

My next victim to hit the dance is Zander. Swoozie hands him his Scare Pair envelope, and when he opens it he fist-pumps and shouts, "YES!" then high-fives his friends before going into the gym.

Taylor and Drew come in together. She's in a short sparkly sheath dress and high heels, but Drew's still taller than her by a couple inches. They remind me so much of the way I saw them in the future that I feel all warm and happy inside. Tee gets her Scare Pair envelope from Brody and I sincerely hope whoever she's paired with doesn't have high hopes for a love connection, because Taylor's one hundred percent taken.

Reenzie and Sean come in soon after that. They look dazzling, of course, like they're ready to be anointed prom king and queen. I give Reenzie her envelope and Meegan gives Sean his. When he opens it, he glares at me and his face turns to stone.

"Is this a joke?" he asks.

"I didn't do it!" I object. "It was the computer!"

"I'm not dancing with you." Staring daggers at me, Sean crumples the Scare Pair card in his fist. "Reenz, I'll meet you inside."

He stalks into the gym. Reenzie scrunches her brows and leans close. "For real now—did you set yourself up with him?"

"Reenzie. He hates me. Why on earth would I set myself up with him?"

Reenzie smiles. "You're right. He totally hates you. Here, why don't you take my Scare Pair."

She hands me her card and I look at it. "Derek Montzer. The nose picker. That's really sweet of you, Reenzie."

She smiles. She has no idea I'm being facetious.

"I'm gonna let you keep him, though," I say. "I'm sure he's looking forward to your dance. Don't be a ghoul!"

Reenzie grimaces, then heads into the gym after Sean.

By now almost everyone has arrived, so I volunteer to stick around and hand out the last cards while the rest of the sisterhood goes into the gym.

"I'll stay too," Gus says. "Doug Church already told me he has a boyfriend he met online. Whole dance concept, complete waste of time."

Gus is fun, and the two of us are having a good time dishing about which computer couples we think will succeed and which will crash and burn, when Tom Watson comes out of the gym and beelines for Gus.

"Seriously hating you right now," Tom says.

Tom's bookishly adorable, with thick-framed glasses and the uncanny ability to wear a vest over a button-down striped shirt, red tie, and pressed jeans and make it look not just semiformal but high fashion.

"What did I do?" Gus asks.

"You sicced Anton Graff on me! I just broke up with him last week!"

"No clue what you're talking about," Gus says. "The computer did everything."

"The computer gave me Jack Rivers. Anton has his own little extra card with my name on it." He points at Gus. *"J'accuse!"*

"Okay, put that thing away, 'cause I want no part of it," Gus says. "Whatever crazy forgery Anton made is on him. More importantly . . . Jack Rivers is *gay*?!"

"I know, right?" Tom says excitedly. "And he's really cute. I think this might be his coming out party."

I am dying listening to their conversation. It's perfect! Jack has a secret crush on Tom; Tom thinks Jack is totally cute. . . . This will be exactly the encouragement Jack needs to get over his fear and embrace his true self!

"Mija! You will not believe the *mishegoss* this boy put me through!"

Ames is a self-proclaimed PuertoMecuadorbano Jew. Her mom's side is a mix of Latina ancestries, and her dad brings home the no-bacon. When she speaks Spanish, I'm with her. When she pulls out the Yiddish, she loses me.

Right now she's strutting down the hall in heels so high I'd break my neck if I tried to take a step, and she's poured into a skintight tiger-stripe dress that by all rights should be a crime against fashion but on her looks spectacular. Rows of bracelets clink up and down her arms as she walks.

Jack is several feet behind her. He wears a rumpled blue suit and doesn't even attempt to keep up.

"He lost his car keys inside his house," Ames explains. "*Panzon!* I had to wait around for almost an hour before he found them *in the freezer*!"

"Because that's where I got the pizza I had for dinner!" Jack explains as he catches up and joins us. "It was way in the back and the baggie it was in was all iced over, so I had to use my keys to chop it out. I left them there by accident."

"How old was that pizza that you had to *chop* it out of the freezer?!" Ames shoots back. Then she says, "You know what? Never mind. Autumn, give me my man."

I hand her the envelope with her name on it. She rips it open and reads it in a blink. "Michael Watley? *Dios mio,* yes!" She tosses the card over her shoulder and slinks into the gym, singsonging, "It's your lucky day, Mikey!"

Behind Jack and me, Tom clears his throat. We both turn. Tom stands a couple feet away, an adorable smile on his face. I can't help but smile back. I know what's going to happen and I can't wait.

"Excuse me," Tom says to Jack, "but it would be my honor to personally deliver your Scare Pair card. I think you'll see why."

I scan Jack's face for the excitement I know he must be feeling. I can only imagine his racing heart and his sweaty palms as Tom approaches him.

I look for those things, but I don't see them. Honestly, the closer Tom gets, the more Jack looks like he smells something gross.

He takes the envelope from Tom. Tom leans forward as Jack rips it open, like it's Christmas and he's just waiting for Jack to unwrap the best gift ever.

Jack pulls out the card. He stares at it. He scrunches his brows.

"What is *this*?"

Tom casts a quick glance at Gus, then back at Jack. He looks a little uncertain now and laughs nervously. "It's your Scare Pair card. I've got the matching one."

He holds up his own card, but Jack sneers, "I can't be hooked up with you. You're a *dude*."

The word drips with scorn, and Tom understands immediately. He purses his lips and nods. "Got it. Some kind of computer glitch. No worries."

"No worries?! No *worries*?!" Jack's voice floats high and out of control. "This is sick, that's what this is. This is somebody's sick joke!"

"Okay, enough with the 'sick' stuff," Gus says. "It's a mistake. It happens."

Both Tom and Gus look completely disgusted, and I know I have to do something quick. This is supposed to be Jack's big watershed moment. I can't let it fall to shreds.

"Gus is right!" I say, jumping between Jack and the guys. "I mean, the whole Scare Pair thing is just about meeting new people, right? So forget the fix-up part. I mean, it's a funny mess-up, right? You guys can go in to the party as friends and laugh about it!"

"You are a sad person," Tom says. "You can hang out here if you want. I'm going to go in and dance. Want to join me, Gus?"

"Love to."

No! I want to scream as the two of them walk into the gym. *You have it wrong! Jack's gay! I swear! I don't know why he's acting this way!*

Jack, meanwhile, is turning into the Incredible Hulk—a description he'd appreciate under pretty much any other circumstance. His face is fire-engine red, his fists clench and unclench, he snorts through his nose, and he's pacing back and forth across the hall.

"Jack, calm down," I say gently. "This doesn't have to be a big deal."

Instead of answering, Jack *roars*—this horrible, guttural noise—and punches his fist into a wall. Immediately he yelps and clutches his hand to his chest.

"Jack!" I gasp. "Are you okay?"

I put my hand on his back, but he shakes me off. "I'm going home," he mutters. "Tell Ames to get another ride."

He storms down the hall. I take a few steps after him, then stop and clench my fingers in my hair, no idea what to do. I'm still trying to figure it out when I hear loud, high shrieks from inside the gym. I run inside. It's pitch black, lit only by strobes and red, green, and orange gelled lights, plus fog shrouds the room. Still, it's impossible not to see what's going on. Ames is in the middle of the dance floor, on the back of Corbin Foster. It almost looks like Corbin's giving her a piggyback ride, except she's flapping her arms, trying to push Ames off her, while Ames yanks at Corbin's hair and swears at her in a string of Spanish so filthy, Eddy would stand up and cheer. Zander's right in front of the scrum, applauding and cheering her on.

"Girl fight!" he cheers. "Keep it up!"

Mr. Winthrop, our faculty chaperone, races to Ames and pulls her off Corbin. I run over, too, and Taylor and Drew meet me there. Ames kicks and struggles in Mr. Winthrop's grip, while Corbin darts to the safety of Zander's arms.

"You need to stop, Amalita," Mr. Winthrop says. "You're already facing a suspension for fighting. Don't make it worse."

The word "suspension" makes Ames freeze. She looks up at Mr. Winthrop plaintively. "Pleeeease don't suspend me. You suspend me and *soy muerta*. And I'm sorry, but you saw that girl. She was all over him. You *know* Zander's mine."

Mr. Winthrop frowns. "Really? 'Cause that's not the scuttlebutt I've been hearing. Why don't we go sit down and you can give me your take."

Unbelievable. Ames just imploded and Mr. Winthrop's using it to make sure he's solid on the latest gossip.

"Actually, Mr. Winthrop," Taylor says. "I was thinking Drew and I could just take her home."

"I'll come too," I say, but Taylor shakes her head.

"We're good," she says, and smiles shyly up at Drew. "We were going to leave soon anyway."

Drew smiles back at her. Their connection is so obvious I can practically see it sizzle. I may have inadvertently destroyed Amalita's and Jack's lives, but at least one thing went well tonight. I nod, and Taylor puts an arm around Ames and leads her out of the gym. I talk to Mr. Winthrop for a bit and try to convince him not to suspend Ames. He agrees to strongly consider it, but only if I give him the scoop about what was going on with J.J. and me in Mrs. Foreman's office the other day.

No, he doesn't actually say it that way. He acts like they're two totally different issues, but I know him well enough to get what he's after. We go chat in a corner and I give him just enough to satisfy his need for news: that it was just tutoring, it maybe got a little flirty, but it's all up in the air and I'd appreciate his discretion because Carrie doesn't know anything about it, and J.J.'s still very much with her.

"You sure about that?" Mr. Winthrop asks.

He nods to the dance floor. Despite Amalita's scene, the music never stopped, and now people are back out like nothing ever happened. A slow dance plays, and the first couple I notice is Zander and Corbin, though I can't imagine why Mr. Winthrop's pointing them out. Reenzie and Sean are dancing, too, but that's irrelevant to our conversation.

Then I see it. Carrie and Keith Hamilton sway in each other's arms. They're just under one of the green-gelled lights, so they're not hard to see. They're pressed tightly together. Keith is taller than J.J., and Carrie has to stretch her arms long to wrap them around his neck. Her head tilts back to gaze up at him, and as they talk and laugh I can't help but notice that his eyes constantly move from her face to the cleavage bursting from the sweetheart neckline of her dress.

"Is this the Scare Pair song?" I ask Mr. Winthrop, and he shakes his head.

"That was a half hour ago," he says. "They've been at it ever since."

I scan the dance floor for J.J. and Mariah, but I don't see them. "Where's J.J.?"

Mr. Winthrop nods toward the wall next to the dance floor. It's too dark for me to see anything but shadows . . . until a strobe light blinks on and I see J.J. in its fractured glow. He leans against the wall, arms folded, his face a wooden mask.

I'm completely torn. It's awful to see J.J. so obviously hurt and angry, but at the same time this is *exactly* what I wanted to happen. And not just selfishly so J.J. can be free. Breaking them up will save them both from a horrible, dead-end, unhappy future. It's like with Sean—yes, I'm making J.J. miserable now, but in the long run I'm saving his life!

As they dance, Keith leans down and kisses Carrie high on her neck, right by her ear. Carrie doesn't pull away. She smiles and tilts her head to the side, giving Keith more room to play. Just before the strobe stops flashing, I see J.J. stalk out of the gym.

Mr. Winthrop nudges me. "If I were up in the air with a boy and I saw him run out all upset like that, I'd go after him."

I'm completely grossed out by getting love advice from a teacher . . . but he's right. I run out of the gym and see J.J. pacing back and forth, taking deep breaths as he runs his fingers through his hair and clenches them tight.

"J.J. . . . hey."

He looks at me with unfocused eyes, then takes a deep, determined breath. "I need to walk," he says. "You want to go for a walk?"

I feel a thrill and do my best not to sound inappropriately excited. "Sure."

He walks us down the hall and out the door. Neither of us says anything, and I let J.J. lead the way. It's warm out, but there's a light breeze blowing, and I think about how nice it would feel to have J.J.'s arm around me. He keeps his hands in his pockets, though, and his head down. I stay by his side as we walk the path past the lawn where we all eat lunch, then down to the track. There are no lights, but the moon is full enough that I see J.J. in a shimmery glow.

"You okay?" I finally ask.

He shakes his head.

"The sick part is she told me she had a crush on him," he finally says, looking down at his shoes. "She told me that back in freshman year, when we dated the first time. And now she fixes herself up with him, like it gives her an excuse to do whatever she wants, like it doesn't even matter. . . ."

He shakes his head and keeps walking.

I shouldn't try to make this better. I *want* him upset with Carrie, for a million reasons. But I can't help it.

"It was the computer," I say. "She didn't fix herself up with him at all."

Okay, it's a half-truth, but maybe it'll help.

"Whatever," J.J. says. We're at the bleachers now, and he leans against them. "The computer fixed me up with someone I used to have a crush on too. And you know what I did? Spent one dance with her, then went looking for Carrie. Because she's my *girlfriend*. Did you even see her in there with him?"

I nod, but I'm not really listening. I'm staring at the way the moonlight hits his face. He looks so sad and broken. I'm dying to reach out and touch him. Comfort him. Maybe put my hand on his cheek, or—

"I don't get it, Autumn," he says. "She knew I was there. Who would do that right in front of me?"

I know exactly what I want to reply, but every brain cell screams at me not to do it.

Brain cells are overrated.

"I wouldn't," I say. And before my annoying brain can weigh in again, I wrap my arms around his neck and lean in to kiss him. He's surprised at first; then he kisses me back. His arms pull me closer and I hear the sound of the ocean in my ears because everything else is gone. There's nothing in the world but J.J., me, and this kiss. I never want it to end, and I can tell—I can *feel*—that he doesn't either. He's in love with me just like I'm in love with him, and he has been forever, just like he told me in the future.

Suddenly he pushes me away. He holds my shoulders at arm's length and stares at me like I'm a demon trying to possess his soul. "What are you doing?"

"I want to be with you," I blurt. "I was stupid last year. I never should have broken up with you, and—"

"*I* broke up with *you*," he reminds me, "'cause you didn't have the guts to tell me how you really felt."

The words hurt, but they're true. "I know," I admit. "But I was wrong. And hanging out with you again . . . I *know* this is real. And I know you feel the same way. And—"

"Stop," he says sharply. "You don't get to say that. You don't get to say any of this. Do you have any idea how long it took me to get over you? I was in love with you. I *begged* you not to go out with me unless you knew it was what you wanted, and you didn't care."

"I *did* care. It's just—"

"*Don't*. Whatever you're going to say, I don't want to hear it. I can't trust it. I will *never* be able to trust anything you say again."

"That's not true!" I say, but of course I can't explain how I know that, so I just gaze up at him, begging him with my eyes not to be mad and to give us another chance.

Instead of coming closer, he backs away, like he's repulsed. He shakes his head.

"I'm going home," he says. "Don't follow me."

He walks away. I stare after him until he disappears into the night.

I shouldn't have kissed him. I pushed him too fast. Just like I pushed Jack and Amalita.

I flop down onto the bleachers and pull the locket out of my dress. The *zemi* glows in the moonlight.

"Please tell me I didn't ruin everything," I say to it. Then I open it. I close my eyes while I move the dials, trusting the spirit inside to tell me where I need to go. When I open them, I see the dials are set for November 28, ten years from now.

Okay.

I snap the locket shut, close my eyes again, and think hard about the future I want to see.

12

ten years and one month later

I'm in a dark room.

Not totally dark. There's a screen in front of me with a picture projected on it. It's a picture of a bunch of people in caps and gowns, throwing their caps into the air. As I peer closer, I recognize Reenzie and Sean, right in the middle of the front row.

So the picture's from *my* graduation.

The picture fades as the lights flick on and people applaud. I look around and see the room's full of round tables where people eat and drink.

"Wasn't that great? Thanks to everyone for sending in your pictures for that slideshow."

The voice comes from the front of the room, where Carrie now stands at a podium in front of the projector. She's clearly older than I know her now, but she looks even better—more confident and together. She wears her hair in a short pixie cut that accentuates her cheekbones, and her sleeveless black cocktail dress is simple and sophisticated. She's also in great shape. Her stomach is flat, and I can see the muscles in her arms as she applauds with the group. If she had a baby while she was in college, there's no sign of it now.

When the applause dies down, Carrie speaks again into the mic. "As reunion chair, I'm so thankful you all could make it. Have a great evening, enjoy the food and the music, and I hope I get the chance to personally catch up with each and every one of you."

Everyone claps again, and as Carrie prances off the stage, she nods to a DJ in the back corner who cranks up the tunes. It's a Kyler Leeds hit from our junior year—one off his *As You Wish* album, the title track of which Kyler actually wrote about J.J. and me.

I take it as a sign. J.J. has to be here, right? I follow Carrie, figuring she'll lead me to him, but she beelines to a table with Gus and the Senior Social Committee girls, all of whom get up and hug her, congratulating her on the great speech and presentation.

"This is great!" I gush to Carrie. "You don't hang out with us in the future anymore! I mean, no offense, but look at you—this is a *way* better deal for you than J.J. and dropping out of college and babies, right?" I pull out the locket and keep gushing to the *zemi*, "So I didn't screw everything up at all! This is excellent! What happened to everyone else?"

Carrie, of course, doesn't answer, so I go hunting on my own. I walk around the banquet room, peeking at tables. Most of the people look like slightly tweaked versions of the ones I know now. Maybe they're a tiny bit fatter or thinner, maybe their hair's a little longer or shorter or a different color, maybe they dress with more personal style . . . but they're easy to pick out as their high school selves.

Then there's the handful of people who look seriously old. As if they're in their forties, even though almost everyone in the room is under thirty. Like Michael Watley, the super-hot basketball player I gave Ames as her Scare Pair. He has a paunch, wears old-man glasses, and only has hair on the back and sides of his head. If he weren't wearing a name tag, I'd have no clue who he is. Same with Denise O'Bryan, who I swear must have spent every single day between high school graduation and now baking in the sun with baby oil slathered over her. Her naturally light-colored skin is mahogany, and she's so wrinkled she looks like a shar-pei.

Then there's one guy who looks like no one I know but who is also weirdly familiar. I see him coming through the main doors—maybe from the restroom? He's quite heavy and looks even more so because his blond hair is so short and his hairline is so far back on his head. What hair exists is gelled and combed into manicured rows. The guy is stuffed into a conservative blue suit, and his tie and tightly buttoned shirt push the fat of his neck up into his chin. He wears round wire-rimmed glasses. Honestly, he looks more like someone political I'd see interviewed on the news than anyone from my class.

No name tag. Is he someone's guest? Maybe, but I can't shake that feeling that I should know him, so I follow him to his table.

"Jack, honey, what took you so long?" a female voice calls as he gets closer. "You missed the slide show."

"*JACK?!*" I roar incredulously.

Jack smiles and plops down onto his seat. "I don't need to see it, dear," he says. "I lived it. Am I right?"

"*Dear?* Jack *honey*?!" I wheel to the seat next to Jack and point. "She's a *woman!*"

I move closer to her just to be sure. Yup, she's a woman. A really mousy-looking woman with no makeup, limp brown curls, and a super-conservative Laura Ashley dress with a lace-trimmed Peter Pan collar.

"You're *always* right, sweetheart," she says, patting his hand. Then she looks to everyone else at the table. "I wish we'd brought little Tommy. He'd have loved to see those pictures of his daddy all young and sprightly."

"Little *Tommy*?" I gape at Jack. "Tell me you didn't name your child after Tom Watson. Tell me you don't have a *child*! You're supposed to be dating a hot guy named Nathan!"

I hear sniffing and I look around the table at Taylor. She wears a frumpy black dress and no makeup. Her head is down and she looks like she's trying not to cry out loud. I bend down next to her.

"Tee? Are you okay?"

"Sorry," she says to everyone at the table but me. She takes some Kleenex from her purse and dabs her eyes. "It's just . . . Drew and I wanted to have kids. We even picked out names. . . ."

She can't continue and sobs for real, burying her face in her hands. Next to her, a woman with jet-black hair and heavy black eyeliner leans back in her seat and stares at Taylor. "Car crash in the night . . . Your true love is now no more. . . . Death comes to us all." She intones the words dramatically, with a slight French accent, then takes a pause before she adds, "It's a haiku. I wrote it because I knew I'd see you."

"Wow," says a guy across the table with a super-dark tan and teeth so white they have to be veneers. I'm so distracted by the color contrast that it takes me a second to realize it's Sean. He sits next to a woman who looks like a living Bratz doll. "Depressing much?"

The Bratz doll giggles and hugs Sean's arm, while the black-haired woman fixes him with a glare. "Life is depressing. You Americans fool yourselves into thinking otherwise."

"You *are* American," Jack says. "And life is not depressing. Look at me. Great little wife, great kid and another on the way, great job. We're even thinking of getting a Disney vacation home."

He says all this like it's a dream come true, but his smile doesn't meet his eyes. He also doesn't make eye contact with his wife at all when he talks about their great life. He just pats her hand. She smiles and looks at him adoringly, but he doesn't even seem to notice.

"Let's not argue, okay?" Taylor asks between sniffs. "I only came here because I thought seeing you guys would make me feel better."

"There *is* no feeling better," the black-haired woman says. "Life is unfair. My father died when I was fifteen. My grandmother died two years later, remember that? She was running to give me a hug on Thanksgiving when she slipped and fell and broke her hip. Two weeks later, she was dead. You think that's fair?"

As she speaks, I feel something icy fill my chest, and I walk through the table so I can get closer to the black-haired woman and stare at her face. It's gaunt and overly pale and half hidden by her extreme eye makeup . . . but it's also like looking in a mirror. "Are you . . . *me*?"

"Okay, I think Taylor losing her boyfriend three months ago in a car crash is a little more tragic than you losing your *grandmother* ten *years* ago," Jack snaps to Future-Dark-Maiden-Me.

"I lose my grandmother senior year?" I ask, horrified. "Eddy dies *this* Thanksgiving?"

"Can we just stop talking about it?" Taylor asks.

"Why?" Future Me snaps. "It's life, and it's tragic, and Americans don't know how to cope with it. Why do you think I went to school in Paris? Why do you think I dropped out and stayed there instead of coming back here?"

"Because you couldn't hack the real world?" Sean suggests. "So you just stayed away and did the misunderstood starving artist thing?"

"At least I'm not all fake tan with fake teeth and building my life on fakeness!" Future Me shoots back, though I'd probably have a stronger argument without the fake black hair.

"Sean's not fake!" the Bratz doll squeaks. "He's doing his residency in plastic surgery! He's going to change people's lives! And I'm going to be his first patient. I've made a list of all the things I want him to do to me."

She bounces in her seat as she runs down the list of surgical enhancements she wants to have done, while Future Me and Sean keep arguing, Taylor cries, and Jack sneaks furtive looks at the dance floor, where Tom Watson and his boyfriend or husband dance and smile and laugh and clearly have the time of their lives.

I can't hang at this table anymore. Instead I walk around the room, hoping for any kind of good news about anyone I love, but it all bites. According to the gossip I hear, J.J.'s now a hermit who lives in Seattle and talks to no one but his dog. Reenzie's a White House page, which sounds good . . . but she's cut off all her friends because she doesn't have time for them anymore. And Amalita . . . no one knows what happened to Amalita. Every time her name comes up people just frown and shake their heads.

"I don't get it," I say. "All I've done is try to make things better, but everything's a total disaster. How did this happen?"

13

october, senior year

The next thing I know I'm back on the bleachers, the night breeze cooling my face. The Scare Pair dance is still going on, and as a member of the Senior Social Committee I'm required to stay for it all, but I can't deal. I stop at my locker to grab my bag, then walk home, my head throbbing from everything I just saw.

My future with J.J.? His amazing proposal and our road trip around the U.S. and our forever happiness? Never gonna happen. Jack will never come out of the closet. I am going to be a pretentious, depressing disaster. Taylor won't get to spend her life with Drew. And all because I was working so hard to make the future *right*.

I'm plagued by a tangle of bad dreams all night, but in the morning I jump out of bed, completely energized. Yes, the future I saw last night was awful, but it's completely within my power to make sure it never happens. I just have to be smart about it. I tug on the chain to pull out the locket, open it, and look at the top window. It shows the number 5. I've jumped five times, and I have five jumps left.

Next I pull out my old journal—the one that had the *zemi* symbol on it two years ago but is now just a mostly filled lined notebook with a sliced-open cover. I flip to an empty page in the back and make a list of everything I need to change before those five jumps are done:

J.J. hermit in Seattle, not with me.

Eddy dies this Thanksgiving.

Ames still alcoholic?

Drew dies in car crash.

Jack stays in closet.

Sean kind of a tool.

I'm a pretentious, bad-poetry jerk.

I finish off the list with numbers for my mom/Glen and Erick but follow them with question marks since I don't know where their futures are at the moment. Then I look at the list. What should I tackle first?

"Eddy," I say out loud. "Today I'm saving your life."

I check to make sure my debit card is in my wallet. The

money I made this summer is in my account, and while Mom wants me to save it for college, I'm sure she'd approve of the things I plan to buy today. At the same time, I don't want to explain my motivation, so I ask Mom for the car instead of a ride. She's thrilled. She knows Dad's accident is the reason I hate to drive, so I'm sure she thinks my request is a big psychological step forward. She falls all over herself to give me the keys.

I drive myself to Walmart, do my shopping, then walk into Century Acres so laden with bags that I have to lean heavily on one of my other purchases: an old-lady rolling walker, the seat of which I've also covered with bags.

"Autumn!" Eddy and Zelda shout from their matching comfy seats. Then Eddy jumps up and runs my way.

"*STOP!*" I shout.

"It's okay, Autumn," Zelda says. "I'll save her seat."

"It's not the seat," I snap. "Eddy, do not move."

"What? Do I have a bee on me?" Eddy asks.

I place all the bags on the floor, leave the cart, and run to her side, then take her arm. "Lean on me," I say as I gently guide her back into the chair. Eddy looks at me like I have a cucumber growing out of my face.

"Autumn, what's wrong with you?" she asks.

"I want you to be safe," I say. "I got you some things."

I hold up a "stay" finger and run back to the bags. I pull out a small metal stick with a hook at one end and four rubber-capped prongs at the other. Eddy narrows her eyes.

"That better be a messed-up looking cheerleader baton for a midget," she says.

"No, it's a cane!" I enthuse. "It folds up small so you can take it with you anywhere; then . . ." I yank it out to its full height and lean on it, but I'm much taller than Eddy, so I have to hunch over. Still, I try to make it convincing when I say, "See? Super-comfy! And a great way to make sure you're safe when you walk!"

Eddy looks at Zelda and raises her eyebrows. Zelda sighs and shakes her head.

"Wait, there's more," I say, running back to the bags and pulling out items as I show them off to Eddy and her friend. "I have these grab bars with suction cups—you can stick them to any wall and put them all over your room so you can catch yourself if you fall. And I got these racks you can put on the sides of your bed so you won't fall out at night. Did you know that can happen?"

"Oooh, so you want me to sleep in a crib?" Eddy asks.

"Not *exactly* a crib."

"And that cart under all the bags. What's that, a walker?" she asks.

"Well . . . yeah!" I say. "But look how handy it is. It has four wheels, so it's very steady, the grip handles keep you stable, and there's even a built-in chair so if you get tired while you're walking around, you won't fall—you can just sit!"

"Is that a toilet seat?" Zelda asks; then she turns to

Eddy. "Your granddaughter got you a toilet seat. She doesn't think you can handle the toilet."

"No, no!" I object. "I know you can handle it, but the guy at the store said it's easier for people of a certain age to have a seat that's raised a little higher, so you don't have to crouch as low. That way you don't have to struggle to get up and risk a fall!"

"Zelda, will you excuse me and my *nieta dementa*?" Eddy asks.

"Maybe," Zelda says; then she nods to me. "Come here."

I walk over to her. She leans close and inhales deeply.

"Um . . . Zelda . . . are you *sniffing* me?" I ask.

"Looking for harsh perfumes. They never come out of the upholstery. You're clean." She turns to Eddy. "I'll go back to my room and have a nosh."

"Aren't you guys having lunch soon?" I ask. It was why I rushed through my Walmart trip. In old lady land, lunch starts at exactly 11:00 a.m.

"Yes, but I didn't say I was having lunch. I said I'm having a nosh. *Then* I'll have lunch." She waves to Eddy. "I'll come get you when I'm done."

Eddy waves back, then lowers her voice. "The woman eats morning till night. That's why she looks like she has a blimp between her *pechos* and her *caderas*." She pats Zelda's chair and I sit. She waves toward all my shopping. "This all came from someplace, and I don't mean the store. *Dime.* Tell me."

I look around to make sure no one is listening in, which

is crazy because no one around here can hear; then I tell her all about my dad's latest gift and the things I've been seeing. The only thing I leave out is the most vital piece of information, mainly because I don't want to scare her.

A slow smile spreads across her face. "And you saw me *muerta, sí?*"

My face burns red, but she doesn't seem upset. In fact, she leans in closer, elbows on her knees and chin in her hands. "Tell me, how did I go? Another stroke? An aneurysm? Oh, *lo se*! It was the receptionist, *sí?* He went *loco* and pulled out a gun and shot us all in the middle of music time."

I rear back and grimace, horrified. "Eddy, no!"

She shrugs. "Nah. Figured I wouldn't get anything that exciting. Plus you got me all that safety stuff. What is it, broken hip?"

I purse my lips together. "It doesn't matter what it was, because it's not going to happen."

Eddy throws back her head and laughs.

"Eddy, it's not funny! We're talking about your life!"

"Which I've lived, *querida*! So take back all those things. I don't need them."

"But . . . it's my job to change things." I look around again, because I always feel stupid saying the next part, even though it's true. "It's my mission. Peace and harmony, remember? You know it better than anyone."

"I do. But I also know you can't change everything. And some things you can't change at all. One day I will go to be with *mi amor,* your *abuelo.* I'm not afraid of that. And when it happens, it will *not* be your fault. *Comprende?*"

"But if I can stop it—" I begin, but Eddy silences me, putting her hand on my knee.

"I love you, Autumn. I love you for wanting to take care of me, and your friends, and the rest of your family. You will do great things for all of us. Who knows? Maybe just by telling me you've already changed what you saw. I'll be more careful now, because it would be nice to have a little more time. But when things do go wrong—and they will, *querida*—know that it won't be your fault. Okay?"

I look into her eyes, so alive on her tiny wrinkled body. I smile. "Okay," I say. I get up, kiss the top of her head, then put all the bags together so I can return them.

"Leave the walker with the seat," Eddy says. "Zelda and I can take turns pushing each other down the halls."

I wince. I'm fairly certain Kyler Leeds will hate me forever if his Mee-Maw breaks every bone in her body thanks to a wild walker wipeout, but Eddy's right. I can't protect her—or anyone I love—from everything. Still, I can at least try.

While I'm in line returning everything but the cart, I email Gus and apologize for the way Jack acted at the dance. I tell him Jack's usually a much better guy, that he's going through some personal stuff that makes it rough for him right now, and I hope he and Tom can forgive him. I almost don't hit SEND because I know "personal stuff" is code for Jack's fear of coming out. I'm hoping Gus will guess that, maybe talk to Tom, and maybe they can reach out on their own to Jack and try to help. At the same time, I don't want to push too hard. In the end I figure what I'm saying is nebulous enough that it's okay. If it comes back to bite me, I can always say I meant Jack was worried about college or something.

I'm heading back to my car when I get a text from Reenzie.

OMG have you seen this???

Then she sends me a picture. It's Ames, splayed out on her bed. She's lying on her side, propped up on one arm, a smile on her face. That's weird, but fine. What's not as fine is what she's wearing: some super-short slinky nightie with tiny spaghetti straps. I drop my phone and have to rescue it before another Walmart customer runs it over with her cart.

I call Reenzie.

"Tell me you're the only person who has this."

"Why in the universe would I be the only person who has this?" Reenzie retorts. "Why would she send it to me? You think I want that on my phone? You think I want that in my *brain*?"

I'm getting nothing helpful out of Reenzie. "I gotta go," I say, and immediately call Amalita, who doesn't answer. Luckily I have the car. I drive to her house and her mom opens the door a crack when she sees it's me.

"Hi, Mrs. Leibowitz," I say. "Is Ames around?"

She pouts sympathetically. "Autumn, I'm so sorry. Amalita's not feeling well today. She doesn't want to see anyone."

"Okay," I say. I turn away as if I'm going to go, then spin back around before she can close the door. *"Una cosa . . . me gustaría hacer empanadas de Thanksgiving de este año. ¿Tiene una buena receta?"*

She brightens immediately. *"Oh, sí! Sí! Adelante!"*

It's a cheap play on my part, but I didn't see another way. Ames's mother comes from a hodgepodge of Spanish-speaking cultures. The language is her first love, and the food of her heritage is her second. The instant I opened my mouth and asked her—in Spanish—if she had a good empanada recipe so I could make the dish this Thanksgiving, I knew I had her. She brings me into the kitchen, hands me a pen and a notebook, and rattles off recipes and tips in high-speed Spanish for a full hour. She's so excited about it that I kinda *do* want to make empanadas for Thanksgiving and almost forget why I'm here. Luckily it comes back to me before she shuttles me out the door.

"Por favor, ¿Puedo hablar con Amalita? Se acaba de tomar un segundo."

After we've had such a good time together, how can she say no to me seeing Ames for just a second? She pretends to consider, but she's already smiling, and soon I'm knocking on Amalita's door before opening it up and shutting it behind me.

Unlike my own room, Ames's is perfectly neat. Cluttered with jewelry stands and makeup kits and accessory shelves and mirrors and extra clothing racks to hold the outfits that don't fit in her closet, but neat. Her bed is even made . . . with an Amalita-shaped lump tucked right in the middle of her fuchsia-and-black tiger-striped comforter.

I sit next to the lump.

"Ames?"

"Go away, Autumn. I'm never leaving this room ever again."

"Really?" I ask. "'Cause I don't think there's a bathroom in here, and at a certain point—"

Ames flips the covers off her and sits up. She's wearing an amazingly conservative tent of a nightgown, with long sleeves and a ruffled neckline. The remnants of last night's makeup make dark circles under her eyes, and her hair is a frizzed-out fright wig screaming out from her head in all directions.

"You saw the picture?" she asks.

"Yeah, I saw it," I admit.

"Then you know I can never show my face again," she says. She lies back down, turns away from me, and cuddles the comforter up to her chin. I move to the other side of the bed and crouch down so I can look her in the eye.

"What happened?"

She sighs heavily.

"I don't remember sending the picture to Zander. I woke up this morning and my head was throbbing and I was so sick and I checked my phone and I saw it."

She messes with her phone and then tosses it to me. It's an outgoing text to Zander. The picture . . . preceded by a note that says:

> Dance w/Corbin all u want—can she give u
> THIS???

There's no response text from Zander. I wince. "How did you find out other people had it?"

She just raises her eyebrow.

"Other people *did* text you?" I guess.

"Texted, emailed, called . . . some *freshman* sent me a link. At first there were five versions of that picture. An hour later there were thirty."

I hurt inside for her because I know *exactly* how she feels. My first year at Aventura, Reenzie put up a horrible website about me and I was positive I'd have to move away and hide under a rock for the rest of my life.

"I can't believe I did something so stupid," Ames moans. "Now Zander will never want me again."

"Are you kidding me?!" I snap. "This guy sent your private picture to the entire world, and you're worried he won't *want* you?!"

"You don't know how many people he sent it to," Ames retorts. "Maybe he sent it to just one person. Maybe one of his friends took his phone and *he* sent it around. You don't know."

"Ames, for real—"

"Just go, okay?" she asks. "I wanna sleep. I still have a headache."

She burrows back under the blankets.

"Ames . . ."

She fake snores. She's done.

"Fine," I say. "But I've been there, remember? It'll get better. And if you want to talk, just call me, okay?" I rest a hand on the part of the under-the-covers lump I think is her back. She doesn't respond. "Love you, Ames," I say.

I hate to leave her like this, but I don't know what else to do. I spend the rest of the day texting and talking about the situation with Reenzie and Taylor, but it doesn't help. Reenzie's totally unsympathetic. She thinks Ames brought this on herself the second she sent the picture. Taylor and I totally disagree—Ames had no clue Zander would betray her and show the picture around—but we're both still clueless about how to make it better. We figure the best we can do is be there for her while we all wait for it to blow over.

In the meantime, I tell myself, maybe something good will come out of the whole thing. Maybe this will be the thing that takes her off the path I keep seeing in her future and makes everything better.

That's what I'm still hoping the next morning, when I walk into school looking around for Ames. She hasn't returned any of my calls, emails, or tests, but if she does show up, I want to make sure I'm right there by her side.

I don't see her anywhere, but I *do* find Carrie Amernick

waiting by my locker. She's clearly not happy. Her mouth is set in a grim line, her hands are on her hips, and smoke is coming out of her ears.

Immediately, I freeze. Did J.J. tell her about Saturday night? Is that why she's so angry? Did he tell her that we kissed and he realized he wants me back?

"Hey, Carrie," I say warily. "What's up?"

"Your time on the Senior Social Committee," she says in a clipped voice. "*That's* what's up. You completely blew off cleanup duty yesterday."

Prickles of guilt crawl over my skin, having nothing to do with the fact that I threw myself at her boyfriend. "Carrie, I'm so sorry!" I say. "I totally forgot! Some family stuff came up, and then—"

"Don't want to hear it," she cuts me off. "You were fine enough to email Gus. He said he heard from you and you didn't even *mention* the cleanup, never mind apologize for not being there to help."

"I know," I agree. "That's what I'm saying—I totally blanked. But—"

Carrie puts up a hand, stopping me. "Don't want to hear it. You shirk your duty, you're out of the sisterhood. Period." Then she leans in closer and bares her teeth, which I swear she filed into fangs. "We also don't allow sisters who try to steal what isn't theirs. I know what you did with J.J., and it didn't work. We're back together, we're totally in love, and we even made a deal. I won't talk to Keith Hamilton again, and he won't talk to you again. Ever." She stalks away, then turns back, a sweet smile on her face. "Oh. He won't be tutoring you anymore either. Yeah, I know about that."

She turns and flounces down the hall.

I'm stunned, but I actually don't take her that seriously. J.J. might get distant again, but he's not going to stop talking to me entirely. I mean, he can't. We have all the same friends. And besides, he still has feelings for me. I know it. I *felt* it. No way would he avoid me forever.

That's what I think, but then I don't see him all morning. Not even in passing. It's not completely unheard of, but it makes me wonder the littlest bit if he might be specifically avoiding places I'll be.

Lunch cinches it. I grab my tray and bring it to the spot where we always eat . . . and no one's there. I stand there, all alone, holding my tray. I spin around slowly, searching for my group. Taylor's nowhere, but that doesn't surprise me. She told me she was going to try to get off campus and meet Drew for lunch as often as she can. Ames isn't around, but she texted me in the morning to tell me she's playing sick—she's too mortified to come to school at all.

Finally I see J.J., Jack, and Carrie. They're sitting and eating with Kassie and a group of Carrie's other girlfriends far across the lawn.

Is Jack mad at me too? Or is it just that I was there when he freaked out on Tom and Gus and he doesn't want to talk about it? Either way, same thing. He chose Team Carrie.

Reenzie and Sean I find eating with a bunch of the other football players. I don't go over to them. I don't want to seem *that* lame. But Reenzie catches me looking and then pulls out her phone. I get the text:

> More college recruiters coming this week. Sean wants to keep his distance so you don't mess anything up. Sorry!!!!

So that's it. My friends have all ditched me.

"So wait," Jenna asks. "Amalita's been out of school for all this time?"

It's three weeks later, and I'm spending my lunch period on the phone with Jenna. I'm eternally grateful our lunches sync up. It's the only thing that makes the period bearable.

"Yeah," I say. "She convinced her parents she's horribly ill and can barely get out of bed. They've dragged her to a bunch of doctors for all kinds of tests, but she says it's still better than facing everyone at school."

"And everyone else is still avoiding you?"

"J.J., Carrie, and Jack, yeah," I say. "Sean too. Reenzie isn't, but she's always with Sean, so she kinda is. Tee and I are cool, but she's always with Drew, so I don't see her that much, I basically just hang by myself, and work on my grades and college applications."

I sigh. I have more to say, but it's hard, and I'm not sure I want to say it out loud. Finally I do.

"Jenna . . . ," I begin, "do you think this was my dad's plan?"

"What do you mean?" she asks.

"Do you think he knew I'd use the locket to mess everything up and make my life miserable?"

"Autumn, that's crazy. Why would your dad do that?"

I shrug. "I was so freaked out about graduating and leaving. And now . . ." I sigh again. "I don't know . . . I feel like maybe it'll be a relief to go, since everything is so bad."

Jenna takes a second to think. "I don't buy it. Your dad's not like that. He wants you to make the future better, but he'd also want you to be happy *now*."

"You're right," I agree. "I just don't know what else to try."

"Another jump?" Jenna suggests. "Maybe the future will help you figure out what to do next."

"I only have five left," I say. "I want to use them when I know I've made some kind of change. Everything here's been the same kind of awful since the Scare Pair dance." The corners of my mouth curl in a smile. "One cool thing happened, though," I say. "I got my SAT scores."

"You did?!" Jenna squeals. "How did you not tell me?! We've been waiting for this!"

I laugh. There was actually some kind of computer snag with my scores, so it took longer for them to come out than we thought. Jenna's been as anxious as me to hear. "Okay, you ready for this?" I ask. Then I tell her.

"That's *huge!*" she shrieks.

"I know!" I'm grinning now; I can't help it. "My mom's losing her mind."

"How is this not jumpworthy?!" Jenna wails. "Getting into a great college can change everything!"

"I know," I admit, "but it's not like I'm in anywhere yet."

"But still . . ."

I laugh out loud. "You just want me to jump so you make sure you still end up with Simon."

"Yes!" she agrees. "He's perfect for me! I need to know he's still out there!"

"I promise I'll find out as soon as I can," I say. "But now doesn't feel right."

Jenna grudgingly relents, and we hang up so we can both get back to class.

Talking to her always makes me feel better. I sail through the rest of the day, then go home to find Mom in a cleavage-y little black dress. She has a full face of makeup.

"Whoa," I say. "You're all dressed up. I thought we were going to Aglio."

"We are," she says breathlessly, "but I thought it would be nice to dress up for the celebration. Erick's already upstairs showering."

Anything that gets Erick into the shower is good for me, so I'm on board. I run upstairs and shower and primp until I'm all set in a little red sundress. Erick's in nice khakis and a button-down shirt. He looks good. He even eased off the body spray, which I take as a personal congratulatory gift.

"Falls, table for four?" Mom tells the host when we get to the restaurant.

"Four?" I ask as we're led to our seats. "Is Eddy coming?

"No," Mom says. "Not Eddy."

Her voice is shaky. Why is her voice shaky?

"I invited someone else," she continues shakily. "Someone I want you to meet."

My heart lands in my stomach because I suddenly know what she's going to say.

"Mom . . . really?" I ask with dread.

"Really what?" Erick asks. "What's up?"

She looks at him, because I guess that's easier than dealing with me. She takes a deep breath. "Erick, Autumn . . . there's no easy way to say this, but—"

"She has a boyfriend," I say sharply, cutting to the chase. "Glen, right?"

Mom works hard to keep smiling. "Yes. Glen. He's a very nice man. And I'm not saying anything dramatic is happening between us, but we've been seeing each other for a while now, and I just think it's time he met the two most important people in my life. And please don't think for a minute that I'm trying to replace your father in any way. I—"

"Mom," Erick interrupts her, "it's okay. I'm happy for you."

"You are?"

Mom and I ask it at the same time, only she's delighted while I feel like I've been stabbed in the back.

"Sure," Erick says. "Dad would want you to be happy. Ooh, garlic knots."

Erick tucks into the big basket the waitress drops at our table, and I'm stunned while I watch him eat. How can he be okay with this? I finally decide it's only because Erick hasn't *seen* Glen. Once he looks at the guy and sees his helium-head, pipe-cleaner-limbed ridiculousness, he'll change his mind.

"Gwen?"

We all turn to see the man himself. Glen. He wears a gray suit with an unpleasant yellow shirt. His head and face are devoid of the blond hair I'd seen before. It's a slightly better look—maybe Mom got him to shave—but his chin is weak without any facial hair. The top of his head dances with beads of sweat. It looks disgustingly similar to the beads of butter on the garlic knots. I'm nauseous.

"Glen!" Mom lights up at the sight of this guy. She stands and leans close like she's about to hug or kiss him, then looks at me and changes her mind. She squeezes into her side of the booth so Glen can slide in next to her. His eyes widen a little when he looks at me. We *have* met before, kinda, outside Catches Falls. But he lets it go.

"Autumn, Erick, it's a true joy to meet you," he says. "I've heard so much about you both."

He hands presents to each of us. Erick tears his open. It's a guide to training for *American Ninja Warrior*. Erick pumps his fist in the air. "Yes! It's like my dream to be on that show!"

"That's what a little birdie told me," Glen says with a smile to Mom.

Vomit.

"It's a great gift," I snark. "We totally want his life goal to be a gym rat meathead."

Glen pales. Mom blushes. Points to me.

"Autumn, why don't you open your present?" she asks.

I do. It's a book called *Make Freshman Year Rule*, and the picture on the front is two young smiling girls, a blonde and a redhead.

"The girls on the cover wrote the book during their own freshman year," Glen says. "They said it's all the things they wish they knew when they first got to school."

"They kind of look like you and Jenna, don't they?" Mom asks. "I thought that was so cute."

"Very cute," I say, then stare daggers at Glen. "And I'm sure trying to read it won't frustrate me and make me miserable at all."

Glen takes a deep breath, then turns to Mom. "Maybe this was too soon," he says. "This is a family celebration. I should go and—"

"No," Mom insists. "Stay."

He does, which is fine because I'm energized now. I

finally know what I need to do to continue my mission. I'll use this dinner and make sure it drives Glen so far away from my mom he won't dream of coming back.

Glen does what I'd expect. He acts very nice, asks all kinds of questions, and doesn't try to touch my mom in front of us. In return, I start every sentence with the words "My dad," I glare, and I slice down every single thing he says and does. I feel like we're verbally arm wrestling, and I'm totally winning. I know this because Mom drags me to the bathroom before dessert.

"Autumn, I know this is hard for you, but—"

"*Hard?!* Mom, this guy is awful!"

"You're not being fair, Autumn. He's very nice."

"Yes, he is. He's nice. And *boring.* Dad was romantic. He was fun. He was goofy. He was strong. He swept you away every single day of your life!"

Mom's eyes are full of tears, and that's good. I *want* her to remember what she's throwing away. She wipes her eyes and sniffs. When she speaks, her voice is small. "Your father isn't here," she says.

Automatically, I reach for the spot under my shirt where the locket rests. "Isn't he? Isn't he always with us?"

Mom sniffs harder. I put my hand on her arm. "Mom, I'm not saying you can never be with anyone else. But this guy? Dad gave you this magical, exciting life full of love and happiness. He gave that to all of us. Glen can't do that. He's nice, but he's a washcloth. You deserve more than a washcloth."

Mom purses her lips, then laughs out loud. "Remember the meteor shower? When he woke us all up in the middle of the night to drag us onto the deck?"

I nod. "And you said no, because it was too cold, but then we went out and saw he dragged every blanket and pillow from the house outside to make a giant nest."

"And he had hot chocolate," Mom adds. "And we sat out there, all bundled up and warm, and watched the whole sky streak by."

"And he sang, remember?" I ask.

Mom laughs. "Any song he could think of that had the word 'star' in it. And remember his shooting star dance?"

We both imitate Dad's bad disco move, swiveling our hips and pointing our fingers across the ceiling like we're tracing the path of a shooting star. We both laugh.

"I love you, Autumn," she says. "Thank you."

We hug, then go back to the table. Even though we tried to clean up, it must be pretty obvious we'd been crying because Glen leaps out of his seat, concerned. "Are you okay?"

He looks earnestly at my mom, so clearly worried for her. It's pretty obvious he cares about her—maybe he even loves her—but he's no Reinaldo Falls.

I see the way Mom looks at him, studying him, and I know she sees it too. "You were right, Glen," she says. "This is a family celebration night. I think it's best if you go."

Glen blinks, confused; then he seems to understand what she means. "Oh," he says, flustered. "Well, um . . ." He reaches for his wallet but Mom shakes her head.

"It's on me," she says. "Thank you."

She keeps her gaze on him, and I know Glen's waiting to hear the same thing I am. Some kind of "I'll call you," or "We'll be in touch," or something to indicate they're still together and going strong. Instead she says nothing. Glen seems to get it. He swallows hard, and his Adam's apple—which looks like a mini version of his bald sweaty head—bobs up and down.

"Okay," he says. "Good night."

Despite Mom's wishes, he puts enough money down on the table to pay for everyone's dinner. Then he leans toward Mom as if to give her a kiss good night, but she leans away. Not much, but enough. Glen purses his lips but manages a last smile to all of us and then leaves.

"So," Mom says when she settles herself back in the booth, "anyone hungry for dessert?"

"Starving for it," I say.

Why wouldn't I be? The whole world seems lighter and happier. Yes, Mom looks like she's holding back tears, but of course she is—we just talked about Dad, who's the best guy in the universe. Remembering him is always great and hard at the same time. And, yes, Erick is glaring at me, but he just liked that Glen gave him a workout meathead present. He'll get over it.

Dessert is spectacular. Tiramisu with a candle to celebrate my SAT accomplishment. I blow out the candle, but I do it in honor of more than just a score. After weeks of feeling lost, I finally took a huge step to complete my mission from Dad. I told Jenna I'd know when it was time to jump ahead and check on the future, and I absolutely do. The minute we're back home, I shut myself in my room and set the locket for today's date, three years from now. The year that used to mark my mom's wedding. I clutch the locket in my hand, close my eyes . . .

14

three years later

I expect to end up at my own house around Thanksgiving, but instead I'm in a small room. There's a large window with soothing drapes, though I can see the outline of bars on the window. There's a beige carpet, but it looks old and matted down. I see a single twin bed, made up with an old, vaguely pleasant floral bedspread. Reenzie and Taylor sit together on the bed. Reenzie wears a white bathrobe. She has no makeup on, her hair is unwashed, and her face looks drawn and tired. Taylor wears all black, which I hope is a fashion statement and not a bad omen about Drew. Amalita and I sit in matching chairs across from the bed. We're dressed casually, which for me means jeans and a T-shirt and for Amalita means a bright red tube dress, but with only a few pieces of jewelry.

Is this Reenzie's dorm room? Is that why she's the only one undressed?

Taylor looks searchingly into Reenzie's eyes. "Are you okay?" she asks.

"You tell me," Reenzie says. She lifts her hands and her bathrobe sleeves drop down her arms . . . to reveal both her wrists, heavily bandaged.

I run to her side and kneel down "Reenzie? What did you do?"

"It was just so hard, you know?" Reenzie tells Taylor, her eyes filling with tears. "Stanford was all I wanted, but then I got there and it got so hard."

"But you were doing great," Future Me says. "You told us you were on honor roll all freshman and sophomore year."

Reenzie nods. "I was. Straight As. That was my goal— straight As, summa cum laude, top of the class, just like my parents always told me they expected. They kept sending me all these emails about how hard it is to get into the best law schools and how I basically had to be the best or I'd never do it, and I'd never score a top political internship, and I'd never be the next female president."

"No pressure or anything," Future Me snorts.

"They were right!" Reenzie insists. "And I was on track! But this semester . . . nothing worked. Everything I wrote was wrong. And my Political History of the Middle East . . . impossible. Bs and Cs, best I could pull."

"But Bs and Cs aren't bad," Future Me tells her. "*I get

mostly Bs and Cs. Junior year is hard. And it's early in the year. There's time to get better."

"For you, maybe," Reenzie says. "It didn't work that way for me. I had already lost top of the class, but I could still save summa cum laude if I moved quickly."

"So you cheated," Ames says in a matter-of-fact way that sounds pretty harsh to me.

The Reenzie I know wouldn't let anyone talk to her in that tone of voice. This Reenzie just lowers her head sadly. "I bought some essays online. One for the Middle East class and one on the significance of the first African American president on race relations in the United States. Both really good. Guaranteed As. But I got caught. First-time offense is a suspension, community service, and an F, but each essay was a separate offense. They expelled me." She looks down at her wrists. "I wanted to be gone before my parents found out." She lowers her voice to a whisper. "I still wish I were."

"No!" I say it at the same time as Future Me, who moves from her chair to sit next to Reenzie and put an arm around her.

Taylor's eyes are full of tears. "I wish you'd told me how bad it was," she says. "I wish I could have helped."

Reenzie half laughs, half sobs. "Like you needed my problems. Your boyfriend was dying of cancer."

"*Cancer?!*" I blurt. "Now I'm supposed to fix cancer?!" I turn to Tee and throw my arms in the air. "How can I possibly make everyone's future better when you fell in love with the most fragile boy in the universe?!"

"I know," Taylor answers Reenzie, not me, "but I still would have been there for you."

I plop on the floor and rest my head in my hands. Unbelievable. I'd jumped to see how I'd made things better with my family, but clearly my friends still need a lot more.

I feel totally helpless, and I can tell from listening that Reenzie, Taylor, and Future Me do too.

Then Ames pipes up.

"Enough," she says. "No more moaning. I'm sick of it."

"Amalita . . . ," Taylor warns, but Ames ignores her.

"No, it's stupid! You did this to yourself, Reenzie. You cheated. You got caught. That's on you. So, what, you're gonna end it all because you feel sorry for yourself?"

Reenzie, her face twisted in fury, holds up her bandaged wrists. "That was the plan, yes."

"And it failed," Ames says. "So you're here. Now what?"

"Ames, what is wrong with you?" Future Me snaps. "You're not helping."

"Yeah, I am," she says. Then she kneels down in front of Reenzie. "Remember senior year, when I got drunk and sent that picture to Zander? The one that ended up all over? If you think I didn't want to end it all then, you're crazy."

"You did?" Reenzie asks.

"Yeah, I did," Ames replies. "That whole time I stayed away from school, I thought about it every day. I thought it would be easier than facing what everybody thought of me. But you know what? That was dumb."

"Okay, Ames," Future Me interjects, "I only took Psych 101, but I know it's a bad idea to call a depressed person dumb."

"I'm not just saying, Reenzie," Ames goes on, "I made my mess, just like you. And I was the one who had to make it better, just like you."

"It's different," Reenzie says. "You were embarrassed. I ruined my life. I'll have to transfer to some community college if I want my degree. And when I apply to law school, the first thing they'll see is I got kicked out of Stanford."

"Uh-huh," Ames says. "And guess what everybody sees—still!—when they Google my name. That stupid-ass picture. I went into my college dorm and my roommate had it up on her computer screen. When I got out for summer jobs, they've seen it and they ask me about it. And you know what I do? Same thing you'll do when people ask you about all this. I own the mistake and I deal with it."

Ames moves closer to Reenzie now. She kneels down in front of her and takes her hands. "I messed up big-time, and I was ready to throw it all away 'cause I thought it would never get better. But it did. I'm in school. I make and sell my own jewelry. And I have kick-ass friends who are even stronger than me and won't let their own *pendejo* mistakes get in their way. You got it?"

Reenzie doesn't answer right away, but she smiles. "Your jewelry," she finally says. "I'm gonna have some pretty ugly scars for a while. Got any bracelets that can cover them up?"

15

november/december, senior year

I don't hear Amalita's answer because I'm suddenly back in bed.

It's interesting. I jumped thinking about my family, but I didn't see them at all. Does that mean they're okay? Did my intervention with Glen succeed so he's no longer an issue?

I have to believe *yes*. Dad would want me to know if Mom still needed my help. So with her all set, Dad's spirit made sure I saw the people who need my help the most. Specifically Reenzie. And Tee, but the only way I can help her is to keep making changes now, so hopefully I find a future where Drew's okay.

But Reenzie—her I can help. If Stanford is too high-pressure for her, I have to make sure she doesn't go. The hard part is I know she already applied there for Restrictive Early Action. That means if they accept her, she has to go. They're not supposed to make their decision until December, but I want to act fast, just in case.

I head to my computer and write a letter to the Admissions Department at Stanford. I try to channel Reenzie's voice and explain that even though I applied for Restrictive Early Action, I only did so to appease my high-pressure parents. I say that I'm having communication problems with my parents, and they don't understand that Stanford is not really the college for me. Since I can't convince them, I humbly ask the Admissions Department to simply reject me. I sign it, print it out, then go downstairs and grab a stamp and envelope from the desk where Mom pays all her non-auto-pay bills. Snail mail's my only choice for this; email is too easily traced. Even if I set up a fake "Reenzie" email, they'll see it's not the one from her application.

I think I make a good argument. I bet they even get kids all the time who apply because their parents pressure them into it, so I'm sure they'll buy it. Reenzie will kill me if she ever finds out, but I'm okay with that. Better she kills me than tries to kill herself. At least, as long as we're talking metaphorically.

My jump also helped me figure out what to do about Amalita, so the next day after school I come home and make a batch of empanadas using Ames's mom's recipe. I make a ton of them, because Thanksgiving is only a week away and I may as well freeze some and save them for that.

I call Ames's house to make sure her mom's there, and I'm thrilled when she answers.

"Hello?"

"Hi, Mrs. Leibowitz! I made your empanadas! Can I bring some over for you?"

"I don't know, *mija*. Amalita's still feeling under the weather. . . ."

"I don't even have to see her!" I offer. "I just want your opinion on these before I serve them up for Thanksgiving."

That clinches it. She says yes, and I ride my bike over to Amalita's, the empanadas warming my back through my backpack.

"*Muy delicioso*, Autumn," she raves forty-five minutes later when we're sitting at the kitchen table together. "*Perfecto!*"

"It was your recipe," I say humbly. "I just followed it and everything worked out."

I spend some time chatting with her, and I listen while she tells me all about every single dish she's making for Thursday's meal. Then, when she's about to boot me out so she can make dinner, I ask to see Amalita.

"Just for a second," I say. "She's just been sick so long, I'm worried about her."

Mrs. Leibowitz frowns. "I don't want you to catch anything. . . ." She walks to a kitchen drawer and pulls out a hospital mask. "Just in case. And only stay for a minute."

I thank her and pull on the mask, then pull it off once I storm into Amalita's room.

"Hey!" she objects.

She's in the exact same nightgown as three weeks before, which would worry me from a sanitation point of view, except the baby blue fabric is so clean it practically glows, her room smells like lemon and bleach, and Ames herself looks sparkling clean. Her hair is plaited back in twin braids. Lying back against her pillows, she looks like she's about six years old.

"Go away, Autumn," she mutters. "I don't want to see anybody."

"Your mom gave me a mask to come in here," I say. "What does she think you have, Ebola?"

Ames shrugs. "I'm lucky my dad's a hypochondriac. All the doctors say I'm fine, but I just tell him new symptoms so he keeps me home. Right now he thinks I've got walking pneumonia."

"Ames, this has to stop," I say.

"Yeah, I thought so too," she says dully, "but it keeps going on. I saw this one today."

She pulls out her phone and shows me a Vine. It's the picture she sent to Zander, only someone animated it. For six seconds, Amalita dances in her nightgown as hearts fly out of her eyes.

"It's never going to end," she says. "Never."

Her eyes have the same defeated look I saw on Reenzie's face in my last jump. But thanks to Ames, I know what to do about it.

"No," I say. "No more moaning. I'm sick of it."

Ames frowns. "Excuse you?"

"I am!" I say. "You did this to yourself, Amalita. You got drunk. You sent a picture. That's on you. So, what, you're gonna give up on your life just because you're feeling sorry for youself?"

I'm quoting Amalita to Amalita, only she can't possibly know since it's a speech she's going to give to Reenzie three years from now, in a future I've already made sure won't happen. I don't quote it perfectly, and the pep talk I go on to give her is about *my* past, not hers. I remind her again about my sophomore year, when everybody hated me and all I wanted to do was disappear.

"I never thought that would get better," I say. "But it did."

"'Cause Reenzie took the site about you down," Ames says. "This picture is out there forever."

"So what if it is?" I say, channeling Future Ames the best I can. "So what if people Google your name years from now and it comes up? You know what you'll do?"

"Oh, you're gonna tell me?" Ames challenges me. "Like you're psychic now?"

I try not to smile. I see it as an excellent sign that she has the energy to get angry with me.

"Not psychic," I say. "I just know you. And I know you're too kickass to let your own mistake and a bunch of some complete jerkoffs' bullying get in your way. So whenever this comes up, you'll hold your head high and deal. You messed up, sure, but Zander and the losers like him are the *panzons* who took advantage. And if you stay here and hide, or take yourself out of the picture, they win."

Ames is quiet for a second. "I think I should call Zander," she says.

I'm stunned. "Seriously, Ames?! Why?!"

She smiles. "I want to tell him I have family in the Cuban mafia whose business is revenge. If he gets anywhere near me, or does one thing to piss me off, they'll make him disappear."

I grin. "*Is* there a Cuban mafia?"

"How should I know?" Ames asks. "But I bet he doesn't know either."

"If you do call and tell him that," I say, "he'd be *really* happy if you never went back to school and he never saw you again."

"Yeah, I bet he would," Ames agrees. Her eyes dance as she thinks about it, then she catches me grinning giddily and rolls her eyes. "*Callate*," she says. "Go. Maybe I'll see you at school tomorrow. Give Zander one less thing to be thankful for over vacation."

I give Ames a big hug, then dart out of her room and ride home.

Ames does go to school the next day, even though she says it was a nightmare trying to convince her parents she *wasn't* sick anymore. It's an ugly day for her. Lots of people laugh and whisper behind her back—or right in front of her face—but she ignores it all. And she takes a special joy in grabbing every opportunity to get near Zander, who always looks terrified and runs in the other direction. At lunch, she even sprawls on the lawn like always, even though it's the same pose she struck in the picture and everyone notices. I'm proud of her, and I'm crazy-over-the-moon thrilled to have a lunch friend again.

"So," she says, "when were you going to tell me you're head over heels for J.J.?"

"What?!" I blurt, and quickly look away from J.J., since of course I was staring right at him.

"*Mija,* I was hiding and depressed for three weeks, not dead. That boy tells me everything."

I suddenly feel a little light-headed. "What did he say?"

"Oh, look at that. Now you're staring at me and not him."

"Ames!"

She sits up, jangling all her bracelets. "Come on. He loves you."

"He said that?"

"No. *I* said that. *He* said that after what happened last year he can't ever trust you that way, and he's better off sticking with a girl who at least knows she wants to be with him."

"But what about her and Keith Hamilton?" I balk. "She kissed him!"

"*He* kissed *her.* Different. And not on the lips."

I open my mouth to object but she shakes her head, cutting me off with earring jangle. "I know! But that's what he said. And you were straight with me yesterday, so I'm gonna be straight with you. You had your chance with him. You blew it. It's Carrie's turn. Maybe it'll work for her and maybe it won't, but you can't get in the middle. If it's meant to be, it'll be. *Que sera sera.*"

I nod, but Ames has no idea what she's talking about. If I had just let the future be, Ames would be doomed to a future in rehab, Sean would be doomed to paralysis, Carrie and J.J. would be parents before they were out of college, Jack would be closeted forever. . . . The future is *not* set in stone, and it only gets better if we make it better.

J.J. isn't meant to be with Carrie. I know it. I just have to figure out a way to make him know it too. With Thanksgiving break, I guess I'll have time to think about it.

We make the holiday a bigger affair than last year, since Mom decides to have her friend Amanda and a bunch of the other Catches Falls workers and volunteers over. That means the whole weekend and days leading up to the holiday are a giant whirl. We clean the house, make song mixes, make list after list of everything we want to serve, shop . . . it's crazy. Mom loves it, though. I keep an eye on her, just to make sure she's not upset about Glen, but she seems completely carefree.

She, Erick, and I all go to Century Acres together to pick up Eddy. She's waiting in her favorite lobby chair but leaps up when we walk in. She races over to me in quick shuffling steps, then loses her balance and screams as she pinwheels her arms.

Alarms sound in my head. I thought I'd changed the future, but it's Thanksgiving and she's going to fall and break her hip! I run to catch her . . .

. . . which is when she stands up straight and smirks at me. "Gotcha."

"Eddy!" I shout.

"What? I gave you something else to be thankful for," she says. She takes my arm, and as we walk to the car she adds, "Oh, you just missed your boyfriend. Kyler just picked up Zelda. He's taking her on a private jet to the Keys. Any chance we're doing the same?"

We're not, but it's still a great meal, and it's fun having the house full. I Skype Jenna in on the festivities for a while, so it's like she's there, and Eddy goes crazy for the empanadas I made with Mrs. Leibowitz's recipe. We do that goofy thing where we all go around and say what we're thankful for, and I list my friends, and Eddy, and Mom, and Erick. And when I add, "And Dad, because I'll always be thankful for him for as long as I live," Mom reaches over and squeezes my hand while Eddy winks.

That night, though, after Mom runs Eddy home and is hanging out back with all her friends and Erick has retreated to his faux man cave, I get sad. This time last year I started going out with J.J. Yes, it was all messed up and I ruined it all, but that's not the part I think about. I think about the road trip we took when I was devastated about Sean and he wanted to make me feel better. How he drove me all through Florida, taking me to taste the wildest, greasiest, bizarre-est foods at these random places he'd looked up just because he knew we'd have fun trying them. I remember how we put on new personas at each restaurant, just to mess with everyone around us.

It's like I told Mom when I was talking her out of Glen. When you have someone who makes you laugh and is romantic and surprises you and makes you come alive and be happier just because you're together . . . why would you want anything else?

Once I thought I did. Now I know better.

I wonder if there's any chance he's feeling nostalgic too.

I could call him, but that's not as much fun. I'd rather surprise him. Just show up on his doorstep. I run upstairs and toss on distressed denim shorts and a patterned tank. Something very cute but casual enough that I can claim the visit as spur of the moment. I brush out my hair, add product, a little makeup, and cute sandals and slip my phone in my back pocket and I'm ready. I shout out to Mom and her friends that I'm going for a walk, and then I'm out the door.

J.J.'s only a few blocks away, but my heart's racing like I'm running a marathon. I have all these images of how he'll come to the door, surprised for a moment. Then he'll shake his head and say, "Amazing"—only he'll say some kind of anagram for the word. And when I ask why, he'll smile and say, "Because I was just thinking about you." And I'll say, "I was thinking about you too." Then we'll have that nervous excited smile thing for a while, and his parents will call out asking who it is and J.J. will be all embarrassed and answer but say he'll be right back and then he'll come outside and we'll talk in the moonlight until he leans down and—

I hear the shouting when I'm in front of his next-door neighbor's house. Apparently, J.J.'s already in his front yard with someone. And they're not happy.

"It was a *mistake*!" a girl wails.

Carrie. *Carrie* wails.

Carrie made a mistake?

I perk up. This could be very good. I want to listen closer. I want to *see* what's happening, but I can't just stroll out in front of the house. They'll see me and they'll stop and I won't learn anything. I walk onto the neighbor's front lawn and sidle up to the hedges that separate it from J.J.'s. I gently push my way into the plants until I'm right in the middle. I'm covered, but I can see J.J. and Carrie through some leaves. They're lit up by the outside house lights, so I can see he looks hurt and furious. She looks like she's been crying.

"How is that a 'mistake'?" J.J. asks. "You, what, tripped and fell and he caught you with his lips?!"

"That's not funny," Carrie says sulkily.

"No, it's not. Know what else isn't funny?" J.J. pulls out his phone and holds it out to Carrie like it's a crucifix and she's a vampire. It has the same effect too—she shies away and won't look. "It's not funny when Keith Hamilton sends me a selfie of the two of you kissing."

"He wasn't supposed to do that," she snaps.

"Why, because you didn't want to get caught?!" J.J. explodes. "He also said you two have been dating behind my back ever since the Halloween dance! Is that true?!"

I hear his voice crack on the last question, and it breaks my heart. I don't want him with Carrie, I'll admit it, but it's awful to hear him hurt like this.

"I didn't know what I wanted," Carrie says softly. "I needed time to figure it out."

"Have you figured it out *yet*?" J.J. asks.

Carrie doesn't answer. She just looks at him, her eyes big and sad. It's a complete standoff . . .

. . . which is when I get bitten by the world's largest mosquito.

"OW!" I shout without thinking, slapping at my neck.

Carrie and J.J. both look my way. I freeze, hoping they'll decide it was their imagination.

They don't. They both walk right toward me. I love my bright orange hair, but I realize this is one time when it's not really working in my favor.

"Autumn?" J.J. asks.

I'd like to say he intoned the word with surprise and excitement, but it's more like horrified disgust.

"Are you kidding me?" Carrie yelps. "Are you *spying* on us?"

She reaches into the bushes, yanks my arm, and drags me out, scraping me through about a million sharp branches.

"Ow! Ow! Ow!"

"What are you doing here?" Carrie snaps.

I look back and forth between Carrie and J.J. They both look furious. I decide to go with the truth.

"I just came by to say hi," I tell J.J. Then I add to Carrie, "I had no idea you were here, I swear. But then I heard you guys fighting and—"

"You decided to hide and watch?" Carrie spits.

When she says it that way, the truth isn't really so flattering. Time to redirect.

"Hey," I tell J.J., "I'm not the one who cheated on you."

"Yeah, you are," J.J. says stonily. "Just not this time."

For a second I wonder if it's worth clarifying that while I may have *emotionally* cheated on him last year, Carrie actually had a full-on relationship behind his back.

Looking at his face, though, I decide to keep that detail to myself.

"Go home," J.J. says. "Both of you. And do me a favor and stay there."

He turns and walks into his house, shutting the door behind him. Carrie shouts his name and runs after him. She twists on the locked doorknob and pounds on the door. I don't do any of that. It's Thanksgiving. His family's inside. And he made it pretty clear it's the last thing he wants. I walk away and go home.

"I thought you spoke Spanish!" Ames screams into my ear the next morning. "What part of *que sera sera* do you not understand?"

I can't even begin to answer that question, but I assure her I don't want to talk about it. I'd love to go to a movie or something, but she promised the day to J.J., and I'm clearly not welcome to come along. It's okay, though. I spend it with Mom and Erick and I do some homework, and then hang with Ames over the weekend. We even get to see Taylor because Drew's out of town with his family. She is completely smitten with him, and I specifically ramp up a game of Would You Rather so I can ask, "Would you rather have the love of a lifetime, even if it's doomed to end tragically, or a love that's just okay, but you know it will last forever?"

It doesn't really work. Taylor thinks I'm talking about my mom and dad, Ames thinks I'm talking about myself and J.J., and it leads the conversation into all kinds of different places that have nothing to do with the fact that Taylor's boyfriend seems to be a ticking time bomb.

When we get back to school on Monday, I kind of expect our lunch group to be back to normal. Yes, J.J.'s upset with me, but he's tight with Amalita, and Jack always follows him. But neither of them joins us at lunch.

"You won't see him," Ames says when she sees me

looking around for J.J. "He's in a bad place. Kinda wants to be by himself."

I get it. I do. But the thing is, I know I can make it better, and it makes me crazy that he won't let me.

"I see a Lloyd Dobler moment in your future," Jenna says when I talk to her about it after school one night. Jenna has always had a huge thing for '80s teen movies, and when we both lived in Maryland, we watched them all. She's always been a big J.J. fan because she thinks he's my Duckie.

"The *Say Anything* guy?" I ask.

"Really?" Jenna shoots back, insulted. "You seriously had to ask? Of course he's the *Say Anything* guy. You have to do something like he did. Make a statement that reminds J.J. of everything you guys have."

Lloyd Dobler made his statement by holding a giant boom box above his head and playing Peter Gabriel's "In Your Eyes" to his girlfriend, Diane Court. Giant boom boxes no longer exist, I would look ridiculous holding one over my head, and I happen to know that J.J. Austin is not a Peter Gabriel fan.

He's also not a Kyler Leeds fan, but there is that song Kyler wrote that's literally all about J.J. and me. I have it on my phone. And I even have a Bluetooth speaker that would be way easier to hold over my head than a boom box.

I decide the next day will be my Lloyd Dobler day. I warn Amalita in advance that I won't be at lunch. I don't tell her where I *will* be because she won't approve, but I don't want her to feel abandoned when I don't show.

Ames told me J.J.'s in a bad place and wants to be by himself. I've had a lot of time at Aventura High in bad places, and I know all the best spots to be by myself, so I figure if I look hard enough I can find him. I don't bother with the library. It's one of my go-tos, but J.J. likes to move around when he's upset, like at the dance when he went out and walked around. I figure the lower fields are my best bet. I wander down to the track and the bleachers, but he's not there. Then I walk down to the equipment shed by the soccer fields, but he's not there either.

I have one more shot. The lower field bathrooms are in this cement bunker, but one side of the building is completely blocked off by trees. There's a bench against the wall on that side, which is hysterical because it's almost like the school put it there purposely as a completely secluded spot for kids to hide and make out. If they did, it's kind of brilliant, because no one actually uses it for that. Since it's so obviously a make-out spot, everyone figures either

A) someone else is already there and you don't want to walk in on them, or

B) a teacher will come by any second because it's such an obvious place to catch against-the-rules PDA.

Point is, if I were J.J. and I *really* wanted to get away and be alone, it's where I'd go.

I get Kyler's song all queued up on my phone, get the Bluetooth speaker synced, then squeeze my way between the edge of the trees and the cement building.

There's someone on the bench . . . but it isn't J.J.

It's Jack and Tom.

And they're full-on making out.

"Ohmigod!" I squeal.

Jack and Tom jump at the sound of my voice, and Jack leaps off the bench and as far as the clearing will allow. He's bright red, completely disheveled, and hunched over a little. He holds out his hands in twin "stop" signs, scrambling to explain.

"It's not what you think. What you saw, it's . . . it's . . ."

"Wait, hold up," I say quickly. "I'm so sorry—I meant 'ohmigod, this is great,' not 'ohmigod . . . ohmigod.'"

"Huh?" Jack asks.

Tom, who's still on the bench, perfectly calm, explains. "She means she's not freaked out."

"Of course not!" I say. "I'm totally happy for you guys! I knew you'd be great together!"

Jack looks like someone just short-circuited his brain. He gapes at me. "You . . . you *knew*?"

Tom rolls his eyes. "She totally knew. She outed you to Gus."

"Okay," I balk, "I didn't *out* him—"

"'Personal stuff' that makes it hard for him to handle a guy for a Scare Pair date?" Tom asks.

"That could have been anything!" I shoot back.

Tom just raises an eyebrow.

"Wait-wait-wait," Jack stammers. "How did you *know*?"

There's no way I can tell him the truth, so I just shrug. "I don't know . . . I just knew. Or suspected, I guess."

"Does anyone else know?" Jack asks. He looks terrified.

"No," I say definitively. "Not at all. No idea." Then I grin. "But they *could*! No one would care. We'd all be happy for you! See this smile?" I ask, pointing to my face. "Imagine it on all your friends' faces. Oh! Yes!" I gasp as I come up with a brilliant idea. "We can have a coming out party for you! We'll do it at my house! It'll be fantastic."

"Autumn," Tom says, amused, "gay men aren't debutantes. We don't have coming out parties."

"Right. I knew that," I say, "I just want to help. I mean, why keep it a secret when you totally don't have to anymore?"

"No, I *do* have to," Jack says. "And if you're really my friend, you'll keep it a secret too."

"But why?" I ask. "I mean, don't get me wrong—I totally won't tell anyone if you don't want me to—"

"Even though you outed him to Gus," Tom notes.

I'm about to object, but instead I cede the point. "Yes, even though. But just . . . why?"

"Just . . . because. Okay?"

He looks earnestly into my eyes, and I nod. "Of course. Whatever you want." Then I grin again. "But I'm happy for you guys." I run and give Jack a hug, then stand there, smiling at the two of them.

Tom looks at me pointedly. "Autumn? Don't you have someplace to be?"

"Nope," I say. Then I realize what he's getting at. "I mean, yes! Absolutely! Gotta run!"

I zip through the trees surrounding the clearing and twirl around happily as I start back up to the main lawn. I may not have fixed things with J.J. and me—yet—but I fixed Jack's future!

I wonder if this means Nathan's back in the picture.

One way to find out. I choose a cozy patch of grass, plop down with my legs crossed, and pull out the locket. I open it and play with the dials. Three years and six months from now should be good. The summer after our junior year in college. I close the locket, squeeze it tight, and close my eyes. . . .

16

three and a half years later

I'm on the beach. I recognize it immediately—the beach near the Shack, where we go every Friday after the football games. I'm close to the water, and I see a whole group of us is there: Sean, Reenzie, Taylor, Jack, Amalita, and Future Me. We all look good—like ourselves, really. We're on the sand, laughing and talking and I'm immediately happy. It feels easy and simple and it's everything I've missed since we haven't been like that in my time for a while now.

As I listen, I get that we're all miraculously home from college at the same time and trying to get some time in before we split off for internships and jobs and vacations and other stuff we have planned. We're talking about where we want to live when college is over next year, and if maybe we'll all be in the same city again.

"Wanna hear something crazy?" Future Me asks. "I think I'm going to stay in school."

"*Callate,* you are not," Ames says.

237

Ames sounds dubious. I'm more concerned. "Why?" I ask. "Are we failing?"

But Future Me explains it's because she loves her psych major so much, she wants to pursue it professionally and go on to get her doctorate. "So I can change people's lives," Future Me says, and there's a twinkle in her eye that I totally know comes from the fact that she *did* change all their lives, back when she was me.

Of course, this is a line of reasoning that makes my head hurt, so I just smile and hold up a hand. "Yeah, you change people's lives," I say supportively. "Up top."

She does not slap my hand, but Jack chimes in playfully. "How will you change lives, exactly? Outing them like you outed me to Gus Carillo?"

A guy I don't know gasps. "She *outed* you?!"

"Shut up!" Future Me laughs. "I did not out you!"

"Totally outed me, Ben," Jack says dramatically to the guy. "Scarred me for life."

"Can't hold it against her," Ben says. "I'd have lost out if you were still in the closet when we met."

"I'd have come out in college," Jack says. "For sure."

"You wouldn't, though," I say. "I saw. You'd be miserable without my help. So you're welcome." I look Ben up and down. He's got the dorky-cute thing going on, but he seems very into Jack and they look happy together. "Nathan was cuter," I say, "but this guy's good too."

"Oy," Ames says. "You'll never believe what my manager asked me about yesterday."

"The picture?" Taylor asks sympathetically.

"The picture," Ames agrees.

At first when she says "manager," I think maybe she's an actress, but when she keeps talking, I realize she means *hotel* manager. Ames is majoring in hotel management, and for the last three summers she's been working at the same beach hotel in Maine. Her boss had Googled her before, but this time he apparently clicked a few pages in and found the contraband.

"What did he say?" Sean asks.

"He didn't," Ames says. "I didn't let him. When he started in I said, 'Look—am I good at my job?' He said 'Yeah, you're the best.' So I told him that's all that mattered, and if he had a problem with that I'd just quit. So he shut up. And he gave me a raise."

"Yes!" I shout. "Ames, you rule!"

Everyone else seems to agree, but then Sean's face goes dark.

"Oh, hey," he says, "did you guys see in the news about Garth Cheskin?"

"Who?" everyone asks.

"Garth Cheskin. I knew him from football summer camps. He's a quarterback at FSU. Or . . . he was. Took a nasty sack in a game last season." Sean shakes his head miserably. "He went down hard. Ended up paralyzed from the neck down."

"I'm so sorry," Reenzie says, echoing the sympathy on everyone's faces. "Were you guys close?"

"No," Sean admits. "Fell out of touch years ago. But the crazy thing is . . . that could have been me. Remember how badly I wanted to play football there?"

"Remember?!" Future Me asks. "You *hated* me for messing that up."

"I didn't *hate* you," Sean balks.

Reenzie, Jack, Ames, Taylor, and Future Me all laugh out loud, and Sean grudgingly admits he might have hated me a little.

"So what's up with you and Drew, Tee?" Ames asks. "Everything good?"

I hold my breath for a second, even though Taylor's wearing a white shirt and denim shorts, which seems like a good sign.

"Amazing," she gushes. And as she talks, I get their whole story. They've been together this whole time. He graduated a year ago and moved to New York, where he worked on Broadway, then got some big job performing a show in London. The long distance sucked, but Taylor says he's flying home even as she speaks, and the two of them will have two whole weeks together. She can't wait.

Turns out Reenzie's in love, too. She met her boyfriend at Wesleyan, where she applied after Stanford rejected her. When she talks about the school, I can tell she loves it. She says it's just as hard as any Ivy, but the vibe is more laid-back. "Laid-back" was never a term I'd use for Reenzie, but it seems to suit her, and she's on track to graduate top of her class and hit a great law school.

"This is incredible!" I shout. "I changed our futures and it worked! We're all happier! I am a Time Goddess Genius!"

Yet even as I say it, I'm very aware there's one person very obviously not on the beach. I assure myself it doesn't mean anything. This future is so good, J.J.'s absence has to be just a scheduling thing, and he and Future Me are either together or just really good friends but on our way back to one another.

Then there's a lull in the conversation, and Future Me asks, "So . . . anyone hear about J.J.? Is he in town?"

She says it in a tinny, forced-casual way that makes my heart sink, and the way all my friends look at each other and won't meet her eyes is unbearable.

"Oh no," I whisper. "Come on, everything is so good. This *has* to be right."

But it's not. After a painfully long silence, Taylor speaks up. "He's in town, but Naomi won't let him meet up with us."

Future Me's face clouds over even more. "All of us? Or *me*?"

More glance exchanges.

"Wait, I don't get it," I say. "Who's Naomi and why won't she let J.J. see me?"

"Seriously?" Future Me bursts out. "It's been two years! I get it. They're together. I'm not going to get in the way."

"I know, but look at it from her side," Taylor says. "You're the last woman her boyfriend was with before her."

241

"You ask me," Ames says, "she only keeps him away because she thinks if you're together, he'll go back to you."

Future Me looks at Ames intently. "Do *you* think that?"

Ames shrugs, but Jack says what she's thinking. "Doesn't matter," Jack says. "J.J.'s whipped. And it's bad. She treats him like dirt."

"So why is he with her?" Future Me asks, and I can feel her hurt in my own chest.

"You know him," Jack says. "He's gun-shy. After you and Carrie in high school, he never trusted that someone would stay with him. Even in college, when he visited you and you got back together, he was always jealous. He'd freak out that something would happen at a party or someplace, and you wouldn't tell him. Then he met Naomi, and she was at his school and always there and always hanging on him and always doing things with him—"

"*Only* with him," Ames mutters, "'cause she's a *muy posesivo mujer loca* and wants him all to herself."

"Whatever," Jack says. "Point is, whatever we think about her, he's fine with it, so . . ." Now he shrugs too.

"But he's *not* fine with it, right?" Future Me asks. "'Cause if he were, Naomi wouldn't have anything to worry about."

"What do you want me to say, Autumn?" Jack asks. "That he's secretly still in love with you and maybe he wishes things were different?"

"Yes!" Future Me says. "That's exactly what I want you to say!"

"What would it matter?" Jack asks. "He's not going anywhere. I don't know if he loves Naomi. Maybe he does. He says he does. I think he just feels safe with her, and he's messed in the head enough that he won't risk that to go after something more."

Taylor puts out a hand and rubs Future Me's back. "You gotta get over him, Autumn," she says gently. "It's over."

Future Me looks like she's about to cry. I feel the same way. No matter how well I fixed everything else, J.J. and I are still hopelessly broken.

Taylor's phone rings. She answers it, then listens and her face goes pale. My heart sinks lower because even though all my friends and Future Me are asking her what's wrong, I already know.

"It's about Drew's plane," she tells us, her eyes misting over as she tilts the phone away from her mouth. "Something . . . something went wrong."

17

december, senior year

I'm crying now. It's the middle of a school day, I'm on the lawn where anyone can see, and I'm crying.

Was that one Colorado future I saw the only one where I end up with J.J.? And if it is, why did I have to see it? How is it at all fair that I have to live out the rest of my life knowing I *could* have been ecstatically happy, but instead I messed it all up?

No. There has to be a way to get him back.

I keep trying the Lloyd Dobler route. I keep my Bluetooth speaker with me at all times all week, but J.J.'s so good at avoiding me that I never catch him alone. I could show up at his house like the real Lloyd Dobler, but given how happy he was the last time I tried that, he'd probably call the cops and have me arrested for stalking and trespassing, which would *not* look good on my college applications.

At least Jack and I are friends again. It takes a while.

Even though I was totally cool about him and Tom, he's nervous around me all week. Every time he sees me, he gives me these nervous looks and quickly walks away. By Friday, though, he seems confident I won't give away his secret.

"Hey," he says softly when he catches me in the hall. "Thanks for . . ." He looks around to make sure no one's watching. "You know."

"No problem," I say. "How's it going?"

Jack smiles, and it's completely adorable. He looks nervous and happy and excited, and it's like I can feel his energy bring me up just being around it. "Really well," he says softly. "Yesterday my parents were out at some work dinner, so he came over, and—"

"What up, *mi amigos*?" Ames cries as she and Taylor approach from down the hall.

We hear a distinctive stomping of low heels and spin around to see Reenzie. She's clearly on the warpath. I've seen her in this mode many times since I've known her, and the results are never good. My blood chills as I realize *why* she might be on the warpath.

"I'm going to hit my locker," I say, already moving in the other direction. "Want to make sure I have everything before class."

"Nobody moves!" Reenzie roars. "Not until you answer a question. Who hates me?"

"What, you want the whole list?" Amalita asks.

"You mean, like, who has *ever* hated you, or who hates

you *now*?" Jack asks. "'Cause they're different. I mean, I hated you freshman year, and no doubt Autumn hated you sophomore, and—"

Reenzie silences him with her hand in the air. Her other hand shows us her cell phone. "I just got a call from the head of the Admissions Office at Stanford. They told me they got a letter—*from me*—asking them to reject me because I don't really want to go to the school. They called to make sure I sent it, because it sounded like the complete opposite of what I said in my application."

I work really hard to make my eyes wide and surprised. "Wow," I say, trying not to let my voice waver. "*Did* you send it?"

"No, I didn't send it!" Reenzie roars. "I would *never* send it, and the only person who would *think* to send it would have to be someone who knows I applied early to Stanford!"

She glares daggers at us, one at a time.

"Which is *everyone*," Taylor reminds Reenzie. "You shouted it out loud on the lunch lawn the day you sent it in."

Reenzie's face softens a little. "I guess. Doesn't really matter anyway. I told the admissions person the letter was a complete fake . . . and they told me to expect good news in a couple weeks!"

Taylor squeals and jumps up and down with Reenzie. I try to look happy, too, but all I can think about is Reenzie, pale and spent, her wrists wrapped in gauze.

"It's terrific," I say with as much enthusiasm as I can

muster, "but . . . you know . . . I hear that school is really high-pressure. You sure you want to go?"

"Why?" Reenzie's eyes become slits, then quickly widen in horror. "Oh my God, was it *you*? Did you sabotage me like you sabotaged Sean?"

"No!" I lie. "And I didn't sabotage Sean! That was an accident! I'm just saying . . ." I sigh and deflate. All of a sudden I feel like I'm going to cry. I *know* what she's in for, and there's no way I can warn her or steer her away from it. Even if I told her the complete truth, she'd never believe me.

"Autumn?" she asks. "Are you okay?"

I nod, and a germ of an idea pops into my head. When I look back at Reenzie, I know my eyes are watery and I probably look a little desperate and crazy, but maybe I can make all that make sense.

"It's just . . . ," I start, and my voice cracks without me even trying. "I've been meeting with Mr. Winthrop about colleges, and he told me these stories about people who get to a big-deal school and they think it'll be easy and perfect, and when it isn't . . . they sometimes lose it. He said he knew one student who got so overwhelmed by everything . . . he tried to kill himself."

Reenzie tilts her head and smiles sympathetically. "Sweetie, he was just telling you that because you can't get into those schools. He made it sound worse so you wouldn't feel bad."

Ugh. She's not getting it.

"It's not that!" I say too quickly and loudly.

Reenzie raises an eyebrow.

"Okay, maybe it's partially that," I say, "but it got me worried about you. Just promise me that no matter what happens when you get to college, no matter how much you feel like you can't tell anyone if you're having trouble . . . just know you can pick up the phone and call any one of us. We're all here for you."

I turn to Ames, Jack, and Taylor for confirmation, but they're looking at me like I just sprouted a duck bill. I ignore them and look plaintively back at Reenzie.

She puts her hands on my shoulders and looks deep into my eyes.

"I love you. And, yes, if I ever have a freak-out panic attack—which I won't—I will call you."

"You promise?"

"If it means we can end this conversation, yes, I promise."

I nod. It's not exactly what I wanted, but maybe it's enough. Maybe when things get bad she'll remember this and reach out. Maybe I'll find out next time I jump.

The bell rings and we head off to class. "I expect you all at the game tonight," Reenzie says as we go. "Play-offs— it's a huge deal for Sean."

"Which means I'm sure he doesn't want me there," I say.

"Whatever. He accepted a full ride to UNH like a month ago. Division Two school, he'll get actual play time; he's good. Still pissed at you on principle, but he's good."

"What?!" I look at all my friends. "How did nobody tell me this?"

"Didn't come up." Ames shrugs, then turns to Reenzie. "You know I'll be there. We're cheering."

"Autumn, Jack, and I will be there too," Taylor says. "Save us seats. And one for Drew."

"But not one for me," Jack says. "I'm going with J.J."

"And you're not sitting with us?" I ask.

Jack looks uncomfortably at me for a split second before he and all my other friends race off to class.

"So now J.J.'s even avoiding me at places I don't plan on being!" I vent to Jenna as I walk home from school that afternoon. "I wasn't going to this game at all. I *still* don't want to go. Taylor, Reenzie, and Ames are making me."

"Maybe it'll be fun," Jenna offers.

"Fun would be tweezing every hair off my body, one by one," I say. "This is three hours of self-torture. You really think I'll be able to concentrate on the game?"

"Do you *ever* concentrate on the game?"

"No, but this'll be worse. All I'll be doing is searching for J.J., then psychically willing my memories of our future into his brain."

"Maybe it's not all about you," Jenna offers. "Maybe J.J.'s sitting with Jack to help him. So Jack can be near wherever Tom sits, without anyone getting suspicious."

"I *doubt* J.J. knows about Tom," I scoff. "And Tom won't even be in the bleachers. He's an A/V guy. He's up in the booth doing all the music stuff between plays. . . ."

My voice fades away, pushed out by an idea brewing in my head.

"Autumn?" Jenna eventually asks.

"Not Autumn," I answer. "Lloyd. Lloyd Dobler."

I hang up with Jenna and immediately call Jack.

"You know you owe me," I say, and when he doesn't balk at that, I make him promise to text me once he and J.J. find seats, then let me know exactly where they are. I also make him give me Tom's cell phone number, and I ask him to text Tom *himself* to let Tom know that when my call comes in, he should take it.

"Should I be frightened about whatever you're planning to do?" Jack asks.

"Best not to think too much about it," I say. Then I hang up and change into turquoise shorts and a turquoise spaghetti-string tank top, with a wide-collar off-one-shoulder purple tee over the whole thing. Plus purple and turquoise ribbons to hold up my ponytail. It's like Rainbow Dash threw up all over me, but those are our school colors, so everyone looks just as ridiculous on game days. By the time I'm decked out, I figure Jack had time to talk to Tom, so I pick up my phone.

"Tom!" I shout when he answers. "I desperately need you."

"Aw, see, and here I am all taken," he says.

"Not what I meant," I say. "Just tell me if you can make this happen."

He doesn't say anything for a while after I finish, and I worry I lost the connection or totally freaked him out.

"Tom? You there?"

"Oh, I'm here," he says.

"So?" I ask. "Can you help me?"

"Pretty sure you're beyond help," he says, "but I'm a sucker for a good love story. Send me the file, then come to the booth at the beginning of halftime."

I squeal and thank him, then hang up and finish getting ready, which today means sending Tom the file and doing some major anagram research. I barely finish in time for Taylor and Drew to pick me up. I'm thrilled the two of them are so blissfully in love they don't even notice me in the backseat, because I'm a mess. I can't sit still. I jounce my knees, check random apps on my phone, fix my hair, pop mints, and unbuckle a couple times to shift to the other side of the car just so I can move. When we get to the field, I leap out of the car. My heart is pounding so hard it's like I'm being chased by lions, and I still have an hour before the game starts and the entire first half. I have to calm down . . . but I can't.

I think I speak to Reenzie, Taylor, and Drew during the next couple hours. I'm pretty sure I stand up and cheer when the rest of the stadium does. And I definitely sing the fight song two or three times, because our team scores points and we always sing when they score points. But I'm doing it all on autopilot. I'm actually paying attention to the big screens at each end of the stadium. They're not big like NFL screens—at least, that's what Reenzie says—but they're big *enough*, and the A/V team uses them to show big moments on the field, or put up things like "DE-FENSE" to get us to cheer, or little animations of horrible things happening to cartoon guys in the opposing team's jerseys. So I watch the screens and I listen to the sounds the booth projects through the stadium: the snippets of songs, the *ba-da-da-da-da-da!* that gets us all to shout "CHARGE!" and the fight song that plays when we all sing.

The more I watch and listen, the more nervous I get about what I'm planning to do at halftime.

It's important, though. Unless I do something big and daring, J.J. will avoid me until we graduate and any chance of us having a future will be gone. I'm going to do something crazy, but I'll do it for the greater good, and it'll make things better. Just like I made things better for Ames, and Sean, and my mom, and Carrie, and Jack. This is a proven formula that works!

As halftime nears, I excuse myself, ostensibly to hit the restrooms, but instead I head to the A/V booth. I find Tom inside with three other people from the A/V group, all of whom hoot and applaud when I walk in.

"You've got guts, girl," says Emma Stubens, a girl in a red-checked romper and thick-rimmed glasses. "I like that."

Emma walks with purpose in my direction, getting so

close I think she wants to hug me. I awkwardly put out my arms, but she ignores them and clips a small microphone to the spaghetti strap of my turquoise tank. Then she hands me a little box. "The mic is wireless. The box goes in your back pocket. When you hear the music start, flip the switch." She shows me a tiny "on" switch on the box. "Then you're live."

"Ben Yates is already down there with a camera," Tom says. "He's got a great zoom, so he can stay far enough away that he won't spoil anything. You ready?"

I take a deep breath and blow it out. "Yeah," I say. "I'm good."

"Sweet," Tom says. "You're up right after the marching band. Better get in place."

I nod, then thank everyone and rush out of the booth. I check my phone and look once more at the text Jack sent me with his and J.J.'s section. It's on the other side of the stadium from where I am now, but I have time. The air horn signaling halftime just blew, and I can hear the marching band make their way onto the field. I swim upstream through an endless river of people heading for the bathrooms and snacks, then take a position a few rows back from Jack and J.J.'s seats. I tuck myself behind a support beam so they won't see me if they turn around. I peer out to check on them . . . but Jack's there alone. For just a second I freak out and I'm about to call Tom and cancel everything when I realize Jack would have told me in his text if J.J. wasn't there. He's at the game; he just got up for halftime.

I shift anxiously from side to side as the marching band plays and I watch for J.J. What if he doesn't come back before it's time? I can't do this if he's not there. I'll have to call the whole thing off.

Finally, I see him coming back toward his seat, his arms full of a giant tub of popcorn and two sodas. He sits next to Jack just as the band finishes their final note and the stadium erupts with the kind of hoots and applause the marching band never gets unless there's a giant board with graphics telling everyone to "Scream! Real! Loud!"

My heart is thumping so loud it echoes in my ears. There's just two minutes left of halftime, and they're all me.

"And now," Emma Stubens's voice echoes through the stadium, "a special message of love and reconciliation from one of our own. You go, girl!"

I freeze. Why did she say that? I didn't tell her to say that! But now I hear the music, and I see everyone in the whole stadium looking around and craning their necks and twisting in their seats, and I see the big screens filled with *me*. Or more specifically, the pole I'm hiding behind, with wisps of my orange hair and purple-and-turquoise clothes peeking out from it.

The box, I think. *I need to turn on the box.*

I dig it out of my back pocket and manage to flick it on, but my hands are so shaky I drop it, sending a massive *SQUEE* of feedback through the loudspeakers.

"Sorry!" My voice echoes through the crowd as I retrieve the box and slip it in my back pocket. The music has already moved slightly ahead of where I was supposed to start. I have to jump in *now* or I never will. I step out from behind the pole . . . and sing.

"Your eyes on mine, the day we met . . ."

It's the opening line of Kyler Leeds's "As You Wish," the song he wrote to help me express how I feel about J.J. I downloaded the karaoke version and sent it to Tom, so that's what I'm singing to. At the time Kyler wrote it, the song was all about how much I loved J.J. as a friend. For this occasion, though, I tweaked some of the words to make it clear that it's not just friendship I want anymore. Now it's a song that says loud and clear that I've seen the light, and J.J. is the one I want forever.

As I sing, I walk slowly down the aisles, making my way to J.J., and I quickly realize a few things:

1. I'm a horrible singer. Oh, sure, I'm awesome when I'm in the shower belting at the top of my lungs. Or screaming along to the radio? No one better. But now that I hear my voice echoing back to me through the stadium loudspeakers, I hear it's small and tinny and kinda off-key. Plus I'm so busy listening to myself echo back to me that I'm always a little behind the actual music and have to rush words together in bunches to catch up.

2. It is majorly distracting having my face staring back at me, giant-sized, from two stadium screens. Not only is it eerie, but I also keep catching glimpses of myself that make me realize I probably need a consult with a professional hair and makeup artist. I mean, I've always thought I was pretty good at those things, and I get the Amalita Seal of Approval, which is huge, but there's nothing like seeing myself in Jumbotron to get the full effect.

3. I'm a klutz. Which means I can't walk through the aisles and stare at my screen-self at the same time without tripping and stumbling. It happens at least six times, and each time I catch myself on someone sitting in an aisle. This leads to spilled sodas, popcorns, and in one case a spilled hot dog that somehow splatters ketchup and mustard all over my purple T-shirt.

4. "As You Wish" was a pretty big hit for Kyler . . . last year. Now everyone's over it and they think it's pretty cheesy.

All these things combine to make the next minute not *quite* what I had in mind. I'd kind of imagined everything would stop and the whole stadium would hold their breath while they watched me make this grand gesture that any one of them would die to have happen to them. Instead I'm pretty sure no one can hear my tweaked-out lyrics because they're drowned out by people booing, laughing, or shouting helpful notes like "Go home!" and "Train wreck!"

I decide not to hear any of it. I concentrate on J.J. I see him, just a few rows down from me. He's staring, jaw dropped, clearly impressed by what I'm willing to go through just to prove how I feel. I lock eyes with him—which makes me trip even more as I make way to his tier, but whatever, can't be helped—and emphasize all my changed words so *he* will hear them, even if no one else does, and he'll know exactly how much he means to me.

I get to his row—of course he's sitting in the middle—and have to skip a few bars of the song to sidle past everyone else. "Excuse me . . . excuse me . . . coming through . . . sorry, excuse me . . ." But then I'm at his side. He's in his seat, I'm smiling down at him, and I finish the last line of the song (the shortened song—I cut it down since I knew I had limited time): *"Aaaaaas youuuuuu wish."*

Even with everything, I still kinda expect thunderous applause. It doesn't come, but nobody's booing either. It's like now that I've reached my target, the whole stadium really *is* holding its breath, waiting to see what'll happen next.

"J.J.," I say, and the words echo back to me a million times over. I know what I want to say next, but it's hard.

Not because I don't feel it, but because I feel it *so* much I don't even know if I can get the words out without crying. To help me, I think about the moment I saw in the future, with him proposing. I smile and the words spill out easily. "I'm in love with you. I was in love with you even when I thought I wasn't. You're my best friend in the world. And I came out here to tell you that in front of everyone. And to ask you, 'Can iguana wet goo?'"

J.J. looks at me blankly, as does I'm pretty sure the entire stadium.

"It means—"

"'Can we go out again?'" J.J. says.

Explosive fireworks of happiness erupt inside me. "Yes!" I shout. "We can!"

I lean down to throw my arms around him, but he jumps up and recoils away.

"No," he says firmly, and he's close enough to my mic now that his words echo through the stadium. "I was saying I get the anagram—'Can we go out again?' But I'm not insane, Autumn. I'm done. The answer is *no*." He turns as if he's going to walk away, then changes his mind and leans close again. "And if you really want to do 'as I wish'? *Never* make me hear that song again!"

The stadium erupts into cheers and applause. *Now* J.J. turns his back on me, pushes his way through the aisle, and storms out of the stadium, the camera on his back the whole way. I'm still staring after him in shock when the air horn blows and the football teams race onto the field to start the second half.

"Sit down, loser!" shouts some burly guy who doesn't even go to our school. "I'm trying to see!"

"Sorry," I say. My voice does *not* echo through the stadium this time. I guess Tom cut the power to my mic. I slip into the seat next to Jack that J.J. just vacated and try to make myself as small as possible.

"I wish you'd told me ahead of time," Jack says. "I'd have told you it was a bad idea."

I nod, staring down at my lap. In my peripheral vision I see the people next to and in front of me laugh and stare, but if I don't focus on them, I can drown them out a little.

"Want to get out of here?" Jack asks.

I do, desperately, but I feel like standing up would just get everyone's attention, and I can't take that right now. I shake my head.

"'Kay," Jack says. "Let me know if you change your mind."

He turns his attention to the game, and I keep mine in my lap. It's torture to sit here. I wish I could just close my eyes and blink myself home so I could pull an Amalita and burrow under my covers for three weeks.

Then I realize. I *can* close my eyes and go away. Maybe not home, but someplace else. Maybe someplace that'll show me things don't turn as bad as I think. I wait until the group right around me turns back to the game, then pull the locket out from under my shirt. I open it but keep it cupped in my hand and don't look when I fidget with the dials. I know Dad will make sure I go someplace I need to see. After a few seconds, I close the locket, squeeze it in my hand, and think only about my dad, reaching out his hand to guide me.

18

fifteen years in the future

Dad is truly looking out for me. I open my eyes in a super-clean, white-and-stainless-steel modern-looking kitchen, and right in front of me are two flat computer screens, built into the wall. The one on top shows a calendar. It's early December, same as when I left, but it's fifteen years in the future.

"No wonder the kitchen looks modern," I say. "Or since I'm in the future, is it actually retro?" I lift both cupped hands to the sides of my head and make an explosion noise while I stretch my fingers out and move them in either direction: Mind. Blown.

The panel below the calendar is a photo album, I guess. Or a screen saver that shows pictures. I watch the slideshow for a bit. It's mainly pictures of me and Erick as kids, some of us in my now. There's others of us older, like me graduating college in my cap and gown—it has to be college because the cap and gown are blue, not black like the ones we wear at Aventura. Plus I look older. Then there's one of me, Reenzie, Amalita, and Taylor. How old are we there, twenty-six? I do the math and figure I'm in my thirties in this future.

My *thirties*. How crazy is that?!

I keep watching the screen, and I see lots of pictures of kids. These two dark-haired toddlers crawling all over a grown-up Erick. Are they his kids? And the two redheaded girls . . . one who looks maybe seven holding hands with another who's maybe five. Could they possibly be mine?

This has to be my mom's place. No one else would have this many pictures of Erick and me and—I guess—our families.

"Autumn, it's ten in the morning," my mom's voice rings out, as if to confirm my thoughts. "I don't need a drink."

"Well, if we're having this conversation, I do," I hear my future self say.

My instinct is to hide as I hear footsteps coming closer, but that would be ridiculous. I'm invisible to everyone here. I stand my ground as Future Me walks into the room.

"Holy crap, I'm gorgeous!" I shout.

I can't help it. It's insane, the body that walks into this kitchen. And I can see every inch of it because Future Me's wearing skintight jeans and a super-clingy black, low-cut top. I gape and move closer as Future Me opens Mom's fridge and brings out a bottle of champagne and a container of orange juice. "Sure you don't want a mimosa?" Future Me calls.

"Ten in the morning, Autumn," Mom says again. "I only keep that stuff in there for you."

Future Me rolls her eyes and mixes a drink. As she does, I check her out more closely. There's something off, but I can't quite figure out what it is. Then she lifts her head to look at the slide show of pictures. She's standing perfectly still now, facing me and smiling, and I gasp out loud.

"Oh my God, what did you do to us?!" I shout.

I wasn't wrong at first glance. Future Me has a *killer* body. But it can't possibly be real. I couldn't get that much cleavage if I shoved every sock I own into the strongest push-up bra in the universe.

"And what is up with your *face*?" I wail. "How are lip implants still a thing and why did you do them???"

Future Me doesn't answer. She just smiles with those balloon-animal lips that are seriously not attractive on anyone and certainly not on me. Even my hair, which at first glance looked gorgeous and natural, I can now see isn't my real color. It's some kind of crazy mix of orange and blond and spreads in waves down below my shoulders. It's pretty . . . kinda . . . but I know my hair doesn't grow like that. It has to be extensions.

"Autumn, for real?" I ask her, but of course she ignores me.

Future-Me leads me into the main room of what seems like a beautiful condo. One whole wall is glass, and through it I can see the ocean. We're right there practically on the sand, but judging from the view we're several floors up. The room is light and airy, and my mom is sitting on a puffy cream-colored couch. It's weird. If I'm in my early thirties, then she's in her late fifties, but she looks much older. Her brown curls are threaded with gray, and she's curled on the couch under a crocheted afghan. Surrounding her—on the walls, the end tables, and the coffee table—are framed pictures of my dad. Sometimes alone, sometimes with Mom, sometimes with all of us as a family. It's like she's built a little shrine to him and is all curled up inside it.

Future-Me sits on the other end of the couch and takes a big sip of her drink. "Okay, let's talk about it."

"Is it true?" Mom asks. She nods to a magazine on the coffee table. I sit on the floor to get a good look at it. On the cover is a picture of Kyler Leeds, and I swear, I always thought he was hot now, but he is *smokin'* in fifteen years. Like, it's unbelievable. I guess he's a movie star now because the picture shows him looking lustfully at some equally gorgeous young woman and the headline reads: KYLER LEEDS AND DINA FLORES, with the subheadline SPARKS FLY ON THE SET AND OFF—ARE THEY LEAVING THEIR MARRIAGES FOR EACH OTHER?

Future-Me sighs. She dips her finger into her drink, then licks it clean. "It's true."

I look back and forth between Mom and my Future Self. They both look so pained and sad I have to laugh out loud. "Seriously? We're this upset about Kyler Leeds? I don't even care this much about him *now*!"

"I thought you went through counseling," Mom says.

"I thought when the baby was born, he promised no more cheating."

Future-Me laughs ruefully. "Mom, I married a superstar. Of course he cheats. It's part of the package."

I literally fall over backward as I realize what they're saying. "Hold up—Kyler Leeds is my *husband*?! Those kids in the picture—they're mine and *Kyler Leeds's*?!" I gasp as something even more vital strikes me. "I've seen Kyler Leeds naked?!?!?"

"I just think you deserve better, Autumn," Mom says.

"Are you kidding?" Future-Me says. "I have everything in the world. I have nothing but money, we go on fabulous vacations, I have great help for the kids . . . I bought you this condo, right? And I have a great home. . . ."

I noticed the whole time Future-Me says all this, she can't meet Mom's eyes. When she finally does, she crumples and tears well in her eyes. When she speaks again, she sounds small and broken. "I don't know, Mom," she says. "You say I deserve better, but I don't know that there's anything better out there. I mean, Kyler was supposed to *be* my something better. Remember how we started dating?"

"How can I forget?" Mom asks. "You framed the article. It's right there on the wall." She gestures across the room.

"Are you kidding me?!" I shout. I leap up and run to the wall, where a huge glass frame holds a several-page feature from *People* magazine, detailing my great romance with Kyler Leeds. I immediately devour every word. Turns out it all started with my big performance at the football game.

Apparently a lot of people filmed it on their cell phones, and it went so hard-core viral that Kyler saw it, and felt so bad for me he "rekindled a friendship sparked by their grandmothers." Friendship turned to love, the article says, which reached a crescendo my senior year of college, when Kyler reenacted my big stadium moment and proposed to me in the stands. Unlike J.J. Austin, however, I didn't turn him down. We got married the summer after I graduated, we have two kids, and according to *People,* life has been a fairy tale since then.

According to the conversation between Future Me and Mom, however, he's been cheating on me the whole time.

"I worry about you, Autumn," Mom says to Future Me. "The things you do to yourself to try to get his attention . . ." She gestures up and down my body, and Future Me's face grows even tighter than it surgically is. "Whatever I do to my body is for *me,* not him," she says. "I like it."

I snort. "Not unless you've had a brain transplant, you don't."

Future Me shakes her striped mane and smiles. She puts a hand on Mom's knee. "Enough about me. I'm worried about you. You're in L.A., right on the beach. You're still young. There's a million things to do. I invite you to parties all the time and you never come. You just sit here by yourself unless your grandkids are around. You need to get out there and live, Mom. You could meet someone!"

Mom smiles and gestures to the pictures all around her. "I did meet someone. Your father."

"Mom . . . ," Future Me starts, but Mom shakes her head.

"I had my time. I had amazing years with the love of my life. No one else will ever compare to that. You said so yourself, remember? When I tried to date that man Glen? Remember that?"

Future Me nods. Mom's eyes suddenly get wistful.

"I ran into him recently—did I tell you that? At Disneyland. I was with the girls. He was there with his wife and daughter. It was perfect, actually, because Maisy and Lily wanted to ride Tower of Terror and they didn't want to do it alone, but you know I can't do that one. Turned out Glen's family was going on it, so the girls went with them. Glen's not a thrill ride person either, so he stayed back and we talked. It's funny. He said he thought I was the one he'd marry. And he said he still thinks of me whenever he eats anything pumpkin flavored."

Mom laughs, but it's sad, and I see her eyes are far away. Future Me must see the same thing, because she looks pained. "You really liked him, didn't you."

There's a little too much silence before Mom answers; then she scoffs. "No! Besides, I'm perfectly happy with the way things turned out."

As she gets to her feet and walks away, Future Me calls out, "Where are you going?"

"To make a mimosa!" Mom chirps. "I can't let you drink all alone, can I?"

19

december, senior year

When I open my eyes, everyone around me is booing. For a second I think it's because they saw what I saw, and they're booing me for being a terrible daughter and ruining my mom's last chance for happiness. Then I realize the other team just scored a touchdown and our chances of winning the playoff are slipping away.

I grab Jack by the arm. "If you ever—*ever*—hear me say I want to get any kind of plastic surgery, you have my permission to kick me in the head."

I want to also tell him never to let me marry Kyler Leeds, but he won't really believe that's an option for me anyway, plus I'm fairly certain I can remember that on my own. I wait until the next big play is happening, then slip out of my row as best I can and walk home. Erick's there with a group of friends. They're all piled on the couch, watching something disturbingly familiar on the TV: me, singing loudly and off-key as I stumble-walk through the stadium toward J.J.

"Seriously?" I explode. "Already?"

Erick's friends respectfully stop laughing. Erick's mirth is unabated. "Are you kidding? It's already up from, like, twenty different angles. This one's the best."

"How did you even know to look for it?" I ask.

"I have you on Google Alert," Erick explains. "Only a couple of the videos call you out by name, but once I had one, I looked up the others. So good."

"I'm not insane, Autumn," J.J. says on the screen. "I'm done. The answer is *no*."

"Harsh," Erick says. Then, as if only now realizing I'm a real person this happened to, he looks concerned. "So . . . like . . . are you okay?"

"Where's Mom?" I ask, ignoring his question.

"Up in her room," he says. As I walk upstairs, he calls after me, "If it helps, you're getting tons of hits! You could totally get on *Tosh.0!*"

I climb up the stairs and knock on my mom's door.

"Come in!" she calls.

She's in a pair of gray silky pajamas, propped up in bed and watching TV. She smiles as I come in.

"Hey, Autumn!" she says. "I thought you'd be out late tonight. Wasn't there a game?"

"We were losing." I shrug, as if the state of the football game had anything to do with why I usually stay or go.

I notice the picture on Mom's night table. A framed shot of her and Dad. I know it's on their honeymoon because they told me, but it's so close on their faces it could be anywhere. Mom's laughing about something and Dad has this satisfied smile—probably because he's the one who made her laugh—and they look so young and happy and in love that it hurts.

I think about Future Mom with her shrine of Dad pictures surrounding her all the time.

"Want to watch with me?" Mom asks, scooting over and patting the bed. "I figured I'd hang up here and give Erick and his friends some privacy."

I hop onto the bed and scrunch low so I don't tower over Mom. I pretend to watch the cooking show that's on; then I ask, "Mom . . . do you ever see Glen?"

"Glen?" Mom repeats as if it were the silliest word in the English language. "No. He called me once, after our dinner, but I made it quite clear I wasn't interested in pursuing anything."

"Really? 'Cause I was thinking . . . maybe you should call him again."

Mom turns and looks at me quizzically. "You *want* me to call him?"

"I'm just saying . . . maybe I was a little harsh when we all got together. I mean, I don't want you to . . . you know . . . miss out on someone just because I got a little weird about it."

"Oh, baby . . ." She leans over and kisses my head. "I love

you for worrying about me. But you were right. And honestly, I knew it too. I had the most wonderful man in the world in your father. There isn't anyone else out there who could possibly hold a candle to him. Certainly not Glen."

She sounds convincing, but I remember the way Future Mom looked when she reminisced about Glen, and I know she feels more than she's letting on. I try to press her on the subject, just to see if she might reach out to him again, but she's firm. The Glen chapter of her life is closed. She even deleted all his contact information.

I guess the good news is I know my mom listens to and respects what I have to say. The bad news is my advice led her down a path that will make her miserable. I think about it after I tell her good night and go into my room. My very first jump was to her wedding. Everything there seemed wrong: my friends, me, Erick . . . but especially Mom and Glen. I was positive that's why Dad wanted me to see it— because everyone in my little corner of the world was on a crash course toward disaster, and I had to stop it.

But now I think that was a mistake. I think he sent me to the wedding because Mom getting married was the one thing that was *right* in our future.

I pull out the locket and gaze at the *zemi*. I imagine the triangular face morphing into the smiling face of my father.

"I should've known," I tell him. "You love her. You want her to be happy . . . even if it means moving on." I sigh and throw myself back against the pillows. "I can fix it, though," I tell my dad in the *zemi.* "I'll get them back to-gether again. I promise."

I kiss the *zemi,* tuck the locket back under my shirt, and pull a pad of paper and pen from my nightstand so I can make a list of everything I know about Glen. It's very short. I know he likes animals because he showed up at Catches Falls before he knew my mom, I know he likes pumpkin-flavored food, and I know he shops at the Trader Joe's near us. That's it. During our one dinner together, he only asked about us and said nothing about himself, so that's all I've got.

I'll make it work. I promise myself that until I make this right, I won't even think about any other future problems. It's not that hard, really. Ames, Taylor, Reenzie, Sean, and Jack seem to be on a pretty good path. My future with J.J. is a giant catastrophe, but I don't get my true love until Mom gets hers. Besides, I have no idea what to do to make the J.J. situation better right now. Better to give it some time before I try anything else.

Operation Glen starts at Trader Joe's. He shops there, so I stalk there. I ride my bike over every day after school. I leave the minute it ends, and I'm happy to escape. Ever since the football game, school is pretty much a night-mare of people mimicking my bad singing, asking me if we can go out again, or papering my locker, backpack, and once even *me* with their versions of "iguana wet goo." My friends stick by me and have my back, but I'm still way happier getting to school the second it starts, spending every free moment in the library, and leaving immediately after it ends.

At Trader Joe's, I sit outside and watch people come in and out. I bring all my books and my laptop so I can get my homework done and work on the Common App for colleges. I hang until it gets dark, taking the occasional break to go in the store and get snacks, use the bathroom, and case the place in case Glen snuck by me at any point.

When I start the plan, I'm a little worried the store managers won't like me sitting around outside and will make me go away. They don't bother me, though. Instead, a disturbing number of people—and more every day—come up to me on their way in or out and ask me if I'm the YouTube girl with the Kyler Leeds song. I can't escape it anywhere. A bunch of the people who stop know me by name. Some even ask for my autograph. I try to smile and be nice, but it's completely mortifying, especially when they want to chat. They laugh about the video like it's a movie they saw instead of my actual life, or say things like, "So how did it feel at the exact moment you realized he meant no?" And of course they all want to know where I stand with J.J. now.

It's a massive testament to how much I love my mom that I don't run to my room, hide, and never come out again.

Over the weekend, Mom recruits Erick and me to put in some work on the new location of Catches Falls, which severely cuts into my stalking time. I'm back at it the next week, though, and I'm in the store trolling for snacks when an overweight middle-aged balding guy in a Hawaiian shirt with a Manager name tag pulls me aside. I assume I'm in trouble for loitering or something, but he just wants to know if the whole YouTube video was a setup.

"'Cause my buddy and me, we think it's some kind of viral campaign for a new TV show, and maybe you're here every day to do publicity," he says. "Like there's a hidden camera watching to see how people react to you. 'Cause if there is, I thought, you know, maybe I could appear on camera. Do some kind of funny bit with you. I was in a theater group in sixth grade, you know."

"Did not know that," I say. He has this happy, expectant grin on his face. He's so excited I almost lie and tell him he's right, but then he'll expect to be in a viral video and I can't help him there. "Sorry, but it's not a publicity thing. The video was real."

"Aw, come on," the guy goads. "No one would do anything that embarrassing unless it was a setup. You can tell me the truth."

I blush bright red, but no matter how many times I tell him the truth, he doesn't believe me. "Even if it was real," he insists, "you must be doing some kind of follow-up. Why else would you be here every day for a whole week?"

I see no way to shut him up except the truth. "I'm looking for a guy," I begin.

"J.J.?" he asks. "Or another one?"

My face burns. I grimace. "Another one. Not for me,

though, for my mom. And no," I add when he opens his mouth, "it's not for a video."

I tell him the basics: that I got in the way of my mom's relationship, I regret it, and I really want to get them back together again. "But honestly," I conclude, "the only real thing I know about this guy is that he shops here. So I'm looking for him."

"Every weekday afternoon?" the manager asks.

"It's all I've got," I say.

"But what if he shops in the morning? Or on weekends?"

It's an obvious question, and I'd be lying if I said I hadn't thought it a million times myself, but it suddenly makes me so exhausted and overwhelmed I want to cry. It must show, because the manager looks stricken.

"No, no! It's okay!" he hurriedly says. "I just meant you should have told us here and let us help!"

"Let you help?" I echo.

"Sure! We're pretty good with all the regulars here. Tell me what the guy looks like and I'll let you know if I've seen him. We can ask everyone else on duty too. Even if he doesn't shop during my shifts, maybe he shops on theirs. Then you'll know exactly when to find him."

Suddenly this overweight, balding manager looks like an angel from heaven. "You'd do that for me?"

"Course we would. You're a celebrity!"

I don't know about a celebrity, but if my personal mortification helps me get Glen and Mom back together, maybe it's worth it. I describe Glen to the manager, whose name turns out to be Earl. The description doesn't ring any bells with him, but a couple cashiers and the woman handing out taster samples all think they've seen him before. He usually shops in the late morning, and usually on weekdays, but he hasn't been in yet this week. I'm seriously considering skipping school for the rest of the week to stalk in prime Glen-time, but Earl has a better idea. He takes my cell phone number and says he'll share it with the rest of the staff, along with a physical description of Glen. Whenever Glen *does* show up, someone on duty will call me. I'm incredibly grateful but also a little dubious. Are they actually going to help, or did Earl just engineer a way to get the phone number of "the YouTube Girl"?

On Wednesday I find out. I've been sneaking my phone with me into every class and keeping it in my pocket on vibrate, just in case. I'm in the middle of physics when it goes off. Subtly, I check the text.

It's Amber at Trader Joe's. He's here! Exact description, plus I asked his name to be sure.

Keep him there!!!! I text back.

I hide my phone again, then start moaning. Loudly. And I double over in my seat.

"Autumn Falls," Ms. Grotnick snaps. "Contain yourself."

"Can't!" I croak. "I think I ate something bad for breakfast. I think I might—"

I start coughing and hacking like I'm about to throw

up. I make the most hideous noises I know how to make. Everyone else in class stops making jokes and moves to lab desks far away from mine to avoid the splash zone.

"Go!" Ms. Grotnick says. "To the nurse's office. *Now!*"

I grab my things and run and don't stop until I get back to my house and on my bike. I might have a problem later if Ms. Grotnick follows up with the nurse, but I can always say I got sick outside and felt so bad I went home to bed. From the time I got Amber's text to the time I arrive at Trader Joe's, exactly twenty minutes have gone by. I run in the door a hot sweaty mess just as Glen is entering a checkout lane. Since breaking up with my mom, he's let the blond fuzz grow back around the perimeter of his balding head, but his face is still clean-shaven.

"Glen!" I shout.

His eyes are magnified by his glasses and already look large, but they go cartoony when he sees me. Instant beads of sweat appear on his upper lip and head.

I take a moment to marvel over this guy being the one who's perfect for Mom, but hey, to each her own.

I run to his cart and cling to the edge.

"Glen, I need to talk to you."

I peer down at his cart. It's filled with peppermint bark, dark chocolate candy canes, Merry Mingle candies, and pretty much every other red-and-white wrapped item in the store. "You are a man who loves seasonal merchandise," I note.

"You don't need to talk to me, Autumn," Glen says,

and despite his instant fear response when he saw me, his voice is kind and reassuring. "I've stayed away from your mother, and I will continue to stay away from her."

"NO!" I wail.

Then I realize other people in the store are grinning and pulling out their phones like they're going to film me. Apparently once you make one mortifying video, people look forward to more. I take it down a notch and ask Glen to meet me outside the store so we can talk in his car. He looks around at the other customers and seems to get it immediately, which makes me think even he has seen my football game travesty.

Once his bags are loaded and we're in his car with the radio on, I tell him what I came to say.

"Glen, I'm sorry. I messed up. It's my fault Mom broke up with you. I was a brat. I told her you were nothing compared to my dad, and she'd be throwing away her time by spending it with you."

"Wow." Glen blinks several times, then wipes his glasses on his shirt. "That's . . . quite an argument."

"It's a *bad* argument. My dad is the most incredible man in the world. That's why I know he doesn't want my mom pining for him. He wants her to be happy. And I really think you can make her happy." I take a breath and add hopefully, "You *do* still like my mom, right?"

Glen smiles. "Autumn, I'm proud to say I fell head over heels in love with your mother. Nothing's changed for me. But I've tried calling her. I understand how hard this is for you and Erick, and I was willing to back up and take things very slow. She wasn't interested. She wanted a clean break."

"Because I got in her head," I say, and I keep going when he opens his mouth to object. "Believe me, I don't know what she said to you and I don't care. I *know* she wants to be with you. I know you two can have a future together. A really good one. Just . . . will you give it another chance?"

Glen shifts in his seat; he's so tall the top of his head bumps against the ceiling. "I'll call her right now if you want me to, but I'm telling you—"

"No!" I shout. "A call won't be enough. She'll say no, but I swear it won't be because she doesn't want to be with you. If you're going to get her back, we need to plan something bigger. Something she can't possibly say no to."

"I can't sing in a stadium, if that's what you're thinking." Glen grins impishly. It's the most personality I've seen out of the guy, and I kind of like it.

"That was a rare failure in a history of life-changing genius," I say. "Trust me on this one. I will come up with something brilliant, and you will sweep her off her feet."

"I'll get my dustpan ready," he says with a super-dorky eyebrow waggle that again makes me wonder for my mom's emotional sanity, but at least he's on board. We exchange phone numbers and I promise to be in touch soon with a genius idea.

Unfortunately, I seem to be out of genius ideas. Plus Christmas break starts next week for Erick and me, and even though we haven't booked any kind of trip, Mom wants to go away like we did last year. Since every day Mom and Glen aren't together is another day that something can go horribly wrong, I'd love to do something before we go. I'm ready to settle for a romantic dinner at the fanciest restaurant in town when I get a phone call on my cell from a private number, which of course I answer because I'm too curious not to.

"Hello?"

"Autumn?" a guy says in an over-the-top sexy voice. "It's me. Kyler Leeds."

I roll my eyes. "Jack, shut up. I've been really good to you lately, and—"

"Autumn, for real," the guy says in a far more normal voice. "It's me. Kyler."

"Seriously?" I ask. "Then why are you talking in that breathy I'm-a-hot-pop-idol voice?"

"Uh, because I'm a hot pop idol?" he asks.

"Whatever," I say. And then I scream into my pillow because, yes, he and I have been legit kinda-friends for a long time now and I can give him a hard time about things, but still. He's Kyler Leeds.

"You totally just screamed into your pillow, didn't you?" Kyler asks, and I can hear the smile in his voice.

"As if, Ego Boy."

"Uh-huh," he says, clearly amused. "I called because I saw your video of my song."

"I'm not sure it was a video *of your song*," I say.

"Whatever. The video's huge, everyone's watching it,

and it got 'As You Wish' back on the radio. It's a hit all over again, and since I have you to thank, I thought maybe I could take you out when I come to town for Christmas."

For a second I tingle all over—*Kyler Leeds wants to take me out!* Then I remember my last future jump and I gasp. This is how it started. Kyler asked me out because of the video, we dated on and off through college, he proposed my senior year, we got married, had kids, and I became Plasti-Cheating-Victim Autumn Falls!

"Autumn?" Kyler asks when I don't say anything.

"I am *not* going to marry you," I say sternly.

"O-kay," Kyler says. "Did I ask you to?"

"No," I say. "And you won't, because I'm changing the future."

"You are a seriously weird chick. Has anyone ever told you that?"

"It's happened," I admit, "but that's not the point. The point is I have to change things up, so I can't go out with you."

"You're turning me down," Kyler says, amazed. "No one turns me down."

"Look, it's not you," I say. "I just don't want to get lip implants."

"That wasn't going to be part of the plans," Kyler objects. "You did me a solid, even if you didn't mean to, and I want to pay you back." He puts his super-sexy voice back on and adds, "Believe me, I can make you a night you'll never forget."

Inspiration lights me up inside. "Yes!" I scream.

"That's more like it," Kyler says.

"No!" I say. "Not for me. If you really want to thank me, I need you to make an unforgettable night for my *mom*!"

"You're fixing me up with your mom?" Kyler asks. "Autumn, I—"

I roll my eyes and explain everything, leaving out all things locket and time travel. "I need to send them on a super-romantic date that's totally beyond anything they could imagine. Can you help me?"

"Sure, just . . . you realize this is the second time you've given up a night with me to someone else," Kyler says. "I'm either really impressed by your selflessness or I'm getting a complex."

"So what should we do for their date?" I ask. "I need something insane—the kind of thing I'd only see in a movie or on TMZ."

"You watch TMZ?" he asks, disgusted.

"Shut up," I say. "Not the point."

The two of us plot together. Kyler knows some absurdly posh resort in St. Thomas in the Virgin Islands, and while I have to admit I have no clue where that is, Kyler tells me all I need to know is it's about two and a half hours away from Aventura in his private jet. It also costs something like my entire college fund per night, but Kyler says he'll make about a gazillion times that in publishing royalties now that "As You Wish" is so crazy huge again, so he's willing to spring for a room, an incredible meal, and all their expenses for an overnight trip. It sounds perfect, but I have a slightly queasy feeling in my stomach.

"Are we sure we want it overnight?" I ask. "I mean, we could just fly them out for dinner."

"Sure," Kyler agrees, "if you want it to be way less than perfect."

"But I feel like I'm sending my mom and Glen to a *Bachelor* Fantasy Suite, and we all know what happens in those."

"How about a non-fantasy suite?" Kyler offers. "Two bedrooms. What they do with them, you never have to know."

I can agree to that without getting totally grossed out, so it's a go. Kyler has "his people" make some calls, then texts me later and tells me the best day for it all to happen is December twenty-third, exactly one week away. Kyler will make sure she's back by late afternoon the twenty-fourth, so we'll have her for Christmas Eve. When I hop on the phone with Glen to tell him everything, he doesn't believe it at all. He asks me at least eight times if I'm arranging some kind of viral video prank on him. I'm not sure he believes me when I say I'm not, though I assure him I *will* launch a viral prank on him if he's too afraid to show up for the date.

The next week is serious torture. Christmas break starts, so Erick and I are hanging with Mom a lot. We help with Catches Falls, we make a ton of Christmas cookies to wrap up as gifts for friends, and we put up and decorate our tree. It's a total miracle I don't spill.

December twenty-third, while Mom is in the kitchen making breakfast, I sneak into her bedroom and pack a suitcase. I toss in a couple bathing suits, a casual and a fancy dress, two pairs of shorts and tank tops, sunglasses, sandals, heels, and a ton of toiletries and makeup.

At exactly ten a.m. I peer out the window and see a limo pull up out front.

At exactly ten-thirty a.m. I see Glen's car pull up behind it. I run down the stairs to watch everything unfold.

The doorbell rings.

"Autumn, can you get it?" Mom calls. "I'm doing laundry."

"Can't, Mom," I say. "I'm in the bathroom!"

Erick, who's on the couch and plainly sees me, looks at me like I'm an aardvark. I make a very clear "shut up" face to him and he shrugs.

"Erick?" Mom calls.

I frantically gesture to Erick, who calls, "Sorry, Mom! I'm"—he flounders for some excuse, then clearly gives up—"lazy."

The doorbell rings again.

"Honestly," Mom huffs as she stalks into the foyer. "You kids . . ."

She throws open the front door.

Glen's there. He is wearing a tuxedo and carrying a bouquet of red roses. Points off for cliché, but points on for effort. He looks good . . . for Glen. His head is completely bald again, and something about his shirt collar makes his head look slightly less like a giant balloon about to fly away from his body.

"Glen?" Mom says, confused. She immediately starts fidgeting with her rumpled hair, old capri sweatpants, and ancient rock concert tee. "What are you doing here?"

"You wouldn't talk over the phone, so I thought maybe we could work things out in person."

"Glen . . . I don't think that's a good idea."

Those are her words, but she's blushing and smiling and keeps touching her hair like she wishes it looked better. She's interested; I know it.

"If that's true," Glen says, "if you're really not interested and don't want to see me again, I understand. I'll go away and never bother you again. But before you do, you should know that limo outside is for our date. I believe it will be pretty remarkable. Especially since Autumn put it together."

"*Autumn* did?" Mom spins around. She's surprised I'm right behind her.

"Hi, Mom."

"What did you do?" she asks.

"I arranged a do-over," I say. "But this time it's all Autumn-approved. This guy's pretty dorky, and he's no Dad . . . but he's also not a washcloth."

"Excuse me," Glen says, "a *washcloth*?"

"You're *not* a washcloth," I say. "It's a compliment."

"Ah," Glen says, rocking back on his heels.

I turn back to Mom. "I know I didn't see you guys together for long, but I feel like he makes you happy. And I want you to be happy. Dad would too."

I don't mean to get teary. I really want her to go on this date and not feel sad. But I am, and she is, too, and I'm kind of worried the date won't actually happen. Then she pulls me in for a hug. "Thank you, Autumn," she says. "I love you so much."

"Hey, how about me?" Erick calls from the couch. "I was cool with it right away."

"I love you, too, Erick," Mom laughs. Then she turns to Glen, and the two of them smile at each other like embarrassed middle schoolers afraid to ask each other to dance. It's sweet. Weird, but sweet.

"I guess I should go get dressed," Mom says.

"Wouldn't hear of it," Glen says. "You look perfect the way you are."

Mom snorts, but Glen says he's serious, and while they debate whether or not she's fit for public consumption, I run up and grab the suitcase. As I thunk it downstairs, I tell Mom she should just go. Everything she needs is in the bag if she wants to change after the flight.

"Flight?!" Mom echoes. "And a suitcase? Where exactly are we going?"

"It's a surprise," I say. "You'll be back tomorrow, and I'll stay with Erick. Call and check as much as you want, but we'll be fine. I promise."

Mom's completely flustered and finds a gazillion reasons to object, but in the end she lets Glen escort her on his arm to the limousine. I watch through the window until the car is out of sight.

"Sweet!" Erick says, leaping from the couch. "Party time!"

I tell him we can't have a party because I'm supposed to be responsible for him, but I do agree to drive him and a couple friends to the Aventura Mall and the movies. When we get home after, there's a limo in front of the house.

My heart sinks. Did Mom's date fall apart? Is she back already?

I run out of the car and up to the door . . . but someone's sitting on the stoop. It's a guy my age. He's in jeans, a simple T-shirt, a baseball cap, and sunglasses, but none of that hides the fact that he's insanely hot. He's listening to his phone through earbuds. Behind the sunglasses I can see his eyes are closed, and he sings softly.

"Kyler?" I say.

"Kyler Leeds is on our stoop?" Erick gapes behind me. He pulls out his phone. "This will get me major girl cred."

I grab his phone before he can take a picture, then turn back to Kyler, who clearly has no idea we're there. I lean closer and can totally hear the music. I laugh, then pull out one of his earbuds. "Are you seriously listening to your own songs?"

"Course I am, it's great music."

I scoff.

Kyler shrugs. "Okay, if that's how you feel. 'Cause I have

287

my guitar in the car and I thought maybe I'd play something for you, but if you're not into it—"

"Omigod, seriously?!" I burst. "Of course I want you to play! Can I choose the song?"

Kyler's grinning at me and I grimace as I realize what he just did. "You suck," I say.

"That's not what you *really* think," he says.

"So, Kyler," Erick says, swaggering up to him. "I've got a pull-up bar in the house. Wanna see who can do the most reps? Maybe shoot a little video of me whupping your butt?"

Kyler grins. "Why? You think girls'll like it if you do?"

"They will *worship* me," Erick says.

I'm about to tell Erick to shut up, but watching Kyler do pull-ups wouldn't be so bad. Especially if he did them shirtless.

"Sounds fun!" I say.

"Sorry, we have other plans," Kyler says. "I'm having a Christmas Eve *Eve* party at my beach house tonight, and I happen to know you're both free. So hop in the limo and let's go."

"To a rock star beach house party?" Erick asks. "Hell to the yes! Can I bring a friend?"

"A girlfriend?" Kyler asks knowingly.

"So she can drool all over you?" Erick asks. "No way! My friend Aaron."

"Sure," Kyler says. "Call and tell him we'll pick him up on the way."

"Sweet!" Erick runs to the limo and dives inside.

"For real," I check with Kyler. "A party at your house."

"Yeah," he says, "How long you need to get ready?"

I toss my hair over one shoulder. "You're not going to be like Glen and say I'm gorgeous just the way I am?"

Kyler lowers his head and looks at me over his sunglasses. I look down at my kickaround terry shorts and tank-with-bandeau.

"I'll need about an hour," I say.

"Got it."

Kyler heads for the limo while I unlock the front door. I wheel around before I go inside.

"Oh! Can I invite Ames and Taylor?" I ask. "You've met them. They're awesome. And they would *die* to go to a Kyler Leeds party."

"Sure," Kyler says. "But if they stalk my house afterward, I'm moving."

"Noted."

I fly into the house, then call Taylor with my cell and Ames with the home line, then hold them both to my ear so I can tell them at the same time. We scream together for exactly three seconds, because we all have to jump immediately and get ready. I make a lightning-fast hour-long transformation in which I shower, blow-dry, flat-iron, product, makeup, and change into a simple but superflattering red halter dress and heels. I fill Schmidt's bowl with kibble and give him a goodbye pet before I fly out the door and join Erick and Kyler in the limo. They're laughing and watching an action movie while they chow on sodas and popcorn, and they're both highly amused by the acrobatics it takes me to climb into the limo while wearing a short, clingy dress.

Once I'm in, we pick up our guests: first Aaron, then Taylor, then Amalita. I'm impressed with Tee and Ames. They keep the crazy freak-out to a minimum and really get along with Kyler. I'm sure it helps that they both look amazing, but they also have intelligent conversations with him that have nothing to do with how cute he is and how much they'd secretly like to marry him. Taylor talks to him about singing techniques and performing onstage, while Ames chats with him about the Miami Dolphins. I knew she watched a lot of football last year when she was dating our team's star player, but apparently she got really into it and still keeps up.

Kyler's house is, of course, ridiculous. Hidden behind a gate so you'd never know it's there, it is three stories right on the beach, lots of space, windows everywhere. The party is already raging when we get there. Dim lights, loud music, lots of people dancing. Aaron and Erick immediately run off, no doubt to hopelessly try picking up one of the supermodels in the room. Tee, Ames, and I are a little more intimidated, but Kyler drops us with Wade, who I recognize as a dancer from one of Kyler's videos. Wade hugs us all right away, makes us completely comfortable, and takes us around to introduce us to everyone. We're in the middle of a conversation when I notice someone on the dance floor.

"Excuse me," I say, and walk across the room to a tiny old woman in a chocolate-brown sweat suit. She stands directly in the glow of a red spotlight . . . and twerks.

"*Eddy?!*" I cry.

She spins around and gives me a huge hug. "Autumn! We were hoping you'd get here soon!"

"We?"

"You didn't think Kyler would have a party without Zelda and me, did you? Now help me get her on the floor. She's an old wet blanket."

Eddy gestures to Zelda. Kyler's Mee-Maw is very close by, but I couldn't see her before with all the spotlights. Now that I'm looking, I see she's hunched deep in the pillows of a dark couch, her arms folded tightly over her chest.

"Zelda!" Eddy yells. "Get up and dance with me!"

"I will not," Zelda says. "You look ridiculous. Autumn, tell your grandmother she looks ridiculous."

"You're jealous," Eddy says. "You wish you had moves like mine. I'm going to go out to the balcony and be with someone who appreciates me." She links her arm through mine. "That's you, *carina.*"

She leads me outside and we find a free spot against the balcony rail. It might be Christmas Eve Eve, but it's still seventy degrees and humid. A light breeze sweeps off the ocean and I turn so it can wash over my face.

"*Muy hermosa*," Eddy says, smiling. Then she moves closer and beckons so I'll bend down to her. "And how are things with you and your mission?"

"Pretty good, I think," I say. "I did something today that I think will make a big difference."

Eddy widens her eyes, waiting for me to continue, but I feel weird about it. Eddy and my mom get along great, but still, Eddy's my dad's mother. She might not like the idea of his wife going out with someone new.

"*Querida.*" Eddy pats my hand. "It's okay. I know. Zelda told me what you did for your mother."

"And you don't mind?" I ask.

She makes a *pfft* sound and waves the idea away. "I love your mother. My Reinaldo, he loved her more. He'd want her to be happy." She narrows her eyes, as if she can peer inside me. "But I think you already know that, no?"

I nod. "I think this is what he wanted me to do."

"Then *es bueno.*" She smiles impishly and nods to the chain around my neck. "And how does it turn out?"

I smile back. I look around to make sure no one's paying attention, then pull out the locket and open it. I have only two more jumps, but I don't hesitate. I set the locket for the exact same September date of my first jump, three years in the future. With a last smile to Eddy, I squeeze the locket shut, then concentrate as I close my eyes.

20

three years later

Everything is similar but completely different.

I'm at a wedding—that's obvious from the giant tiered cake next to me with the bride and groom on top—but it's no stuffy ballroom with a bad DJ. This ballroom is open on every side, seamlessly pouring out to a beautiful green lawn and beach dotted by twinkly lights and tiki torches. A seven-piece band plays onstage, and couples twirl in beautiful gowns and tuxes. The song ends almost immediately, and the bandleader announces a toast from the maid of honor, the daughter of the bride, Autumn Falls.

I remain standing as everyone files off the floor and see Future Me take the stage. The last time I saw Mom and Glen's wedding, I looked horrible and I was such an emotionally shrunken mess I couldn't even speak. Now I stand tall in a beautiful, sleeveless, soft-pink maid-of-honor dress. My hair is its natural orange and lustrous, not brown and lank. I look poised, together, and happy, and when I gaze out toward the head table, there's nothing but joy in my eyes.

"Mom . . . Glen . . . I'm so honored to speak here at your wedding."

The speech goes on, but I don't want to stand and listen, I want to look around. I walk to the head table where Mom and Glen sit close. They hold hands as they listen to Future Me speak, and both their eyes fill with happy tears. There's an empty seat next to Mom's, which I guess is mine, and Erick's in the seat next to that. He's no longer fake-tan orange with bulging meathead muscles. He looks good, and I get a down-to-earth vibe from the curly-brown-haired girl next to him. I can tell by their pushed-together seats and the way she's cuddled against his side that they're together, but I get the feeling it's a good match. For high school, at least.

Hmmm. Erick has a date, but there's just the one empty seat for me. No boyfriend. At least, that's how it seems. Any good boyfriend would be with me at my mom's wedding. If I were with J.J., he wouldn't miss it for the world.

Is J.J. even here?

I look around the room. With everyone sitting, it's easy to spot people I know. I see Eddy and Zelda, and Amanda with the Catches Falls gang. Then someone interrupts my toast by tapping a glass with their fork, and I see it's Amalita. My heart pounds a little and I beeline for her table, wondering if I somehow messed things up and she's going to make a scene, but she just wants Mom and Glen to kiss.

When they do, she raises her glass of sparkling water to them, then sits back down.

Ames is at a table with all my friends, and my heart lifts looking at them. Not just because they're all there, but because they seem so right. Taylor's with Drew, who's perfectly alive and well. Jack's with Ben, the guy I met in the future at the beach. Reenzie and Sean are both there with dates I don't know, but they seem friendly and normal and great. Best of all, Jenna's there, laughing and chatting with all my Aventura friends like they've known each other forever. And she's with Simon, so I know she's on track for life.

They're all so happy and excited, and their energy buoys me. I walk right into the middle of the table and stand there, like I'm a centerpiece, so I can soak up every one of their conversations. . . .

21

december, senior year

. . . but then suddenly I'm on the balcony with Eddy again.

"You're smiling," Eddy says. "Is it good?"

"It's good," I say. "Really good. Everybody I love is really happy."

Yet even as I say it, I feel my smile strain. I keep thinking about that single seat between Erick and my mom and the table of all my friends except J.J.

I can't help it. Tears well up in my eyes, and I feel like an idiot because I'm crying over something that never really happened. I never had happily-ever-after with J.J. for real. It was a possible future, that's all. A fantasy.

Is it crazy that I've never been happier than I was in a fantasy?

Eddy looks concerned. "*Querida,* what is it?"

I shake my head and blink away the tears. "I'm sorry. It's good, really. I did everything I was supposed to. Peace and happiness, done."

"Then?"

"I think I got it right for everyone except me. I saw a future that felt so right, and I wanted it so badly . . . but instead I just messed it up." I sniff and tell Eddy, "Maybe Daddy knew. Maybe he gave me these gifts so I could at least make other people happy, since I'm really bad at doing it for myself."

Eddy rubs my arm. "No. No, *carina*. You have the power to spread happiness, yes. But you're also meant to *be* happy. I feel it, and your father felt it too."

"But I've seen how things end up," I say. "It doesn't work out for me. Not the way it could've."

"It doesn't work out *yet*," Eddy says. "Is the locket all done?"

"No. I have one more jump," I admit. "But, Eddy, I've tried *everything*."

"Ah!" Eddy says, her eyes lighting up. "But have you tried *nothing*?"

"Huh?"

"Sometimes you don't have to move mountains to change your future," Eddy says. "Push too hard, and you can knock things over. Be true to yourself and follow your heart. Then things come to you."

"Eddy, you don't understand. I *did* follow my heart—"

Eddy cuts me off with a snort. "That video? Hah! That wasn't your heart. That was your anxious brain!"

I can't believe it. "*You* saw the video?!"

"Everyone saw the video! The staff showed it to us on the big screen during movie night. You were a huge hit!"

"Fine. Then you know. J.J.'s perfect for me and I terrified him out of my life."

"*Impossible!*" Eddy bursts out. "If he's really perfect, you *can't* scare him away. If you can, then what you saw in the future was just a perfect *moment,* not a perfect life."

"I guess," I admit. "But how do I know for sure?"

"You follow your patient heart, not your anxious brain. What is truly meant to be will be. *Que sera sera.*"

It's the same advice I got from Amalita, but it somehow sounds wiser coming from my grandmother, even if a second later she hears the music kick up and shouts, "A rumba! We dance!"

With a surprisingly strong grip for a tiny old woman, she yanks me back inside to the dance floor, but I quickly slip away. If it were up to me, I'd go home now and think about what Eddy said, but I could never do that to Ames and Taylor. We hang out all night, and in the end I'm glad we do. With them it's easy to forget the ache in my heart and have a great time—especially when Taylor and I get the joy of watching Ames turn down an NBA star flat.

That night, after Kyler has the limo drive us all home, I promise myself I'll take Eddy's advice. Even though I've had a peek into the future, I can't live there, because it just makes me crazy. I used the locket well. I made changes in all my friends' and family members' lives. Now I just have to be patient and wait for my true future to come to me. Up in my room, I take the locket off. "Thank you, Daddy," I say to the *zemi.* "Thanks for letting me help. I love you."

I curl the locket into a silver heart-shaped jewelry box that sits in my bookcase. It's a gift Dad gave me when I was five and I thought it was the most special thing in the universe. It'll make a good home for the *zemi*.

The next day, Erick and I both sleep in until the middle of the afternoon, when Mom and Glen burst through the door. We troop downstairs and see they're both seriously glowing with happiness.

"You think *you* had a good night?" Erick asks them. "Aaron and I danced with *supermodels*!"

Clearly, Mom wants to know everything, so we swap stories. I'm blown away by Mom and Glen's—Kyler went way beyond what he said he'd do. The two of them had some crazy oceanfront suite, with ridiculously decadent meals and spa treatments. He even arranged for a guitar player to serenade them at dinner—with a Kyler Leeds song, of course.

"It was all heavenly," Mom finishes as we all sit together on the couch, "but the best part was just spending the time with Glen." She looks up at him as she says it, and I'm not surprised to see that same dopey-eyed gaze between them that I've now seen at two of their weddings. Then she turns to me and Erick. "Thank you. Both of you."

Glen gets up to go home once we've all swapped stories. Erick invites him to come back tomorrow, but Glen says he won't. He says he's taken enough of our mom's time, and we deserve to have Christmas as just the family, which I think is pretty cool of him. I still grab a Sharpie after he leaves and draw a big smiley face on a big round Christmas tree ball, then say, "Look! It's Glen!" but I'm cool with him nonetheless.

The week after Christmas is pretty hectic. I finish up all my college applications. Erick, Mom, and I also prep for our second annual New Year's Eve party, only this year we're holding it at the new Catches Falls location, since it's finally ready to open. My heart aches when I remember the party last year. How J.J. showed up at my door in a tux and looked so broken but hopeful at the same time, and all because he loved me. I'd give anything to see that look on his face again. This time, though, I'd throw myself into his arms and kiss him and let him know he didn't have to worry about me hurting him ever again.

This year I don't even invite him. He told me he didn't want to see me anymore, so I'll listen. I'll come at life from my patient heart and not my anxious brain. I don't invite him . . . but I do send him an email. It's short. Just a picture of the two of us from back when he was tutoring me in history. It's a selfie I took when we were goofing around, and we both look awful. We're way too close to the lens, and he's at this weird angle where he looks like a sunken-cheeked zombie and I'm making a face that mushes my chin deep back into my neck. It's truly a hideous picture . . . but I love it because it's what we're all about. Or what we *were* all about. Just being ourselves and having fun because the two of us together *meant* fun, no matter what was going on.

Under the picture I write:

If what we had is all we'll have, I'm still so grateful
for the ride.

Before I hit send, I check myself. Is this another desperate ploy to get him back?

No. It's not. It's me being honest. This is how I want him
to remember me, not the moment in the football stadium.

I hit send.

That's two days before New Year's. I don't hear a reply,
and I'd be lying if I said I didn't check my email a million
times a day just to be sure, but I don't actually expect to
hear anything, and I don't.

The party itself is really beautiful. The dogs haven't
been brought into the new Catches Falls location yet, so
it's just this giant wide-open space perfect for an event.
Our guests are a lot of the same people from last year, only
now they include some of Mom's deep-pocket investors
and potential investors. Them and, of course, Glen. Reenzie comes with Sean, who apologizes for staying mad at me
so long. He's really excited about UNH and says the truth
is I did him a huge favor when I accidentally locked him
in my attic. Jack and Tom show up separately, and I dutifully pretend I invited Tom on my own. Personally, I still
think Jack should just come out and everyone would be
fine with it, but *que sera sera*—he'll do it when he's ready.
Taylor comes with Drew and Ames arrives solo, so I declare
her my date for the evening. We hang and mingle with

everyone else at the party, and we clap and cheer when Mom makes her announcements, thanking everyone for their help in getting this place off the ground.

At a certain point, we all end up drifting outside. The dog-bone-shaped wading pool hasn't been filled yet, and it's way too tempting to resist. Even though we're majorly decked out, we all climb in and sit inside, our backs against the cement curve of the bone end and all our legs stretching out toward one another.

"So this is it," Jack says. "All our applications are in. The rest is out of our hands."

"Out of *your* hands," Reenzie says. "Sean and I know where we're going."

"Nowhere near each other," Taylor says, cuddling closer to Drew. "Doesn't it freak you out?"

"Nope," Reenzie says. "We agreed to break up after graduation."

"Because I'm going to be a big football star and I can't possibly resist all the women throwing themselves at me," Sean says playfully.

Reenzie swats him. "You're the one who wants to stay together!"

"We'll *all* stay together," Ames says. "No matter where we go or what we do after this year. Swear it, right now."

I feel a pang in my stomach because we're *not* all together; there's one of us missing even now. I don't want to think about that, though. I love everyone with me in this dog pool, and I want to concentrate on them. "I swear," I say; then I flinch as I think of the future. "Just . . . um . . . Drew?" I add. "Be careful with yourself."

"What?" he asks.

I don't elaborate, and luckily I don't have to because Amalita distracts everyone by trying to make us repeat a ridiculous friendship oath, but we all laugh so hard we can't even get through it.

"Yo! Dog pool people!" Erick calls while we're still laughing. "It's almost midnight! Mom wants everyone inside!"

We pile in and take a spot as Mom grabs her standing microphone once more. She's smiling giddily and her face is flushed, like she's had a little too much champagne. "And now," she says, "as we get ready to count down to a brand-new year, I give you a special treat. A musical interlude, if you will."

She waggles her eyebrows and I laugh out loud. My mom does *not* get tipsy, so this is hysterical to me.

Then I hear the opening guitar chords of Kyler Leeds's "As You Wish." A murmur of appreciation runs through the crowd. I'm amazed. "Kyler's here???" I mouth across the room to my mom.

She just smiles and gives an exaggerated shrug. Clearly tipsy.

Or maybe not. Just then, a guy strolls out from the staff area in back. He wears jeans, sunglasses, a leather jacket, and strums a guitar slung over his shoulder. He *could* be

Kyler Leeds . . . if you had no idea in the universe what Kyler Leeds looked like and imagined him longer, lankier, paler, and with much darker hair.

It's J.J.

My skin prickles all over and my heart leaps against my chest. I turn to look at my friends, and they're all grinning like my apparently-not-so-tipsy mom. I even see Erick looking at me with a loopy smile on his face. He gives me a double thumbs-up.

They all knew.

J.J.'s at the mic now. He stops strumming, but the music keeps going. "It's a backing track," he admits. "I don't know how to play guitar." He yanks off the sunglasses. "Can't really see in here with these things, either."

He takes off the guitar and gently puts it and the sunglasses on the floor, then quickly stands up and stammers, "I, um, I do have a song for you, though. Here goes."

J.J. takes a deep breath, closes his eyes, and holds it in until the music gets to the right spot . . . then sings.

Like, really sings.

How did I not know J.J. could sing?

I'm so amazed by how great he sounds that for a second I don't hear the words. I just assume he's singing Kyler's song. But then I hear, *"If what we had is all we'll have, I'm still so grateful for the ride."*

I shiver all over. It's exactly what I said to him in my email. He's singing Kyler's song, but he changed the words, just like I did for the football game. Only his are a million times better and sweeter and all about the little details he noticed about me from the very first time we met until now. His eyes are on mine the whole song, and they pull me closer. I don't even realize I'm moving until he sings the last note and I'm right there in front of him. He moves away from the mic to step even closer to me. I'm drowning in his longing gaze, and the space between us is on fire.

"I didn't know you could sing," I say.

J.J. smiles. "I can do anything when I'm with you. You know that."

Keeping his eyes on mine, he gently runs a hand along my jawline. I melt as he touches me and close my eyes so all there is is his skin against mine. He twines his fingers in my hair and when I feel him lean close, I turn up my face and press my lips against his.

We kiss for maybe an eternity. I don't know. All I know is I never want it to end, but when it does everyone around is clapping and hooting and J.J. and I are both bright red, but neither one of us can stop smiling. We curl our arms around each other as all our friends surround us, talking a mile a minute about the song and how great J.J. was and how hard it had been for them to keep their mouths shut the whole night. Then Jack notices something out the window.

"Dude," he says to me, "is your brother filling the dog bone pool?"

I run to the window, bringing J.J. with me because I don't want to let go of his hand. Erick totally turned on the tap, and now he and all his eighth-grade friends are splashing around in the shallow water.

"Oh, we so have priority on the splash pool," I say. "Who's in?"

Everyone's in, and we pile out the door. But before we get to the pool, J.J. catches my arm. I stop and face him. The moonlight shines on his face and I can't help myself. I throw my arms around him and kiss him. When I pull back, we keep our arms around each other.

"I love you, Autumn," he says.

"I love you too."

"I have a question for you."

He says it so seriously, and there's so much intensity in his eyes that I can't help thinking about his proposal. I start to hyperventilate a little. I mean, I want that to happen, but *now*?! We're still in high school!

"Yeah . . . ?" I say. My voice warbles; I'm terrified.

"Yeah," he says. Then he takes a deep breath. "Autumn Falls . . . will you go to prom with me?"

I'm so relieved I almost fall to my knees. "YES!" I cry. "Absolutely! Now come on!"

I drag him to the pool. Our friends have already booted Erick and his crew to the big grassy lawn and we splash and jump in the water under the moonlight until we're completely exhausted. When we all leave, J.J. and I kiss good night like we'll never see each other again, even though he's coming over for New Year's Day brunch. Glen drives Erick, Mom, and me back, and I text J.J. the whole time, even though I know he's driving and won't respond until he gets home. His texts arrive when I'm lying in bed—goofy things that make me laugh out loud, but then he finishes with:

Going to bed. I love you. Can't wait until
morning . . . and every other morning after that.

I text him back:

Me too. Love you.

Then I just lie in bed and stare up at the ceiling smiling.

Suddenly I get an idea. I grab my phone again and look up the date of our prom, then go to my bookcase. I take down my silver jewelry box and take out Dad's locket. Looking at the *zemi*, I say, "I think I'm ready for my last jump." Carefully, I open the locket and set the dials for the date of my senior prom. I climb back into bed, shut the locket, and close my eyes, squeeze it tight.

22

may, senior year

The DJ rocks. I'll just start with that. Pretty much everyone is dancing, and I have to hand it to Carrie Amernick and her Senior Social Committee sisterhood, because the place looks amazing.

I'm glad I'm invisible and unbumpable in the future, because I'd never be able to make it across the dance floor without getting pummeled by every jumping, dancing, slamming member of the senior class knocking me over otherwise. Now it's great. They pass right through me, and I get to check everyone out.

I laugh when I see Mom and Glen in a corner. They're just off the dance floor, on a patch of carpet where they won't get pummeled. I guess they're chaperoning. Mom does a fairly decent job with the hip-hop moves, but poor Glen is like a puppet. The fact that Mom seems to find this charming stuns me, but I guess it bodes well for their future.

A slow song starts, and while Mom and Glen and several

other couples pour into each other's arms, nearly everyone else clumps off in groups to cool off and hang. I find all my friends. Ames is with Paul Northrup, a guy I know from English class; Sean's with Reenzie; Taylor's with Drew; and Jack and Tom . . .

"You're holding hands!" I scream. "I'm so happy for you!"

I hug Jack even though my arms go right through him and I only stumble forward, but I don't care. I'm that happy. And I'm even happier when I see J.J. and me. It's four months from now and we're totally together. Near-Future-Me is tucked there under his arm, and we both look blissfully happy.

"So?" I ask the group of them. "Tell me everything! It's spring—you know where you're all going next year! Are we close? Will we see each other in school?"

I've jumped enough to know that nothing I say in the future makes any difference at all. They can't see me and they can't hear me. Yet miraculously, I see Future Me's eyes go wide for a second, like something just clicked inside her head. Is she remembering her past, when she was me and I was her and I asked the question? I don't know, but she jumps in and changes the conversation so we're all talking about college and where we'll be in the fall. Reenzie and Sean's plans haven't changed, but Taylor's going to Northwestern, where they have a great theater program, and Drew transferred there, too, so they'll be together. Jack got a full scholarship to CalArts based on a graphic novel he's apparently been writing and drawing since middle school, so he's set. He won't be anywhere near Tom, who's going to school in Maine, but they seem cool with it.

As for J.J. and me, we're going to two different schools, but they're both in Boston, so we'll see each other all the time.

Fast music kicks up again and my friends and I pile out to the dance floor. I watch us and I can't help but smile. We all look so . . . well . . . peaceful and happy.

"Autumn."

I hear the man's voice clearly behind me, even though the music's very loud. I assume he's calling Future Me, but she doesn't even register that she heard anything.

"Autumn."

The voice is closer now, but Future Me still doesn't turn. And there's something very familiar about the voice.

"Autumn."

He's right behind me, but I'm suddenly shivering all over and I'm afraid to turn around because my heart will literally shatter if I'm wrong. I bite my lip and turn, and the whole world stops.

"Daddy?"

It's him. My dad. His dark hair. His tan skin. His brown laughing eyes and smiling face and he's *right there in front of me*!

"Daddy!"

I throw my arms around him and they don't sweep through him like smoke. My dad is *here*. He's *solid*. He's holding me tight and rocking me back and forth and my face is buried in his chest and he feels like him and smells like him and sounds like him and I'm crying and laughing and I can't stop any of it.

"I don't understand," I finally say. "How are you here?"

"The *zemi*," he says, pointing down at the locket clutched in my hand. "You know what it does, right?"

"Holds a little piece of someone's soul?"

Dad nods. "Just like in the diary and the map. I was there too. But look."

He nods back to my fist. I open it and look at the locket. It's smooth on both sides. The *zemi* is gone. I grin.

"Where will I find it next?" I ask. "Something in my college dorm room, maybe?"

Dad's still smiling, but there's something sad in his eyes and he doesn't answer. I feel a pit start to open in my stomach.

"You *will* come back in something else, right?"

He shakes his head. "You don't need me anymore, *carina*. It's time for me to move on."

"No!" I wail. "I *do* need you! I don't have all the answers. I don't know if Reenzie'll be okay at Stanford or if Drew will get into some kind of horrible accident . . . and I'm going to a whole new school with new people! What if they don't like me? What if I miss home? What'll I do if I don't have you there to help me?"

Dad looks down at me, his eyes full of love. "You'll do fine," he says. He brushes my hair out of my face and smiles. "You know why I named you Autumn Falls, right?"

I've heard the story a million times, but I want to hear it again from him. "Maybe."

He laughs. "I named you after my favorite season. Twice. Because I knew just like it, you had the power to bring peace between extremes."

"Peace and happiness to my little corner of the world?" I ask.

"Exactly." He shakes his head, like he's as amazed as I am that we're face to face. "You were a little girl when I left you. Now you're all grown-up. You're so confident, so caring, so wise. I'm so proud of you, Autumn. You're everything I knew you'd be and more."

"If I am, it's only because you've been helping me." I fling my arms around him and hold him as tightly as I can. "Please don't go."

He hugs me back. "I won't. You might not have me in an object, like a diary, or a map, or a locket, but I'll always be with you, and I'll always be smiling at what I see."

Dad pulls back just enough to touch his forehead to mine. I stare at his face, trying to etch it into my mind so I never forget a single detail.

"I love you, Daddy," I say.

"I love you too."

He pulls me close again, and I hug him as tight as I possibly can, tight enough to hold on to him forever. . . .

23

january, senior year

. . . and then I'm in bed. Alone. Sobbing.

Sobbing . . . but not entirely sad. I'm happy too. I made my dad proud. I had him by my side for three years after he left, and I made him proud.

I put the locket back around my neck. He's not in it anymore, but I'll wear it always just the same. It'll remind me that no matter where I am, and no matter what happens, I'm not alone.

I look around my darkened room, lit only by the moonlight streaming through the window. "I love you, Daddy," I say.

And I know he hears me.